The Second Trial

# The Second Trial

## ROSEMARIE BOLL

Second Story Press

Library and Archives Canada Cataloguing in Publication

Boll, Rosemarie, 1957-

The second trial / by Rosemarie Boll.

ISBN 978-1-897187-72-2

I. Title.

PS8603.O463S42 2010      jC813'.6      C2010-900609-7

Edited by Doris Rawson
Copyedited by Robin Crombie
Cover and text design by Melissa Kaita
Cover photo © iStockphoto

Printed and bound in Canada
Second Printing 2010

*Second Story Press gratefully acknowledges the support of the Ontario Arts
Council and the Canada Council for the Arts for our publishing program.
We acknowledge the financial support of the Government of Canada
through the Book Publishing Industry Development Program.*

 ONTARIO ARTS COUNCIL
CONSEIL DES ARTS DE L'ONTARIO       Canada Council   Conseil des Arts
for the Arts    du Canada

Published by
SECOND STORY PRESS
20 Maud Street, Suite 401
Toronto, Ontario, Canada
M5V 2M5
www.secondstorypress.ca

*To my husband, Ron,*
*who has supported me through many trials*

# PART ONE

# The First Trial

# Chapter 1

## Tuesday

The police officer kept his eyes locked on the thirteen-year-old boy. "You're going to have to move," he said.

Danny crossed his arms. "No."

Sergeant Sandhu faced the boy squarely. "Your father – your dad's a violent and dangerous man, Danny. Your mom can't trust him and neither can you." He paused. "If he gets the chance again, we all believe he'll hurt your mom – very badly. Even kill her."

Danny tried to swallow, but his throat was as dry as cotton. "I was in the courtroom," he replied. "He said he wouldn't. He said he'd never hurt her again."

"I know, but he's said a lot of things that aren't true," replied the police officer.

"You're *wrong!*"

"I wish I were." The officer looked deep into Danny's eyes. "I know this must seem like a bad dream to you, and you want it to end. But you have to understand something. The decision about *what's* going to happen has already been made. I'm sorry, but that's something you don't have a choice about."

Danny flicked imaginary lint from his sleeve. "So why even bring me here?"

"Because your mom wants you to have a say in *how* it's going to happen. You and your sister, Jennifer."

"Yeah, right." Pause.

Sgt. Sandhu sighed. "If you don't take part now, you'll regret it for the rest of your life. Because this *is* the rest of your life we're talking about here."

"They're getting a divorce, and he said he'd never do it again! This is crazy! This is *nuts*!"

"No, Danny," Sgt. Sandhu said, his mouth grim. "This is reality. We're way past happy endings. The decision to give you new identities and relocate you wasn't an easy one. But it's the only safe one because we can't afford to make a mistake. If we don't do anything and your dad kills your mom, well...dead is forever."

The words came at him like sharp blows. *Kill. Dead. Forever.* He twisted in his seat and his eyes darted to the door, the escape from this nightmare.

"There's no running away, Danny. We have to do this. It's time."

Danny launched himself from the chair and flew out of the office and into the hallway. The elevator took forever to reach the ground floor.

His pupils shrank to pinpoints in the sudden sunshine of the downtown street. He hunched his shoulders and kept his head down so that the peak of his baseball cap blocked out anything more than a few paces in front of him. He jostled passersby, ignoring their grunts of surprise and anger. Long blocks of heated cement disappeared under his pounding feet, until he veered south toward the river valley.

The broad river split the city in two. Danny dropped onto a vacant bench overlooking the steep-sided valley. His head throbbed, and he felt like he was going to throw up. He hung his head and massaged his temples. His thoughts were puzzle pieces that would never fit together again. *What had happened to his parents? What had happened to his family? What was going to happen to his life?*

# Chapter 2

## Sunday

Two days earlier, the summer sun had been setting into an orange nest when his mom entered Danny's room. He'd been stretched out in a confusion of bedsheets and blankets. He'd wedged a pillow against the headboard and propped his new video game on his chest. It pinged and buzzed with each deft flick of his thumbs. His mother stepped around abandoned T-shirts and sat at his feet.

"Danny, we have to talk," she said, touching his knee. "Tomorrow's Monday. The trial starts." She swallowed. "You have to decide whether you want to come or stay home."

His fingers kept twiddling the game.

"Jennifer can't come. She's too young. She'll stay at Grandma and Grandpa's for a couple of days."

His eyes stayed on the video game while his thumbs stabbed the buttons.

"Your dad's going to be sentenced. The prosecutor will ask for a long sentence." She let the words hang in the air. "Your dad's lawyer will say what he has to say, and Dad...he might say something too."

Danny drew up his knees. His mom blinked back tears. "If you come, you'll hear things that..." She hesitated and swiped a tissue across her eyes. "...things you never dreamed you'd hear. Things I never wanted to tell anyone, but now it's time to tell the truth." She held up her head and told him about the victim impact statement she was going to read in court. Still fiddling with his video game, he listened to her outline a story about a buried life he'd never suspected. She told him his father had hurt her many times over many years, not just the few times he knew about.

"I thought it best that no one knew. I thought I could protect you and Jen, Grandma and Grandpa, and maybe even myself, from the truth. I couldn't tell my friends, I couldn't tell the neighbors, I couldn't tell the people at work. If I did, then I'd have to admit to myself that I was living a lie.

"Now I know that the only person I was protecting was your father. I was protecting him from dealing with his violent anger. I was protecting him from the truth that he is an abuser."

Danny squeezed his game until his knuckles turned white.

"You don't have to come," she continued, "but everyone thinks you should. The prosecutor, Sgt. Sandhu, the counselor, Grandma and Grandpa." She paused while her fingertips brushed the rash on her neck. "I won't tell you that you *have* to come, Danny," she said. "No matter which way you decide, it's going to be hard. But if you do come, you've got to know – it will be the *hardest* thing you've done in your life."

Danny knew there'd been problems. It had been eight months ago – nearly Christmas – when his father went to jail. He and his little sister had gone to bed. But his bedroom shared a wall with his parents' room, and his father's rising voice stirred him awake.

"We are *not* going to your mother's for Christmas again! You know I can't *stand* those people! We need to have our *own* Christmas. No one's gonna tell *me* where to sit and how to behave!"

"But Paul," Catherine pleaded, "it's been four years since we were there for Christmas. Jennifer was only four and –"

"I don't care if she was still in diapers. We're not going! Can't you get that through your thick skull?"

Danny heard his dad pacing like he always did when he was angry.

"If you touch that doorknob," Paul growled, "I'm going to kill you. I've got my gun right here, under the bed. You know I've got my gun, don't you. Wanna see it? I'll shoot you right here. *Right now.*"

Danny heard the bedroom door crash open, frantic footsteps, and then a sickening *crack*, followed by muffled thumps. Buddy, his border collie, barked wildly. His barks were interrupted by the sharp slam of the front door.

Danny wanted to stay in bed, pretend nothing had happened. He'd overheard arguments at night before, the words inaudible but the tone unmistakable. He'd noticed his mother at dinner, hardly saying a word while Dad carried on about sports, stupid politicians, and the irritating neighbors. Danny knew his parents didn't always get along, but that wasn't so unusual, was it? His friends' parents argued. Some even divorced. Yet tonight his dog's whimpering signaled this was no simple argument, no "accidental" shattering of dishes on the kitchen floor. Something more was wrong, and it bathed him in cold sweat. He held his breath, clutched the covers around his neck, and squeezed his eyes shut. His heart beat with such violence he thought it would burst. Then his mind registered another sound – sobs, muffled by a pillow – and he knew Jennifer had heard it too.

The dog exploded into his room and leapt onto the bed. Then he jumped to the floor, barking at Danny, his head lowered and haunches raised. Just as suddenly, he turned and darted away. Danny threw off the covers and scrambled after him, but he paused in his doorway. A shattered lamp lay outside his parents' bedroom, its shade buckled and cracked. He stepped around the glass shards and stopped dead at the top of the landing. He wasn't prepared for what he saw at the bottom: his mother lying motionless, her nightgown twisted around her thighs, and her face covered by a snarl of hair. Two fingers of crimson blood oozed from her scalp and seeped into the carpet. Buddy paced alongside her, making deep-throated sounds and gently nuzzling her body.

Mom didn't move. Danny sped down the stairs and hurtled over her body. He landed well past the spreading stain and sprinted for the kitchen phone. He dialed 9-1-1, but when the operator answered, his pounding heart swept away his breath, and all he could do was cry.

They'd spent that Christmas after the assault with his mother's parents, Grandma and Grandpa Wilson. Mom's arm was still in a cast, and because of her broken ribs, she slept sitting under a patchwork quilt in a recliner by the fire. Her pain was like an unwelcome guest at a party – unmentionable, but unforgettable.

Grandma and Grandpa had gone all out. They burned cookie-scented candles, played Christmas carols, and Grandma baked the special Scottish shortbread Danny loved. Everyone helped decorate the tree, and Danny had to admit it was a good Christmas, even without his dad.

But by Easter, Mom's injuries had healed and his memory of her pain faded. When she tried to get him to decorate Easter eggs with his sister, he scoffed and said he was too old. He started fighting with both of them. Just about anything could spark him to anger. Most of the time Mom wouldn't yell back. He couldn't understand why she didn't seem to feel as alone without her husband as he felt without his father. He wanted Dad back. He wanted things to be just the way they used to be. One night, while his mother was on the phone, he tiptoed into his parents' bedroom. Most everything was as it should be, except that their wedding photo above the dresser was gone.

He circled the foot of the bed. A floor-to-ceiling closet with mirrored doors was built into the opposite wall. The right side was his mom's and the left side was his dad's. He slid open the left side. Dad's suits and shirts hung in the closet, dry-cleaning plastic still covering some of them. His dress shoes were lined up, clean and shiny, just the way he liked them. Italian silk neckties hung from a rack at the end of the closet. Danny reached over and stroked Dad's McMillan silk hunting tie, the modern tartan – yellow and red stripes over green, blue, and purple plaid. It was identical to the one hanging in his own closet. Everything was in order. Mom hadn't actually thrown him completely away. It was a sure sign Dad would be back in Danny's life.

Then Mom started seeing a lawyer. A couple of times he found her at the kitchen table filling out forms, and he could guess what they were about. She had tried to talk to him one night, but he scowled and stalked off to the TV room to watch some reality show. He didn't even like the show much, but with Buddy's warm head resting in his lap, he could lose himself in the lives of people whose troubles seemed larger than his own. When Mom nagged him, he turned up the volume.

Danny hated the idea of a divorce. He'd been furious with his mother for wanting it, furious with his dad for causing it, and furious with the world and everything in it. People called them broken homes, didn't they? But there was nothing broken about his home, except that his dad just happened to be in jail for a bit. Broken homes happened to other people. In broken homes, parents fought about visiting rights and money. Kids from broken homes had two frantic Christmases spent elbowing for space and attention with half brothers and stepsisters. Some people called them single-parent families as if they were special, but Danny knew he had two parents and he wanted them both. Together. At the same time. When Dad got out everything would be okay again.

After the arrest, some kids at school had said crude things about his dad being a criminal and how his mom must have deserved it. Danny cut them off. Soon, turning his back on people became a habit, and even his friends walked away. He refused to join any teams or after-school activities. Life became just one tedious day after another.

Until the trial.

# Chapter 3

## Monday

The wide courtroom doors shut behind them. Danny and his mom found seats on a long bench. His mouth tasted bitter, and he longed to have his mom wrap him in her arms and tell him, "*Don't worry, Danny-boy, everything's going to be okay.*" But she just sat beside him, her back rigid. He relaxed his fists and tried to slide his hands under his knees, but the cold sweat on his palms stuck to the wood. His hands lurched forward, jarring his arms like the time Dad had let him drive the SUV and he'd released the clutch too fast. Dad had laughed as the vehicle jumped forward. "*Take it easy, son, relax, don't lose your head, just relax and it'll come.*"

Danny pressed his palms onto the scratchy black trousers he wore for school band performances. He let out the breath he didn't know he'd been holding.

They sat to the right of a carpeted aisle that divided the courtroom. The teak benches, the color of autumn leaves, reminded him of church. Earlier that morning, Mom had introduced him to Sandra Johnson, the prosecutor. The prosecutor had shown him the courtroom to acquaint him with the setup. He knew His Honor Alexander Cunningham would sit in this windowless room and preside over the unraveling of Danny's family.

Danny's eyes moved across the courtroom. There it stood – the prisoner's box. *Prisoner. Prisoner.* Danny tried to keep his hands loose and his breathing regular, just the way Dad had taught him to relax before a soccer game. *Pris-on-er. Pris-on-er.* His heart beat out the rhythm of the word. His father in the prisoner's box, his father in jail, his father a convicted criminal, his own father now in the final play of this…game? *Was* it a game? Which side was he on? Which side *should* he be on? Maybe it didn't matter. How could it matter, when there weren't any rules, and the game could end only in a loss?

People started filing in. His mom slid a little closer to Danny, as if she'd just remembered she was his mother and that mothers need to take care of their sons. She glanced at him sitting there awkwardly in his long-sleeved white shirt. He was dressed up – dressed for a school Christmas concert, for church, or for a funeral. Today, at age thirteen, Danny wanted her protection, but she'd said he was now a young man and she could not protect him – no longer wanted to protect him – from the truth.

The door behind the prisoner's box swung open. A guard with a holstered gun slung from her wide black belt loomed in the doorway. Dad came out wearing his tailored gunmetal blue suit. He'd buttoned down the starched collar of his white shirt over a navy and black silk tie. Although Danny couldn't see them, he knew his father's leather shoes were polished as black as ravens. Dad *looked* normal: sharply dressed, his head up, stepping politely past the guard. He looked just the way he did every morning on his way to work.

But nothing was normal.

Mr. Miller, Dad's defense lawyer, approached his client and spoke too softly for anyone to overhear. But it wouldn't have mattered if he had shouted across the courtroom. Danny couldn't have listened even if he'd wanted to, couldn't have talked if he'd needed to. He was unable to move, his eyes frozen on his dad.

"Order in court! All rise!" called the clerk, startling Danny into action. He leapt to his feet, his throat as dry as ashes. The judge entered briskly and took his place behind the raised bench.

"Good morning, counsel, ladies and gentlemen. You may be seated." The judge settled a pair of reading glasses low on his nose and sorted through some papers. He glanced up, and Danny could see his thick eyebrows arch above the black frames. "We're here to sentence Paul Frederick McMillan for his vicious assault on his wife," he said. "This is his third conviction."

*Third conviction?*

"I'll hear from the prosecutor first," the judge said.

Sandra stood before the judge. "Your Honor, Mr. McMillan is a dangerous man. He's been convicted three times for assaulting his wife, and either he can't, or he won't, change. He's a threat to his wife, a threat so serious, that for *her* the verdict in this case means life or death. Your Honor, this court must declare this man a dangerous offender and put him behind bars for *at least* seven years. He is a vicious man with hatred smoldering in his heart. He's beaten his wife and burned her; he's broken her bones and torn out her hair. Even though her physical wounds have healed, she still suffers serious injuries that linger on. These are not flesh-and-blood injuries that can be measured by X-rays, or by healing

time, or by the lengths of scars. They are blows to self-esteem and
confidence, damage to dignity and personal security, destruction of
morals and values. These are the injuries that don't heal. These are
the hurts that are never forgotten. Fear. Unending, crippling, and
ulcerating fear. This is the legacy of the sickness that is domestic
violence."

Sandra paused before turning from the judge to call her first
witness to the stand. The elderly man rested his cane against the
witness box and then sat in the black swivel chair. He laid a coil-
bound report on the table in front of him.

The clerk swore him in, and Sandra walked toward the witness box. "Dr. Hamilton," she said, "please tell us about yourself."

"I am a forensic psychiatrist, and I work with violent offenders. I assess them on behalf of the court. I evaluate the level of
threat in violent, high-risk relationships. I work with a team of
experts: police, prosecutors, lawyers, and community services such
as women's shelters. We try to prevent crimes such as stalking,
assault...and murder."

Danny felt as if he'd been slapped.

"How do you do that?" the prosecutor asked.

"I create a risk profile. I look at the offender's history, attitudes,
mental health, family, social circumstances, and so on. I classify
the offender's threat level."

"You examined Mr. McMillan?"

"Yes."

"As a result of your work, what did you find?"

"Mr. McMillan is a violent bully bent on attacking his wife."

The word *bully* catapulted Danny's mind back into Grade 2,
when James had flattened him with a punch. Two other kids had
knelt on his back, ground their knees into his ribs, and pinned him

down while the schoolyard bully forced a handful of dirt into his mouth. The sudden pain had made him cry out, and the dirt had crept back into his throat and made him gag. The boys' laughter floated above him as the soil worked its way into his eyes, his tears unable to wash away the sting of dirt and disgrace. Today in the courtroom, Danny blinked – *his dad was like James?*

The psychiatrist was still talking. "Mr. McMillan isn't your usual schoolyard bully. Those types of bullies use physical strength to stay on top and get what they want from their victims. They want to impress other people and obtain social standing amongst peers and even teachers."

"What type of bully is he?"

"He's a *selective* bully. He targets only his wife. The more she cowers, the better he feels. Over time, she becomes more easily scared. This makes him feel even better about himself, and the situation just keeps spiraling down. It gets easier and easier to make her afraid, and soon a mere stare is enough."

Danny remembered one time when Dad had stared at Mom at the dinner table. Danny's plate was heaped with pot roast and mashed potatoes awash in gravy, and he was outlining the Grade 4 science project on water systems he was working on.

"Is Brian going to be your partner?" Mom asked. "You worked together so well last time and –"

"Would you like to see the new water treatment plant?" Dad interrupted.

Danny's eyes went wide. "Could I really?"

"I don't see why not. I'm out there every couple of days anyway."

"Well, it can't be during school hours," Mom said.

"Why not?" challenged Dad, giving her a long, hard look.

Her head dropped. "I just don't think he should miss school, that's all."

Dad snorted. "Then we'll take the whole class. Simple as that."

Danny was delighted. "Really? Wow, that'd be great!"

"Sure. We'll do it." Dad had turned to Mom. "Why don't you call his teacher tomorrow? I'm sure even you can figure out a way to set it up."

Danny turned to his mother. "Pleeeease? Could you?"

"I'll see what I can do," she mumbled.

"Yes!" Danny pumped his arm. "Wait 'till the kids find out!"

Mom had made the arrangements. Two weeks later, a yellow school bus buzzing with students bumped its way to the plant. Dad's broad grin greeted the children, and Danny flushed with pride. His classmates giggled and shrieked as they strapped on fluorescent-orange safety helmets that constantly slumped over their eyes. Dad didn't scold the boys when they ran around bonking the girls' helmets in a noisy game of tag. The students learned about viruses, bacteria, protozoa, and the new ultraviolet technology that zapped them all. Danny stood close by his dad throughout the tour.

Back at school, the students made a giant thank you card. Everyone signed it. Danny wrote "*THANKS DAD!*" in bold letters across the top.

It had been a great day. But nobody had thanked his mom. She hadn't even been invited to come along.

Danny's attention was brought back to the courtroom as the prosecutor walked back and forth behind the counsel table. "Dr.

Hamilton, to anyone looking at the McMillan family from the outside, let's say through the living room window, it seems like a solid, respectable, and happy family. How can a family appear so normal on the outside and be so rotten on the inside?"

"It's not as unusual as you might think. The public often thinks of batterers as being from low-income families. They believe the batterers were themselves the victims of childhood abuse or neglect. The public also tends to think abusers have serious mental health problems – they are psychopaths, alcoholics, drug abusers, or career criminals. But this isn't always so.

"Violence also happens in what we might call privileged households. These people have higher than average incomes, both partners are usually well educated, and both partners seem confident, socially at ease, and happy. We call this type of bully an upscale domestic abuser."

"How does an upscale abuser behave?"

"Well he – and it is almost always a man – he dominates his victim by criticizing her – sometimes publicly, but always strongly or even viciously. He also makes decisions – even important ones – without her input. He controls her access to money, and he keeps her from contacting her support group, her friends and family. He wants *control*, and that means cutting her off."

Danny's mind went back to spring break in Grade 3. Dad had promised to drive the family to Drumheller to see the Tyrrell Dinosaur Museum. "Catherine," Paul directed, "you get our bags packed and we'll leave in the morning."

Sleep had eluded Danny. He pulled out his favorite dinosaur books – *Giant Dinosaurs, The Complete T-Rex, Time Flies, A Pebble in my Pocket* – and surrounded himself in bed. He flipped through every picture. He wanted to sneak downstairs and telephone Grandpa. Grandpa was a retired geology teacher, and Danny was used to spending a lot of summer days with him. He wanted to ask where to find fossils, but knew his dad wouldn't approve of the phone call. They didn't talk to Grandma and Grandpa much anymore.

The day had dawned clear and cold: a perfect end-of-winter day. They spent Monday exploring the museum and the treasures of the gift shop. Danny fingered bits of fossilized dinosaur bones, a balsa wood T-Rex skeleton, and a spider trapped in amber. They stayed in a hotel with an indoor pool. Mom watched from a deck chair as Danny and Jennifer splashed as much as they could get away with. Dad stayed in the room and watched the hockey game on TV. On Tuesday, they drove to Dinosaur Provincial Park where they hiked along the clay trail to the fossil beds. Although the sign said it was illegal to take fossils from the park, Danny picked one up and slipped it into his pocket.

"Put that back, Danny," Mom ordered sharply.

"Let him keep it, for God's sake, Catherine. Don't be such a stickler."

Danny had grinned at his dad. He kept his hand in his jacket pocket, twirling the long, smoothly-ridged cylinder of cool rock around and around in his fingers.

The prosecutor continued. "Does this type of bully follow a pattern?"

"Absolutely. A pattern of escalating violence. Mr. McMillan's first conviction was ten years ago. He struck his wife in the face, twice – with a closed fist. He gave her a black eye and badly bruised her face."

Danny looked at his mother. She stared straight ahead, her face rigid and emotionless. *Ten years ago.* He'd been just three years old, and his sister Jen hadn't been born yet. He remembered nothing. But he saw that his mother remembered; the knuckles of her interlaced fingers were white.

"Then the next assault – at least the next assault he was *convicted* for – was only four years later, and it was violent. He flung her into a coffee table, broke her wrist, split open her palm, and pulled out her hair by its roots. And he kept threatening her with more." He shifted in his seat. "For the bully, it's a bit like an escalator ride. Once you get on that bottom step, there's nowhere to go but up."

*Escalator. Mom's escalator accident.* Danny had been happy and excited about starting school that year. Every day, Mom took Jennifer and him to Annie's day care a block from his elementary school. Annie's sons, Tom and Julian, were his best buddies. Tom was in Grade 2 with Danny, but Julian was in Grade 4, so this year the three boys were old enough to walk to school on their own. Jen was just three and stayed with Annie for days of toddler games and naps.

After school, Annie usually let them play in the yard, but one November day they stayed a long time before Annie called them in. Even though the boys usually played in the family room, Annie sat Danny in a living room chair. Jennifer lay on the carpet, Barbies and Barbie clothes strewn about her like autumn leaves. Annie explained that Mom had had an accident. She'd been on the escalator in the mall. Someone had bumped into her, or she'd lost her balance, or something. Annie wasn't sure which, but Mom had tumbled down. She'd broken her wrist and cut her palm on the metal stairs while trying to stop her fall. Some of her hair had gotten caught in the side of the escalator and had been torn from her scalp. But Annie assured them their mom would be okay. She said once Dad had fetched Mom from the hospital he'd come to get them. In the meantime, Annie would take all of them to a Chinese restaurant for supper.

It was almost bedtime before the doorbell rang. But it wasn't Dad who came to pick them up, it was Mom. Her arm hung in a sling. Her jacket sleeve only partly covered the plaster cast on her right wrist. She curled her fingers against the thick white gauze taped across her palm. She was wearing a navy silk scarf, her favorite, the one patterned with golden sunflowers, knotted under her chin.

"Where's Paul?" Annie asked sharply.

In a rush of words, Mom explained there had been a last-minute crisis at work and Dad had had to leave the hospital and go directly to the airport. He'd be gone for the next few days.

"What kind of a crisis could be that important?" Annie challenged. "Why can't he take care of you? Who's going to take care of you?"

Catherine had cut off Annie's questions and told her not to worry. She said she'd be home from work for a while anyway, because she couldn't type, so she'd get Danny to school herself. She had hustled the kids into the car and told them their dad was sorry he'd missed saying good-bye, but he'd be sure to bring them each something nice when he got home in a couple of days.

"Danny, help your sister into her car seat," she said. "And then buckle yourself in." Catherine started the one-handed drive home.

"Mom, what about your seatbelt?" he had asked.

"I'll be fine."

And now Danny knew she hadn't been fine at all.

◣

"Dr. Hamilton, what can you tell us about a bully's ability to change his behavior – to get off that escalator?"

The psychiatrist stroked his chin. "Well, generally, once a bully, always a bully, because he lacks the desire to change. The best predictor of future behavior is past behavior. If he's done it before, he'll do it again."

"Doctor, given this pattern, what do you predict about Mr. McMillan's behavior?"

The psychiatrist ticked off his conclusions on his fingers. "Mr. McMillan has an established pattern of violence. The violence always occurs, shall we say, behind closed doors, in an intimate relationship, and out of sight in the family home, where it's likely to be repeated. He's an upscale domestic abuser, a bully. He was, is, and likely will continue to be an abuser. He is a dangerous man. When someone acts violently, that event establishes the *minimum* violence he is capable of. He will most certainly re-offend with increasing violence. There is no limit."

"So, this is a high-risk relationship?"

"Yes."

"And what category are we in?"

The psychiatrist looked at the prisoner. "We're in the category of homicide prevention."

# Chapter 4
## Monday

The defense lawyer rose to cross-examine the psychiatrist. "Dr. Hamilton, isn't it true that Mr. McMillan apologized to his wife?"

"Yes. In fact, he has quite often shown remorse."

Danny nodded to himself. His dad *had* been sorry, he'd seen it himself. Mom wore that sunflower scarf for a few days, but a few weeks later, before Dad got home, she'd had her shoulder-length hair cut short. She combed it over the bald spot. Even though Danny now knew his father had been in jail, not on a business trip, he remembered him returning with a triumphant smile and gifts for everyone. It wasn't even Christmas yet, but he'd brought a stuffed mountain gorilla with arms long enough to reach around Jen, a hockey jersey for Danny, and long-stemmed red roses for Mom. He stroked Mom's short hair – "I didn't know you'd cut it," he murmured – and Mom wore her scarf again for the next few days. Because of her wrist, she wasn't back at work.

"I'll take two weeks off," Dad had said, riffling his hands

through Danny's hair, "so the family can all be together again. I promise you a Christmas you'll never forget." They'd see the latest Christmas movies, drive through Candy Cane Lane, and go to the mall so Danny and Jen could sit on Santa's knee and ask for all the toys they wanted. They'd drink mugs of steaming hot chocolate piled with clouds of whipped cream. Dad promised tobogganing, skating, and building snowmen in the park, but when the time came he didn't explain why he thought it was too cold for Jen and Mom, but not too cold for Danny and him. Of course, Mom wouldn't be getting her cast off for another couple of weeks, so she couldn't come anyway. In the end it was mostly just Dad and Danny. That was the year Dad started teaching him how to play hockey, and it was great.

But best of all was the Christmas present he found in a cardboard box under the tree on Christmas morning – a border collie puppy, glossy black and shiny white and wildly playful. He couldn't keep his hands off the dog and let Jen rip open the presents containing the dog's bed, plastic dishes, a leather collar and retractable leash, mouse-shaped squeak toys, a rawhide bone, puppy treats, and an orange Frisbee.

Split logs burned in the corner fireplace, and the aroma of roasting turkey was thick enough to taste. Danny chatted endlessly about what to name the dog. By the time Dad helped Mom lift the turkey out of the oven, Danny had decided on Buddy. Later, when Mom insisted, he pulled himself away from the puppy long enough to sit at the table. Danny and Jennifer bolted down their food while Buddy whined for attention from his cardboard box.

It had been a perfect Christmas.

The defense lawyer flipped through the psychiatrist's report. "You've said the best predictor of future behavior is past behavior?"

"That's true."

"But people *can* change their behaviors, can't they?"

"We'd better hope so, or we'll all be in trouble."

"Yes, no doubt. But, given that Mr. McMillan is not a psychopath, an alcoholic, or a drug abuser, doesn't it stand to reason that he *can* change? That he is teachable?"

"Well now, that's not so clear. We do know that the anger management training and marriage counseling he took after the first conviction weren't successful."

"Did you offer him any therapy?"

"No, that's not my job. My job is to assess people, not to treat them."

"So he hasn't been offered therapy to control his emotions?"

"Not to my knowledge."

"He hasn't been offered therapy to teach him to have compassion for his wife?"

"That's correct."

"He hasn't been offered therapy to help him control his anger or change his pattern of behavior?"

"Well, he's already had one anger management course, and it failed to change anything. Sometimes offering offenders more courses just makes them better at taking courses."

"Now, would it be fair to say there are *strong* patterns of behavior and *weak* patterns of behavior?"

"Well, yes, the more incidents there are, the more obvious the pattern is."

"So, in this case, those would be the two convictions in 1992 and 1996?"

"Yes, certainly those, but also all of the other times his wife told me about when I interviewed her."

"How strong is Mr. McMillan's pattern?"

"I would say it is a strong pattern."

"But in coming to that conclusion – that there's a strong pattern of behavior – do you rely on all of the…let's say, *other* instances Mrs. McMillan says happened but were never tried or proven in a court of law?"

"Yes."

"And, Dr. Hamilton, *hypothetically* speaking now, if you ignored everything Mrs. McMillan says except for the three *proven* assaults – would you still say Mr. McMillan's actions establish a pattern of behavior?"

"Yes, I would."

"But wouldn't you agree with me the pattern of behavior is *much, much* weaker than if you include all the other alleged assaults?"

The witness paused. "Yes, I'd have to agree with that. But it's still a pattern of behavior."

The lawyer shifted forward and read from a paper. "Mr. McMillan told you he owns a successful commercial insurance agency? He makes a good living and provides all the comforts that make life pleasant?"

"Financially, the family had a good standard of living, yes."

"Every summer, he took them camping and fishing? They've been to Disneyland and Hawaii?"

"Yes."

"Do you agree he offered his children lots of activities and filled their lives with opportunities? That he always did his best for his children?"

"On the surface, yes."

"And Mr. McMillan is under a restraining order – he's not allowed any contact with his wife or his children for the indefinite future?"

"Yes."

"And the hidden gun? The gun with the tag? It was removed the day after the December assault? He's not allowed to have a gun anymore?"

"Yes."

"And they're getting a divorce?"

"Yes."

"And when you interviewed him, he said he loved his wife? And he was very sorry for what he did?"

"Yes, he said those things."

"Thank you, Dr. Hamilton. Those are all my questions." Mr. Miller returned to his seat.

"Any redirect, Ms. Johnson?" asked Judge Cunningham.

"Yes, Your Honor," Sandra replied as she stood. "Dr. Hamilton, what do you think of Mr. McMillan's parenting skills?"

"Mr. McMillan thinks of himself as a model father, but he doesn't understand what he does to his wife also affects his children. He's not a good parent." The psychiatrist looked at Danny. "In fact, I would say he is no better than a child abuser."

Danny's face flushed, and he wished he could sink into the ground and hide from view. The prosecutor continued her questioning.

"Is it unusual for an abuser to show remorse after an assault?"

"Not at all. In fact, it's part of the standard cycle of domestic violence. Violent men express a lot of sadness and remorse afterwards. It's one of the ways they lure their victims into staying, or coming back into the relationship if they've already left. Then, the cycle starts again."

"Now, you said you know there's a restraining order, a gun prohibition, and a divorce. In your experience, do any of these things make any difference to an abuser's behavior after release?"

"If anything, they can make the behavior worse. The most dangerous time for a woman is immediately after a separation. It doesn't matter what any paperwork says. In fact, going to court can anger the abuser even more. If Mr. McMillan were released today, this would be the most dangerous time for his wife – the time he is most likely to seek her out and hurt her again. He's like a...like a spider. He spins a web and lures his victim into it. The spider's silk is thin, almost invisible, but incredibly strong. The prey becomes ensnared, and in the isolation of the web – the privacy of the home – the spider encases the victim in silk, wraps the silk tighter and tighter, and then injects her with poisonous venom. Eventually he consumes her."

"Dr. Hamilton, in your forty years of experience in forensic psychiatry, how would you rate Mr. McMillan's threat to his wife?"

Dr. Hamilton stared hard at Paul. "My gut tells me that Mr. McMillan is one of the most dangerous men I have ever met."

# Chapter 5

## Monday

"Madam Prosecutor, I understand you have additional evidence."

"Yes, Your Honor. Over the last few months, Mrs. McMillan has written a victim impact statement." She pulled a sheaf of handwritten pages from a folder. "She's here today, sir, to read her statement."

Justice Cunningham replaced his reading glasses and examined his copy. "Madam Clerk, please mark the victim impact statement as Exhibit 8."

"Exhibit 8," repeated the clerk, thumping her rubber stamp across the corner.

"Go ahead," the judge instructed.

"The Crown calls Catherine McMillan."

Catherine stood, squared her shoulders, and patted Danny's knee as she left her seat and walked to the witness box. The clerk swore her in.

"Mrs. McMillan, you may be seated," the judge said.

"I prefer to stand."

"Very well. Ms. Johnson, please proceed."

"Mrs. McMillan, you wrote a statement about the effect this assault and the previous assaults have had on you and your family. Is that statement in front of you?"

"Yes."

"When you're ready, would you please read it to the Court?"

Catherine took the first page in trembling hands. She swallowed and started reading.

"My name is Catherine Marie McMillan. I married Paul McMillan on August 17th, 1986, almost sixteen years ago. When I married Paul, I thought we'd be just a normal couple. We'd raise a family and enjoy our careers. We'd share the good times and support each other in the bad times. We'd grow old together and still hold hands when we were seventy."

Her voice gathered strength. She looked up at Paul. "When we married, I didn't know Paul had something else in mind when he said 'Until death do us part.'"

Paul pursed his lips and shook his head.

"For the first year or even longer, Paul was the charming, generous, kind man I married. I used to think of him as my knight in shining armor. We had good times. We had friends, we visited with family, and we had fun. We didn't have a lot of money, yet some of my happiest memories are of our camping vacations. We'd sit around the campfire at night with a cup of hot, sweet wine under the brilliant starry sky."

Catherine looked at the judge. "I am trying to be completely honest. I won't say Paul was always a bad man, because he wasn't. Not at first.

"In 1987, Paul started his own insurance business," she read.

"He spent long hours at the office. He worked very hard to make it a success. Paul was always a hard worker.

"But he changed. He'd come home tired and short-tempered. He started criticizing me. Little things, at first – how I wore my hair, how I cooked dinner, how much time I spent on the phone with my family. I'd never had anyone say such things to me, criticize me for things that seemed so unimportant." She shrugged her shoulders. "And they *were* little things. I thought it was just because he was stressed, working too hard. So I tried to change the things he mentioned, to make adjustments, to please him. I thought doing those things would turn the clock back and I'd have the charming man I married – the man I loved. I didn't say anything to anyone, because I thought it was just a phase he was going through.

"But no matter what I did, it was never enough. The verbal abuse went on and on for months, getting worse instead of better. And when I got pregnant with Danny in the late fall of 1988, the abuse became physical."

Catherine took a sip of water and turned the page. "He'd pinch me or push me and then make light of it. If I reacted, if I told him I didn't like it, he'd say I was just being stupid, or too sensitive, and he'd lay off for a while. But soon pushes became slaps and criticisms became threats.

"I didn't understand what was happening. Even though we both wanted children, Paul blamed me for getting pregnant while his business was still struggling. Sometimes money was tight. It wasn't the easiest pregnancy, but I thought if I stayed at my job as long as I could, we'd be better off financially when I took maternity leave, and that would reduce some of the stress.

"That wasn't enough either. I bought things for the baby, and he said they were too expensive. So I went to the secondhand store, and that made him furious. He said that no kid of his would ever wear someone else's abandoned clothes."

She looked up at Sandra. "It didn't matter what I did. It was never right.

"Danny was born on June 13, 1989. Paul was so happy that it was a boy. I arranged for six months' maternity leave. I was happy, Paul was happy, and Danny..." She looked at her son. "Danny was a wonderful baby.

"Still, it didn't take long before I started getting mixed signals. In one breath he said it was good that I stayed home to take care of his son, and in the next he'd nag that I was spending too much. He cut down on the amount he gave me for groceries. I thought I'd better get back to work even before my maternity leave ended, and I started making child care arrangements. That didn't please him either. Somehow, he wanted me to stay home and take care of Danny, *and* he wanted me to work and earn money – all at the same time.

"He was impossible to please. And from then on, things only got worse."

⚖

Danny didn't want to hear any more, but he couldn't tear his eyes away from his mother and didn't dare glance at his father for fear of what he would see – that every word was true. He was unable to get up and leave the courtroom. All he could do was sit and listen as his mom continued.

Catherine looked down and brushed her fingertips along the edge of the witness box. "February 29, 1992. Leap year," she said, looking up at Paul and tilting her head. "Funny. I remember the day it happened, but I don't remember *why* it happened."

Her eyes returned to the paper. "Danny was almost three. He wasn't with me just then, he was playing somewhere in the house. Paul lost his temper and hit me twice in the face – with a closed fist. I had bruises and a black eye, and I couldn't hide them like I'd hidden everything else. He was arrested and convicted of assault."

She shifted her weight and looked again at her husband. "That first blow – that's when I knew Paul would never be the same. I could never, ever turn back that clock. That blow – it turned him into a stranger.

"He told me how sorry he was. He promised and promised it would never happen again. He went to all his anger management counseling. Looking back on it, I realize that was my opportunity to leave him, but it didn't look that way at the time. He had already started to isolate me from my friends and family. Now I had something tangible – bruises – to hide. So I began withdrawing. I felt responsible for it all. I'd already hidden so much from everyone that it seemed impossible to confess."

Catherine looked at her son. "And I had Danny to consider," she said, a catch in her voice. "He was just a toddler. I still thought, then, that Paul was a good father. Besides, he'd made all those promises and I desperately wanted to believe him." She looked at Paul. "I insisted on marriage counseling. He cooperated. We finished the sessions and everything seemed better. He settled down, and we had a normal, even happy, family life. At least that's what I talked myself into believing."

Catherine returned to her notes. "Jennifer was born the next year – September 1, 1993. Paul was disappointed she was not another boy. It made him cross with me, as if I'd had a choice.

Right from the start, he wasn't as involved with Jen as he'd been with Danny. He treated her indifferently, more like a stranger's child than his own. When it came time for me to go back to work, he started in on me again. He didn't want me to work. He didn't like the people I worked with. It was no good having both our kids in day care. By then I'd had the same job for three years, and I liked it. His business was going well and financially things were fine. For me, it wasn't about the money. Work was a place where I felt productive and safe. I felt confident in my own abilities. So I tried reminding Paul that he'd agreed from the beginning we'd both have careers, but it was like trying to reason with a rock. The night before I was supposed to return to work, he told me – no, he threatened me – that if anything happened to the children, it would all be my fault. Then he hit me again.

"We repeated the same cycle over and over. The good times between bad times kept shrinking. Soon there weren't any good times anymore, just times when I pretended life was good. He started hitting me every couple of weeks. He was careful to cover his tracks. He hit me in places where people wouldn't see the bruises. He always beat me at home, always at night, always out of sight. The bruises from one blow would just start to fade when he'd hit me again.

"I was careful to cover his tracks, too. No one understood why I wouldn't wear shorts in the summer, or why I always preferred long-sleeved shirts – even a turtleneck, one time, when he choked me and left thumbprint-shaped bruises. No one knew I had nightmares, or understood why I was always tired." She lifted her left hand and traced her right forefinger along the discolored, thickened line that ran along the edge of her palm up to the wrist. "One time he pushed me into the stove. My hand hit the burner, and Paul laughed and told me to be careful not to burn myself because it would hurt.

"I knew the marriage was broken, but I still thought I could fix it. I kept hoping that as the kids got older and he saw they were fine in day care, he'd stop criticizing me for working." She gave a slight, puzzled shake of her head and looked at the judge. His chair was turned toward Catherine, and he was listening intently, tapping the arm of his reading glasses against his lips.

"It must seem crazy to you," she told him. "Now, it seems crazy to me too. It was as if I saw myself reflected in one of those fun-house mirrors. Somehow *I* had become the horrible person he kept telling me I was. *He* really cared about the kids. *I* was the failure. I told him a thousand times that I was sorry, because it was all my fault." Catherine turned to confront Paul. "But now I know. I know that he'd started using the children as ammunition against me."

Danny ran his fingers through his hair. *Ammunition? Dad would do that?*

Catherine's lower lip began to tremble, and she blinked rapidly as she looked back at her notes. She hesitated, and then plunged ahead.

"November 20, 1996. Danny was in second grade. Jennifer was just three. I was late from work. I rushed through the door and asked him to fetch the children from the day care. He snapped. He screamed at me for being late. He swore and said there was no way he would get the kids. It was my responsibility. It was the price I had to pay for my idiotic, selfish decision to work. He started saying things. The violence of his language matched the violence of his blows." She couldn't control the tremor in her voice. Her eyes filled with tears.

The judge leaned forward. "Mrs. McMillan, would you like a short adjournment?"

She lifted her chin and wiped the back of her hand across her eyes.

"No thank you. I have to finish what I've started."

"Take your time, then. Take your time."

She smoothed the paper with the palm of her burnt hand. "He called me such horrible names, and then he stopped swearing. He looked at me like he never had before — with a murderous look in his eyes. What he said next scared me to the bone. I remember every word. '*If I can't count on you to take care of my kids, I might as well get rid of you. I ought to get my gun right now. You're a piece of shit.*'"

Catherine swallowed. "I tried to run away, but Paul caught me by the hair and pulled me back. I screamed when he pulled a patch of hair right off my scalp. He put his hands on my shoulders… spun me around…and spit in my face.

"We were in the living room. He shoved me backward onto the floor. I must have put out my hand behind me because it hit the coffee table. The table flipped over, and the glass bowl shattered. When I tried to get up I cut my palm on the broken glass, but I couldn't even push myself up because my wrist was broken.

"I thought he was going to start kicking me, so I used my feet to push myself along the carpet away from him. But he just left without saying another word. I waited a minute or two, because I was afraid he might come back. I sat with my hand in my lap because…because I didn't want to stain the carpet with blood. But I knew this time I had to call for help. The police came and took me to the hospital.

"The police laid charges, and the hospital social worker urged me to leave Paul. She talked to me for a long time. She offered to take the children and me to the women's shelter. She promised we'd be safe there, and I could take some time to clear my head. The doctor gave me some medicine that was supposed to calm me down, but there isn't a medicine in the world strong enough to dull the shame and humiliation of being beaten by your own husband. All I wanted was to get Danny and Jennifer and go home. By the time I walked out of the hospital, I'd made up the escalator story and called the day care. By the time I got there, I'd made up an excuse about Paul having to take an emergency business trip.

"By then, lying was what I did best. I lied to the children every day that Paul was in jail. I quit my job because I couldn't face my boss or my co-workers. My broken wrist was a convenient excuse – I couldn't write or type, I told my boss. But I didn't let my children know I'd quit. I just told them I'd go back to work when my wrist healed. I repeated the escalator story so many times that I started to believe it myself. It was easier than facing up to the truth of my hidden life."

Catherine looked at Danny. "Since December, 1996, I have raised my children on deceit.

"When their father came back from his 'business trip' he was the old Paul, the one I married. He was nice to us. I blindly hoped we could put the past behind us and move on. I stayed home with Jen and Danny until March. And then the cycle started again. Those 'changes' had just been a smoke screen for the violent man behind it. My new job got me out of the house, and those few hours of routine a day were all that kept me from succumbing to a life of endless beatings, threats, and intimidation.

"More and more, he terrorized me with guns. He started threatening to hurt other people – my parents, the children, even the dog. He said he'd kill them and bury them where no one would find their bodies. He said he'd been studying medical textbooks and he knew how to break my neck and make it look like an accident.

"For a long time, I've cried every day – in the shower, so no one would see, no one would hear, and no one would notice. I'm sorry it's come to this, but I now understand that it's not my fault. I could have told someone and left him sooner. But I was brainwashed and beaten, abused, and oppressed – caught in the trap of domestic violence."

Catherine stood tall. "But I'm not dead yet.

"Since Christmas, with the help of my family and friends, I have faced reality. I've started divorce proceedings. I'm ready to break free from my past. I want a new life for my children and me – one in which I will forget to be afraid.

"I know Paul will do everything in his power to stop me. If he's released, he'll try to make me reconcile with him. When I don't, I sincerely believe he will kill me. I know this truth. Paul has taken away my health, my job, my happiness, my self-esteem. Please don't let him take my life."

# Chapter 6

## Monday

Catherine clutched the wrinkled witness statement in her hand. When her eyes caught her son's, she managed a brave smile.

"Mrs. McMillan, thank you for your statement," the judge said. "Now, I'm sure Mr. Miller has some questions for you." Judge Cunningham lifted his pen. "Mr. Miller?"

"Thank you, Your Honor." He smiled sympathetically at Catherine. "Mrs. McMillan, any time you need a break, just say so.

"Ma'am, in your statement, you claimed your husband physically assaulted you many times throughout your marriage. Is that correct?"

"Well, not during the first couple of years, but since then, yes."

"Can you estimate how many times?"

"I didn't keep count."

"My apologies, I didn't mean to imply that you should have. I just would like an idea – dozens of times?"

"*Many* dozens of times."

"A hundred times?"

"More."

"Ma'am, other than the three criminal convictions, did you tell the police about any of the other incidents?"

"No."

"Did you tell friends?"

"No."

"Family?"

"No."

"Co-workers, neighbors?"

"No."

"Doctors, counselors, psychologists?"

"I might have told the marriage counselor, but that was a long time ago."

"Did you seek any medical treatment for any of these unreported assaults?"

"I couldn't very well do that and still keep them secret, could I?"

"I'm sorry Ma'am, I don't mean to offend. I just need to know what happened."

"I've told you what happened."

"Yes, well, thank you very much. Your Honor, those are all my questions."

Catherine blinked. "That's it?" she asked, looking around for help.

Judge Cunningham put down his pen. "Madam Prosecutor, anything arising?"

"No, sir," she replied.

"Very well." The judge turned to Catherine. "Thank you for your evidence today, Mrs. McMillan. You are excused."

Catherine didn't move. "May I add one more thing to my statement?" she asked the judge.

He looked at both lawyers, who nodded their agreement.

"Go ahead."

She took a deep breath. "Just because I didn't report the abuse, doesn't mean it didn't happen. Paul *wants* me to look like a liar, and I *was* one. His treachery and abuse turned me into a...a *champion* liar. But I'm *not* lying any more."

She looked at Paul. "What about me?" she asked, shaking the impact statement at Paul. "Do I still have to be his victim? Here he's done it again, hasn't he? He pleaded not guilty when he *knew* he was guilty."

Her arm swept across the courtroom. "This whole legal process he's put me through – for him, it's just a way to grind me down again."

She looked directly at the judge.

"And he's never going to stop."

# Chapter 7

## Monday

Danny and Catherine followed Sandra to the courthouse cafeteria. Sandra bought Danny a burger, but when it was time to return to the courtroom, Danny dropped his tray on the conveyor belt where his untouched food inched out of sight.

Judge Cunningham started the afternoon session precisely at 2 p.m. "On June 21st, 2002," he recited, "this Court found Paul Frederick McMillan guilty of aggravated assault and uttering threats against his wife. I've heard evidence for sentencing from both sides. Now I'll hear legal argument. Ms. Johnson?"

"Your Honor," the prosecutor said as she picked up a copy of the *Criminal Code of Canada*, which bristled with yellow stickies. "Today, you must apply the law to the evidence you've heard and formulate a just sentence for Mr. McMillan." She held both her hands out in front of her at waist height, palms up. "All of that evidence, taken together," she said, as she cupped her palms into a vessel, "brands him as a dangerous man – a *very* dangerous man." Stepping toward a podium, she grasped its sides and leaned forward. "He's been convicted three times for seriously injuring his wife. There is a pattern of escalating violence. So… what happens next?"

With measured slowness, Sandra turned until she faced Paul, who continued to sit politely and attentively, his face neutral. "We know what happens next. He's said so himself." A pregnant pause. "He's going to kill her. And he's going to do it with a gun."

⚖

Danny's heart sat like a stone in his chest. Grandma and Grandpa had arrived quickly on that long December night. One of the officers had tried to question Danny, but her words blurred together in Danny's head and he couldn't answer her. The officer stretched a towel over the bloodstain at the base of the stairs and said she'd come back in the morning. Eventually, all the others left, and the house fell silent.

Danny let Grandpa lead him up the stairs and tuck him into bed. Grandpa stroked his grandson's forehead. *Everything's going to be all right. We'll take care of you; don't worry.* After a while Danny's jaw relaxed and he noticed how much his teeth ached. Grandpa stayed with him until he dozed off.

But deep sleep wouldn't come. His father's voice rang in his head like an intruder. *I've got my gun. I've got it right here, under the bed. You know I've got my gun, don't you. Wanna see it? I'll shoot you right here. Right now.*

Buddy lay unmoving at the foot of Danny's bed, his head down, eyes open, on watchful guard. Danny pulled back the covers and slid out. "It's okay, Buddy," he whispered. He crept into the hallway, skirted around the spot where the lamp broke over his mother's head, and tiptoed into his parents' bedroom.

The moon shone through the open curtain and illuminated the carpet. He stepped beside the bed, dropped to his knees, and lifted the edge of the tasseled bedspread. A long, dark shape stretched underneath. The end caught a glint of moonlight as he reached for the object. When he grasped it, it felt familiar. He knew for certain what it was.

The summer after he'd turned ten, he and Dad had gone to fish the Elk River, just the two of them. The sky was brilliant with morning sunshine as the SUV bumped along beside a canola crop that bloomed the color of ripe lemons. They parked as near to the river as they could and fished all morning, catching six rainbow trout – enough for the whole family. Dad gutted the fish, and Danny slid them into a plastic bag and placed them gently into the cooler amid the ice packs and beer cans. Dad lifted the cooler into the back of the truck and reached under a blanket to lift out a narrow, brown, padded bag with two loose strap handles. Resting the bag on the bumper, Dad unzipped it and pulled out the rifle.

"Wanna give it a try? Think you can be a deadeye like your old man?"

Danny was thrilled. He scrambled down the rocky riverbank after his father. The rifle was already loaded. Dad clicked off the safety catch.

"You can just shoot along the water up into the embankment there, where the river turns." He placed the loaded gun in Danny's arms. "Stand in front of me, like this," Dad said, grasping Danny's shoulders and maneuvering him into position. He felt his father's athletic torso braced behind his own small frame.

"Hold the barrel in your left hand – here – underneath. Put the stock against your right shoulder. Move your right foot back and turn your toes out a bit. Use your right hand to grasp the bottom of the stock, and put your finger on the trigger."

The directions came fast and Danny struggled to hold the gun steady. It was heavier than he expected, and the barrel bobbed up and down as he pointed the rifle upriver.

"Now lift up the gun so you can look through the sight, and aim at the middle of the embankment. When you're ready, squeeze the trigger gently."

Danny closed his left eye and squinted down the swaying barrel with his right. He felt his father's arms under his own, his father's head lowered beside his. The acrid smell of gun oil filled his nostrils as he held his breath and pulled the trigger.

He didn't know which startled him more, the loud *crack!* that vibrated through his whole body, or the sudden assault of the gun butt on his shoulder that knocked him back into his father. Stones sprayed from the embankment as the bullet hit, and a flock of starlings lifted off from the trees behind them, squawking indignantly.

"Great shot, Danny." Dad sucker-punched him on the arm. "You're a natural."

In the moonlit bedroom, Danny had pulled the rifle the rest of the way from under the bed. He was kneeling. The rifle lay before him. Then he noticed a white tag, the sort usually used as a price tag, attached to the trigger by a short piece of string. He turned it over and stared.

It read, 'For Catherine.'

The prosecutor motioned toward Catherine, who sat straight-backed and rigid beside Danny. Her body was as taut as a stretched rubber band, and her mouth a tense line over clenched teeth.

"Sir," Sandra continued, "you've heard Mrs. McMillan speak of her fear, and no one can doubt it is real. Dr. Hamilton testi-fied that the most dangerous time is immediately right after the separation. And you've heard him describe Mr. McMillan as one of the most dangerous men he's ever met.

"What does experience tell us?" she asked. "It tells us that battering is the most common way North American women are injured every year. We know most murderers already have criminal records, including a violent offence. We know one-quarter of all murderers use guns.

"It is a continuing failure of our criminal justice system that Mrs. McMillan's situation isn't unique. But today this Court can right that injustice.

"Your Honor, our society owes it to Mrs. McMillan to protect her. Our society owes it to the people close to her – her family and her children – to protect *them* from harm. No one should have to endure the constant fear she will live with every day if her husband goes free. No victim of domestic violence should have to worry for the safety of her children at the hands of their own father.

"Sir, this Court must send a message. It must say, firmly and without hesitation, that all people who commit these crimes will be held strictly accountable. As a society, we cannot afford to be tolerant of domestic violence.

"This message must reach not just those who batter their spouses. It must reach those who abuse their children. It must reach those who abuse vulnerable elders. In short – it must send a signal to all, that our society will protect those who cannot protect themselves.

"Your Honor, I submit that the evidence supports – and justice *demands* – that Mr. McMillan be designated a dangerous offender and sent to jail for at least seven years. Anything short of a long prison term for Mr. McMillan will be a death sentence for his wife."

# Chapter 8

## Monday

Judge Cunningham removed his glasses. "Mr. Miller, may I hear from the defense?"

"Of course." Mr. Miller addressed the judge in a calm and reasonable tone. "Sir, no one doubts the heartache Mrs. McMillan's husband has caused her." He paused. "*However*, it is still the Court's duty to treat him fairly and according to law. And fairness means this Court must follow the rules." He picked up the *Criminal Code*. "And *this* is the rule book. These rules apply to *every* criminal proceeding – including this one. These rules of evidence, developed over the centuries, are the cornerstone of our justice system. Without them, our system of justice would disintegrate." He laid the *Criminal Code* on the table on top of the *Summary of Convictions*. "This is the heart of the matter," he said, cupping his hands as if holding a precious stone. "Even if it seems unfair, the rules say you must ignore everything in the victim impact statement *other* than about the three convictions. Nothing else is admissible." He softened his tone, as if expressing condolence for another's loss. "We're not challenging Mrs. McMillan's sincerity. However, saying those things doesn't prove they happened. Mr. McMillan is being sentenced for *this* crime, not for all his alleged crimes. His criminal record is relevant because the two other assaults were proven in a court of law – but nothing else.

"There are two important legal principles at stake. First, an accused person is entitled to a full trial on every alleged breach of the law. He must be permitted to hear the evidence and test it by cross-examination. Second, the judge must always hear both sides of a story. It can never be fair to make a decision when you've heard only one side. Today, you heard Mrs. McMillan's narrative of this sixteen-year marriage, but not Mr. McMillan's."

He paced a few steps back and forth. "Now what does that mean regarding the psychiatrist's conclusions? He said Mr. McMillan showed a strong pattern of violent behavior. To reach that conclusion, he relied on *all* the things Mrs. McMillan told him. But, when you strip away all the conclusions he based on the *unproven* assaults, his risk profile falls *far short* of showing a pattern of behavior severe enough to label Paul McMillan a dangerous offender.

"Mr. McMillan may be a bully, but that doesn't *prove* he'll assault his wife again. Now, I'm mindful that Dr. Hamilton has a very damning opinion about Mr. McMillan – his gut reaction, he called it. But courts don't run on gut reactions. They run on evidence.

"Also, it's *far too early* to say this man can never change. It's far too early to say society must lock him up and throw away the key. He's *not* an alcoholic or drug addict. Perhaps therapy can give him the tools he needs to control himself. We don't know, because it hasn't been tried.

"Your Honor, Mr. McMillan accepts that his marriage is over. He knows he has forever lost his wife's trust. However, they are the parents of two children, and nothing will ever change that. He wants to remain an active father and participate in raising his children, just as any father would. There isn't any admissible evidence that he's a threat to his children – not in the past, not at present, not in the future.

"Your Honor, the defense believes there should be a firearms prohibition, plus a jail term of two years. The rest belongs in the civil divorce court. Mr. McMillan doesn't oppose a long-term restraining order. The divorce court will also work out the delicate balance between Mrs. McMillan's right to be divorced and end all contact with her husband, and her *children's* right to know and have access to their father.

"In summary, you cannot today sentence Mr. McMillan for what he *might* have done in the past. You cannot sentence him for what someone fears he *might* do in the future. You can only sentence him for the case before you. If this Court gives him seven years, it will be punishing him as severely as murderers are punished. He has abused his wife, yes. But he is *not* a murderer.

"That is all, Your Honor."

# Chapter 9

## Monday

Judge Cunningham leaned back and tapped the side of his pen lightly against his lips. "Thank you, Mr. Miller. Any rebuttal by the Crown?"

"Yes, sir, several points. First, each assault took place in the victim's home. The assaults were a betrayal of everything a home should be – a place of peace, safety, security...a place of love. Mr. McMillan single-handedly changed this refuge into a place of private torment. Behind closed doors that were meant to keep the world *out* and give her a place to get away, he abused his wife. If a person can't be safe in her own home, where can she be safe? So the very private nature of these assaults is an *aggravating* factor in sentencing.

"Second, *none* of these assaults happened when Mr. McMillan was drunk or on drugs. Mr. Miller says this is a mitigating factor and suggests that Mr. McMillan is teachable. However, the prosecution believes it is an *aggravating* factor. His actions, if not planned, were certainly *deliberate*. Given the chance, he will soberly and deliberately assault his wife again.

"Now, the defense suggests Mrs. McMillan will be safe with a restraining order. But a restraining order isn't justice, Your Honor, it's a piece of paper." She picked up a page of the victim impact statement and held it by the top edge, dangling it in front of her. Then she turned toward Paul and positioned it between their faces. "And it won't stop a bullet.

"Third, yes, Mrs. McMillan has filed for divorce. Whether Mr. McMillan agrees or not, it's going to happen. Mr. Miller suggests the divorce and a firearms prohibition will put an end to her problems. We believe it will increase them. Statistics bear this out. The time in which a woman is most likely to die at the hands of an abusive spouse is in the months just after a separation or divorce. For Mrs. McMillan, that time is now. She needs more than just a piece of paper.

"Fourth, Mr. Miller says there's no evidence that Paul McMillan ever abused or threatened to harm his children. What about threatening to kill their mother? Can there be any clearer example of child abuse? How can we possibly consider him a caring and loving father?

"And finally, one last point that is very significant for Mrs. McMillan. She brought it up earlier. She feels that her husband's decision to plead not guilty and force her to testify, when there wasn't a shred of doubt that he assaulted and threatened her, is just another way to torment her, to abuse her again.

"The aim of putting Mr. McMillan in jail for a long time is not to punish him. It's to prevent future violence against his wife. It is done when there is no other way to protect a victim. And that is exactly the case here."

Sandra sat and the judge turned to the defense lawyer. "Final words, Mr. Miller?"

"Yes, sir. Very briefly. It is a basic principle of our criminal law that the prosecution must prove its case beyond a reasonable doubt. The accused needn't *prove* the prosecution is wrong. The accused need only raise a reasonable doubt. We've done just that, raised a reasonable doubt that the *only* way to protect Catherine McMillan is to lock up Paul McMillan for years and years.

"And finally, as frustrating as it may seem to Mrs. McMillan, every person has a *right* to a fair trial. It's not a question of inconveniencing or harassing a witness, or demanding some sort of unfair advantage. It's a right protected by our constitution and every moral principle we hold dear.

"And so, Your Honor, the prosecution's application must be dismissed."

"Thank you, Mr. Miller." The judge straightened his papers. "Before I adjourn to consider my verdict, is there anything more I need to hear?"

"Yes, Your Honor," said Mr. Miller. "If it pleases the Court, Mr. McMillan would like to say a few words."

"He may speak. However, as he's not under oath, and he's not subject to cross-examination," the judge looked at Paul over the top of his glasses, "he must be brief."

Paul stood. He looked straight at the judge. With a polite, calm and respectful voice, he said, "Sir, I wish to apologize to this court, to my wife, and to my family. I know what I did on December 8th was senseless and cruel." He faced Catherine, but she continued to stare straight ahead. Danny looked at his dad, then his mother, and back at his father again. *Should I be listening to my mother's truths, or seeking out my father's truths?* He was trapped between them. His father's words sounded far away, as if they were filtered through cotton.

"I've been in jail for eight months. I've had lots of time to think about my failings as a husband. I've also come to realize the effect my behavior has had on my family." Emotion crept into his voice, a slight quaver.

*Sincerity,* thought Danny. *Yes, he's telling the truth.*

"Catherine, I cannot say how it shames me to hear you say you are so afraid of me that you think I will kill you or hurt our children. I would *never* do such a thing." A long pause, a slight slump in the shoulders, guilt, resignation. "Although I don't want our marriage to be over, I accept that for you it is. I know it's too late to change your mind." He cleared his throat and looked down. Then he raised his head but kept his eyes downcast. "I'm sorry. I promise I'll never hurt you again."

The words settled like an embrace around Danny.

*Everything is going to be okay.*

The judge thanked everyone and called a twenty-minute recess, after which he would deliver his verdict.

# Chapter 10

## Monday

They waited in the lawyers' lounge. Sandra noticed Catherine's down-turned mouth and creased forehead. Danny sat rigid and silent beside her. Sandra leaned over and put her hand on Catherine's knee. "Don't worry, Catherine. Your part is done. You did a good job. It's up to the judge now."

They reentered the courtroom at five minutes to three. Danny and Catherine slid wordlessly onto the same bench. The familiar feel of cool, smooth wood was all that felt real in this sunless room where a stranger could take control of innocent people's lives.

At precisely 3 p.m., the court clerk confirmed that everyone was ready, and then instructed the guard, "Please bring in the prisoner."

In his mind, Danny set aside the word *prisoner* and watched his father enter. Then came the familiar ritual: all rise, stand up, sit down.

Danny heard the door open behind him. *Everyone is already here. Who could it be?* he wondered. He turned to see his soccer coach, Sgt. Sandhu. He was in full police uniform. "Hi Danny," he mouthed. Before Danny could wonder any more about it, the judge began reading from several typewritten pages.

"On June 21, 2002, this Court found Mr. McMillan guilty of aggravated assault and uttering threats against his wife. The Crown has asked that Mr. McMillan be sentenced as a dangerous offender. This is an unprecedented hearing.

"In deciding an appropriate sentence, the Court must remember the purpose of criminal law – to prevent harm to the people in our society. A crime is an act society will not tolerate. So, we punish the offender. This punishment is the signal – to the offender and everyone else – that each and every person will be held accountable for his criminal actions." He turned the page.

"Now, regarding Mr. McMillan, I must ask myself several questions. What punishment will stop him from assaulting his wife again? How long does he need to be in jail to protect the public from further harm? Is there anything the Court can do to encourage him to change his behavior?"

The judge looked at Sandra. "I've heard what the prosecutor thinks I should do." He turned to Mr. Miller. "I've heard what the defense thinks I should do." He turned to Paul, who looked calm and well-mannered in his neatly buttoned suit. "The two proposals are radically different. The defense says he should be prohibited from possessing any firearms or ammunition and be sentenced to a total term of two years. The prosecution says he should be behind bars for at least seven years.

"This is the challenge of sentencing. The prosecutor is right when she says society is entitled to protect itself from dangerous criminals and, more specifically, that Mrs. McMillan is entitled to protection from an abusive husband. It stands to reason that the longer he's in jail, the longer his wife and society will be protected. It's the only way to *guarantee* safety.

"However, Mr. Miller is also right when he says the punishment must fit the crime, and no more. He says a long jail term as a dangerous offender would be punishment greater than this crime deserves.

"Assault is a violent crime. But this isn't simply a case of ordinary assault, if there can be such a thing. When a person is victimized in her own home – behind closed doors and away from the scrutiny of society, by a person who is to be her companion through life – it is more than a crime. It is a betrayal of trust."

The judge addressed Paul. "Society calls it domestic violence or family violence, but it's really *criminal* violence that happens in a home. Mr. McMillan, you have battered and threatened your wife. You did this in a place where she had every right to be safe. You took advantage of her vulnerability and you betrayed her trust."

Paul hung his head.

"You targeted your wife," the judge continued. "Her victim impact statement was a cry of pain and fear, the pain of all the past hurts and the fear of all the future ones. Her world was shattered by your humiliation, intimidation, and violence. The solid ground she thought her marriage was built on became sand under her feet. Fear replaced love. Misery replaced happiness. Shame replaced confidence. I have no doubt your wife genuinely fears you will kill her if you do not stay in jail.

"And how did your crime affect others?" the judge asked. "Your lawyer says you were involved with your children, you supported them, and you enriched their lives by providing them with activities and vacations. Your lawyer suggests you always did your best for your children, that you were a good father.

"Mr. McMillan, I utterly reject that suggestion. It is disgusting to me. How can you possibly believe that beating your wife and threatening to kill her is consistent with good parenting? Suppose your wife's fall down the stairs had turned out differently. Suppose the blow to her head had killed her instead of knocking her unconscious. You would be here today being sentenced for murder, and you *would* be in jail for many, many years." The judge paused, his eyes narrowed, and his voice hardened. "Had that happened, Mr. McMillan, your children would be no better than orphans."

Paul looked up, and his eyes widened. Clearly, he hadn't expected this.

Danny froze. He had never imagined the past might have unfolded differently. He had never considered things could have gone even more wrong than they already had. *What the judge said is true – it is possible. Mom could have died and then Jen and I would be orphans. Alone.*

The judge was still talking. "…reckless, unconscionable, self-serving…" The words hung in the air. For a moment this new truth – *Mom could have died* – seemed more real than the ones Mr. Miller put forward, the ones Danny wanted to believe.

*But it didn't happen. You can't sentence Dad for something that didn't happen. Dad would never let that happen. He said he'd never do it again. Please don't take him away from me forever.*

Catherine straightened, and her hopeful face fastened on the judge.

"…grandparents, brothers and sisters, aunts and uncles," the judge continued. "The misery of domestic violence seeps through a family like a stain.

"I've heard Mr. McMillan's public apology. He s*eemed* to take responsibility for and regret his behavior. He said it would never happen again. But promises are easy to make and hard to keep. As Dr. Hamilton testified, being sorry but then going on to repeat the crime even more viciously is part of an abuser's usual pattern. Genuine remorse may be one step on the journey to reformation, but it is no guarantee he will ever reach that destination.

"In fact, nothing so far has propelled him to action. Putting him in jail after the second conviction didn't work. The counseling didn't work. So far, Mr. McMillan, not one of your actions has convinced me that you can or will take the initiative to change.

"What punishment suits this crime?" The judge pinched his nose and then replaced his glasses. "This is the most difficult sentencing decision of my career," he said. "In making this decision, I am mindful of the worrisome statistics about murder by family members. I am mindful of the lives that will be directly and indirectly affected by my decision. But justice demands that I not try to please anyone or take any side in a case. I must apply the law fairly and impartially, to the best of my ability.

"And the rules of evidence tip the scales in my decision. First, the Crown had no compelling evidence Mr. McMillan is *incapable* of change. Maybe an intensive course of therapy will enable him to make changes. We don't know because it hasn't been tried."

Judge Cunningham turned and addressed Catherine. "The second problem is with the victim impact statement. *If* I could take into account the many assaults and threats you told me about, then there would be enough evidence to prove your husband is a dangerous offender. As Mr. Miller said, courts operate by rules of evidence, not gut feelings. Those rules safeguard the rights of every accused person before the court. They ensure convictions for only those persons whose guilt is proved on proper evidence beyond a reasonable doubt.

"Ma'am, I know it's too late to prosecute your husband for all those other things he did to you, all the other crimes he may have committed against you. I understand you felt trapped and unable to tell the world what was going on, but your years of silence mean that your husband has never had the opportunity to refute your allegations in court.

"That means I must ignore everything you said except about the three convictions. And I find those three assaults aren't enough to prove that Mr. McMillan is a dangerous offender. That application is dismissed."

Judge Cunningham turned to the prisoner's box. "I will now pass sentence. Stand up, Mr. McMillan." Paul stood and adjusted his tie. His lawyer moved to stand beside him.

"Mr. McMillan, I sentence you to jail for thirty months. I will take into account the eight months you have already spent in custody, and I give you two months' credit for each month served. I also prohibit you from possessing a firearm for the next five years."

Judge Cunningham lifted off his glasses and placed them on the bench. Staring hard at Paul, he said, "Mr. McMillan, your conduct has been reprehensible. Make no mistake. If you come before this Court again, convicted of a similar offence, you may well spend the rest of your life behind bars."

Paul lowered his head and mumbled something Danny couldn't hear.

Mr. Miller bowed to the judge and said, "Thank you, sir."

Danny looked at his father, who stood without expression. His mother's head turned slowly toward the prisoner's box, as if gravity were dragging her eyes across the courtroom. Danny saw Dad's eyes lock with hers. A sneer pressed his lips into a thin line. In a second, his face was transformed – like an open hand into a fist.

# Chapter 11

## Monday

Catherine sped past her son and fled the courtroom. In the tight silence, all eyes turned to Danny. Sgt. Sandhu moved protectively beside him, a signal to the others to look away and busy themselves with adjustments to clothes and briefcases.

"Hi, Danny," he said. "I think your mom needs a bit of time alone just now. Why don't you come with me?" He tilted his head toward the door, touched Danny's shoulder, and steered him into the lobby.

"What're you doing here?" Danny asked his soccer coach.

"I've been helping your mom," he replied.

"With what? What's there to help with?" Sgt. Sandhu had been in the courtroom. He'd heard the sentence. *Sure, Mom is upset, but after all it was the right outcome, wasn't it? Even the judge said he was trying to be just and fair....*

"Sandra and I need to talk to you about your dad's sentence. She and your mom will be back in a minute."

Danny moved away and looked out the window. Beyond the tinted glass, the sun softened the pavement. A summer breeze blew across the faces of ordinary people going about their ordinary business on an ordinary day. His mom returned and stood beside him.

Sandra broke the silence. "The sentence was two and a half years – thirty months. The judge gave Paul sixteen months' credit for the time he's already spent in jail. Generally speaking, prisoners serve only a portion of their sentence in jail. Then they're released, under supervision, into the community. Paul's already served over half his sentence. That means he could be released...soon."

"How soon?" Catherine asked.

"Very soon. As soon as the paperwork's complete."

"Your best guess?"

Sandra stepped forward and put both hands on Catherine's shoulders. "One week."

Catherine threw her hands into the air. "I counted on the judicial system to protect us!"

"I know it seems like a failure to you, but –"

"But what?! Am I invisible? He's worked the system and he's won! Where's the justice in that?"

"Domestic violence is a complex problem, and our judicial system is too blunt a tool to fix it. I wish it were different...."

Catherine scoffed. "It's no tool at all. It's a pitiful little stick and Paul just snapped it in half. Now that I'm telling the truth, now that I finally get to tell *my* story, it's like it doesn't even matter. There's no justice for *me*." She looked at Danny. "No justice for *us*."

They all stood awkwardly as Catherine's anger turned into despair.

"Can't we appeal?" she asked.

"A trial judge gets to see the evidence and hear the witnesses firsthand. It isn't likely an appeal court would interfere with a trial judge's verdict."

Catherine's face hardened. "So that's it then. It's over. He's won."

"It's true that the legal part is over. But that doesn't mean he's won. It's time to take the next step." Sandra touched Catherine's elbow and led her to the elevators.

The police officer turned to Danny. "We need to talk some more," he said, "but right now, it's time to go with your mom to your grandparents' house."

Danny shrugged. "Whatever," he said.

Grandma and Grandpa owned a cozy white stucco house tucked into a U-shaped crescent. The garage driveway doubled as the front sidewalk. A pocket-sized wedge of tended grass blended seamlessly with the neighbors' lush yards. Grandpa had never much liked grass, but he cultivated the little patch of Kentucky Blue to keep peace in the neighborhood.

Catherine's green sedan pulled in the driveway. She and Danny hadn't talked on the way from the courthouse. She pretended she hadn't been crying, and he pretended he hadn't noticed.

Danny walked up the driveway. Grandma and Grandpa had been hovering around the front window, watching. The screen door swung wide even before he'd reached the steps. Grandma kept her salt-and-pepper hair cut straight and short. She wore her favorite gardening blouse, but today its pink water lilies looked wrong below her pinched face. Worry lines spread from the corners of her hazel eyes.

"Hello, Danny-boy. Catherine. Come in," she said, her bright voice not fooling anyone. Grandpa stood behind her. Danny slumped under awkward hugs from both of them. His mother began to sob. The tears she'd spared him in the car now flowed freely.

Grandpa's gentle touch directed him toward the back door. "There's somebody outside waiting to see you," he said.

Danny retreated. The moment his hand touched the door handle, Buddy streaked over, his white-tipped tail waving as he squirmed his nose into the crack to hurry the door open. Danny crouched and gathered the dog into his arms. Buddy's head ploughed into Danny's chest and his muzzle lifted to lick the boy's face.

"Hey, Bud, hey Buddy, hiya Buddy, how ya bin," Danny crooned. His fingers dug into Buddy's fur and soaked up the dog's love.

Buddy pulled away and dashed back to the birch tree. He retrieved his Frisbee and dropped it in front of the boy. Buddy backed up two steps and tucked his nose to the ground between his white forepaws. His haunches were raised and his tail flew back and forth in an invitation to play.

Danny heard Grandpa's voice behind him. "Why don't you take Buddy to the park for a while?"

"Okay, sure," he mumbled.

"Do you want to get rid of those clothes and change into shorts?"

Danny shuddered at the thought of reentering the house. He'd already seen his mother cry a lifetime of tears. "Nah," he said, not trusting himself to say more.

"Okay. Take some time. If you're back in 'bout half an hour or so, supper should be ready."

Danny nodded, picked up the Frisbee, and followed Buddy to the back gate.

A wide park ringed the elementary school his mother had attended. A sand-filled rectangle was crammed with kids swinging from monkey bars and darting through a jungle gym. He could already hear the children playing with summer holiday intensity.

Fields and baseball diamonds stretched behind the school. A boys' soccer team was sharpening their ball-handling skills. Two young women called out names and instructions as players snaked through rows of orange pylons on the newly-mown grass.

Buddy tore into the field, crouched low, and then rocketed after the Frisbee. Danny watched him, but his eyes strayed to the soccer players. Their sweat-stained T-shirts were tucked into black shorts. Danny still wore his dress pants and white shirt. He felt like an idiot. He turned his back, picked up the slobbery Frisbee, and flung it in the opposite direction. It glided through the air, slicing a long, thin line between earth and sky, only to be snatched from its course by the border collie's flashing teeth. Danny threw the Frisbee over and over until Buddy's pink tongue dangled limply over the side of his mouth and his chest heaved. "Hey, Bud, let's go get you a drink," he said finally, scooping up the Frisbee. He left without another glance at the team.

On the walk back, Buddy stayed at the boy's side. Danny felt a little more at ease. There were still adjustments to make, yes, but surely the worst was over.

Buddy pushed past Danny and barked at his empty water dish. "No water, Bud?" Danny said. "Just a minute, I'll get you some."

The tap protruded from the stucco wall between the back door and the kitchen window. The window was open, and the smell of Grandma's herbed roast beef wafted into the backyard. He *loved* this dinner: potatoes mashed with extra cream, carrots glazed in sweet butter, new peas fresh from the farmer's market, and puffy Yorkshire puddings in country gravy. His mouth watered. He could hear his mom and Grandma talking. The words made him pause.

"We're going to have to move," Mom said.

"When?" asked Grandma.

"They said it'd have to be soon. Before he's out."

*Move? Why did they have to move? And who were "they"?*

Danny turned on the tap. The voices stopped. They couldn't know how long he'd been listening or what he'd heard. He grasped the hose and filled Buddy's dish. The dog lapped eagerly, before stretching full-length under the weeping birch. Unwilling to return to the tap, Danny threw the hose into the rose bushes and let it run. He sat in the shade beside Buddy and scratched his ears until the dog's eyes closed and his tail came to rest.

The thought of having to move had never occurred to Danny. He'd lived his whole life in the same house. He knew every corner by heart. He'd always had his own room crammed with everything he needed: toys, creased comic books, board games in boxes with split corners, his baseball and catcher's mitt, swimming goggles, the science kits from his grandparents, the familiar wallpaper with hockey stars, soccer players, and his own blue ribbons and gold medals. His room was his space. It was as comfortable as his own skin.

Anger and resentment started growing. He squinted. There was no way he'd move. No one could make him.

Grandpa appeared at the screen door. "Time for supper," he said, and disappeared back into the house.

Danny didn't move. He set his teeth and continued stroking the sleeping dog.

A few minutes later, Grandpa reappeared. He hesitated and then came out to stand beside him. He looked at the boy but Danny refused to look up. Grandpa stood silently a moment and then said kindly, "You've got to be hungry. Come on inside and get something to eat."

Danny followed, but at the last second he veered away from the dining room. He went downstairs to where he and his sister kept some extra clothes. He shed his good clothes and pulled on shorts and a favorite T-shirt.

The others were already seated at the dining room table. Danny slouched into his empty chair. Grandma and Grandpa started some idle chitchat about weeds and the weather, and whether they should water the grass that night. Dishes were passed around the table, and Danny's sullenness gradually dissolved into a full stomach. By the time Grandma served apple pie with vanilla ice cream, he was able to look up and take note of the others. The adults had kept up the fiction of an ordinary family dinner, but no one would look Danny in the eye. Like him, Jennifer remained quiet. *Take a picture and put it in the family album*, Danny thought. *A picture is worth a thousand words.*

Grandpa started clearing the table. Grandma turned to Jennifer and said, "Why don't you go downstairs and pack up your things to go home. You probably want to sleep in your own bed tonight. You too, Danny. There are some clothes down there you should take with you."

Danny had never been particularly close to his sister. There were pictures in the photo albums showing them playing together when Jennifer was young, and of course the whole family on vacations, but once he started kindergarten neither of them had had much time for the other. Jennifer was what he and his friends called a girly-girl – she seemed happy to play with dolls in front of a TV tuned to her favorite shows. She said she wanted to play on soccer and baseball teams, but she never joined. She stuck to Mom. He spent more time with Dad. Their lives didn't often intersect.

Jen sat on the far side of the bed and started twirling her hair around and around her index finger. Danny knew her nervous habit. He had no idea where to start or what to say.

"So. What happened?" she asked.

"Didn't they tell you?"

"I heard Mom crying, so I stayed in the TV room."

Her answer didn't much surprise him. She was good at avoiding unpleasant things – like Dad losing his temper at her or Mom.

"They say Dad'll be out of jail next week."

She paused. "Is that a good thing or a bad thing?"

"I don't know," he shrugged. "I guess it depends."

There was a long silence as they both considered what it might mean for each of them.

"Soooo…are they still getting divorced?"

"Yeah."

"So they'll be divorced and I won't have to live with Dad? Maybe I won't have to see him much."

He stared at his sister. *No*, he thought, *they'll be divorced but I'll still get to see lots of Dad.* "We're going to have to move," he said.

She started. "I don't want to move," she replied.

"Neither do I," he said. "Neither do I."

# Chapter 12

## Monday

His mom gripped the steering wheel tightly. Danny heard her take a steadying breath as she drove away from Grandma and Grandpa's. He rolled down his window and gestured at Jennifer to do the same. Cool evening air swept through the car, and Buddy jumped from side to side, sticking his head out the windows, black ears flapping and nose twitching. Danny pretended to scold him. Busying himself with the dog meant he didn't have to look at his mom.

Although it was almost 8:30, the sun still promised two hours of light when Mom pulled into the garage. She parked beside Dad's black SUV. She'd driven it only a couple of times since Dad went to jail, mainly in the winter when the roads were bad with snow and ice. It still had Danny's hockey gear in it. A couple of times she'd asked him to put it away, but he hadn't. Mom stopped asking. When Dad's secretary had called about the insurance renewal on the SUV, his mother had let it lapse and removed the license plates.

Danny glanced at his equipment. He guessed Dad would keep the SUV and Mom would get the car. And he'd be using his hockey gear again by Christmas.

Mom punched in the security code and opened the door. He and Jennifer dropped their overnight bags in the laundry room, while Mom retreated to the kitchen to make coffee. The red light on the answering machine blinked for attention. She deleted the message without listening to it and dropped onto a kitchen chair.

The kids hurried to their rooms and shut their doors. Danny fell onto his bed and rubbed his eyes until brilliant starbursts shot across his eyelids. Eventually, the heaviness of sleep slowed his heart.

The sun crept westward and the sky eased from crimson to orange. The heatless rays roused him from his fitful sleep. He realized it was bedtime. He tugged his boxers from under the pillow and stood to change. Before shutting the curtain, he opened the sliding window and gazed down.

Wood smoke drifted by and curled in the air. There was Mom, bending over the stone fire pit, fanning the young flames with a rolled newspaper. He'd helped his dad build the fire pit a couple of summers ago and Danny loved it. It was a great way to dodge Mom's rule against playing with matches, and he couldn't believe his luck when Dad once let him use up a whole box to light a single fire. Two years ago, after a winning game, Dad had invited the entire soccer team to roast wieners and marshmallows. After the team had left, the two of them sat staring at the smoldering coals, but by morning it was as if the fire had never existed.

Danny surveyed his room. Although it was just as he'd left it this morning, it seemed different, like an echo of the real thing. He gazed around the room at all the framed photos hanging on his walls. There he was two summers ago, his arms sagging under a huge pink-striped rainbow trout. There was a snapshot of the whole family riding the Horseshoe Bay ferry. They squinted into the sun, and their hair streamed behind them like sails in the wind. Danny opened the top dresser drawer and brushed his fingers across the picture of his soccer team posing with their gold medals, the year Dad had coached them to victory. There was Dad, wearing the red golf shirt the team had bought, with the word *Coach* embroidered above the breast pocket. Danny had put away the picture when his dad went to jail, but sometimes at night, he pulled it out and wished he could be back on the winning team.

There was a ton of stuff in his room. Each object was a piece of his past. He thought more about moving. He realized a lot of it could be picked up and taken with him – memories intact. He'd sweep everything into a big box and move it all to his new house. He'd miss this bedroom, this house, but he could see it was too big for the three of them. He knew, when money had to stretch to cover two households, divorced families often moved to smaller homes. Smaller places were less work, too, and he wouldn't mind not having to cut the lawn or trim lilacs anymore.

Mom had said they'd have to move soon, before Dad got out. Probably she'd make sure they wouldn't have to move too far, so he and Jen could still go to the same schools and have the same friends. They'd have time to settle into the new place before school started. He felt his shoulders relax. Even though his friends had carried on their lives without him, maybe when Dad got out and things were normal again, he'd be able to build some bridges. He'd faked indifference, but he missed his friends.

A sound from outside distracted him – a periodic *fha* – like something heavy but soft landing on the patio. He looked out. A narrow balcony overlooked the yard from his parents' bedroom, and Mom seemed to be throwing something from the balcony onto the patio. Buddy sniffed around the stuffed, black garbage bags. *Mom's probably getting rid of some things she doesn't want to take with her when we move. But I'm not going to throw anything out*, he thought. *This stuff is me. I'm taking it all.*

Buddy barked. His mom had placed a full bottle of red wine and a tall-stemmed wine glass on the patio table. The lively bonfire crackled as the yellow-orange flames licked over the top of the stones and Venus made its first appearance low in the darkening sky. Mom was dragging those bulging garbage bags toward the fire pit, lining them up beside her chair. Buddy stalked the bags, giving them an occasional bark, as if to force them to open and spill their secrets.

Danny watched his mother drag the last bags over. Then she sat and poured herself a glass of wine, took a long drink, grasped the first bag, and opened it. She pulled out something shapeless and dark and threw it on the fire.

It took Danny a moment to figure out what his mom was throwing on the fire.

Dad's clothes!

One by one she pulled out jackets, pants, shirts, socks, ties, even shoes, and threw them on. The smoke darkened to a greasy black and billowed upwards. Crimson flames whipped up inside boiling clouds that swirled higher and higher, obscuring the night sky. Acrid smoke seeped into his room, filling his nose and mouth with bitterness.

She didn't stop until they were all gone.

# Chapter 13
## Tuesday

The ringing phone edged Danny awake. The answering machine kicked in, and a flat, mechanical voice recited the standard instructions to leave a message after the tone.

Before the assault, it had been Dad's voice on the machine.

A man, maybe Grandpa, left an unintelligible message. The machine shut off. Except for Buddy whiffing and snuffling at the foot of his bed, the house was quiet. Where was Mom? Danny wondered. Then he remembered last night.

He got out of bed and walked to her bedroom. The door was ajar, so he pushed it open.

The air smelled of smoke, but as he walked closer to the bed, the smell soured, and was more like rotten fruit. A wine bottle lay tipped on its side, a red stain on the carpet at its mouth. Danny's mother was sprawled on top of the covers, passed out.

Dead drunk.

He backed out of the bedroom and retreated to the kitchen.

The phone rang again. Then the mechanical voice: *Leave-a-message-after-the-tone*. "Catherine? Are you there?" It was Grandpa. "Pick up if you're there." He paused. "Well, call me back when you get this —"

Danny lifted the receiver.

"Catherine?"

"It's me."

"Good morning, Danny-boy," Grandpa replied, the cheerful greeting sounding as artificial as the answering machine. "Where's your mother?"

"In her room."

"Can I talk to her?"

"She's asleep."

"Still asleep?"

"Yeah. Asleep. Drunk. Hung over. Whatever."

"Oh.... Well, why don't we come and pick up the two of you?"

"Whatever."

"Okay. Is Jennifer up yet?"

"No."

"Then give her a nudge. We'll be there right away."

Danny hung up without saying good-bye. He stomped up the stairs and made a point of calling loudly to Buddy. He paused in front of his mother's bedroom but couldn't hear anything inside. He elbowed open Jennifer's door. Her blind was pulled down tightly against the morning sun. "Jen...get up," he said roughly.

She groaned.

"Buddy, wake her up," he instructed. He turned away, knowing the dog would obey, and he returned to his own dark room. Rather than open the curtain and risk seeing the fire pit, Danny switched on the overhead light, stuck a CD into his player, and turned up the volume as high as it would go. The music blasted while he tossed his drawers to find the right T-shirt and shorts. He went into the bathroom to wash up.

He made the mistake of looking in the mirror. Puffy eyelids, dull eyes, and hair flattened on one side, standing up like a feather in the back. He knew he needed a shower, but instead he just dragged a dry comb a couple of times across his scalp. *I feel like crap and I might as well look like crap.*

Jennifer appeared and Danny stretched his leg to kick the door shut.

"Wait," she said. "Where's Mom?"

He pointed at her bedroom.

"Still asleep?" Jen asked, cocking her head slightly.

"Drunk," he said, as he shut the door in his sister's face.

He left the bathroom and stood in his sister's doorway. She sat slumped on the bed, staring at the carpet, her left hand twiddling, twiddling, twiddling a strand of hair.

"Grandpa's gonna pick us up soon," he said with a quick smile, trying to make up for his previous gruffness.

"Oh," she replied.

When Grandpa hurried in, Grandma was right behind him. She hesitated when she approached Danny, but continued straight to Catherine's room.

Grandpa sat on the couch across from Danny, jingling the car keys from hand to hand. "Where's Jen?" he asked.

Danny shrugged, refusing to meet his grandfather's eyes.

"You get Buddy into the car. I'll fetch her."

Danny tugged on his runners without unlacing them. Buddy raced to the back door and returned with the orange Frisbee dangling from his mouth, his tail flying back and forth – happy, happy, happy.

Danny sat in back with Buddy, and Jennifer buckled herself in beside Grandpa. No one said anything about Grandma staying behind. No one listened to the radio newscast. Their silence filled the car.

As soon as they reached the house, Jennifer vanished into the TV room.

"Why don't you take Buddy out back?" asked Grandpa. "I'll join you in a minute."

Danny sat on the weathered park bench under the weeping birch. Buddy stretched out underneath in the shade.

As a geology teacher, Grandpa had always joked that his job was to fill their lives with rocks. Every July he traveled to all kinds of places to study and collect rocks and gems. But he stayed home in August, and Danny would visit as often as he could. Grandpa would show him pictures from his trips and teach him how to identify and classify rocks. His collection filled drawers and spilled into the backyard. He had a story for each rock and although Danny had heard them all, he never tired of hearing them again.

Danny's legs dangled from the brand new cedar bench. "Come on, Grandpa," he said, pointing to a pumpkin-sized rock. "Tell me about this one."

"Well now, that's a beaut. That's British Columbia jade." His words were always unhurried and even, whether he was teaching high-school students or his young grandson. He was never impatient, even when he'd answered the same question a thousand times.

"We picked that up on our way to the Arctic Circle. I think your mom had just finished Grade 1 when we found it. This beauty still shines as brightly as it did when your mom and I dragged it up the hill and into the truck all those years ago." He leaned over and stroked the rock. "Just look at the way the jade catches the sunlight. They used to say rubbing jade across your body would cure stomach problems."

He tugged on Grandpa's hand, leading him toward another rock. "What about this one, Grandpa?"

As always, Grandpa responded with enthusiasm. "Oh, now this one is special. It's both a rock and a tree. Millions of years ago it grew in a different kind of forest. The trees were twice as tall as they are now. It was hot and humid – a tropical rainforest. There were streams and swamps full of fish and reptiles and even clams. When trees fell, they were swept downstream and some ended up lodged in the mud. In time, the trees were covered with layers and layers of mud and sediment."

Danny stayed close to Grandpa and listened.

"Over many, many years, chemicals seeped into this tree trunk and a chemical reaction turned the wood into quartz crystals. As those crystals grew, the wood turned into stone. We call it petrified wood. It's fascinating, Danny-boy. Because it's a rock that used to be a tree, it lets us look into the past and see what a place was like millions of years ago. Anyway, your mother and I dug up this stump up and hauled it home. We placed it here and planted a young birch tree beside it – the present beside the past."

The cedar bench had grayed and the birch had grown up and out, but the petrified wood at its base remained unchanged. Danny and Grandpa sat quietly, each with his own memories. Then, as if he'd grown impatient with the two of them, Buddy ambled over, lifted his leg, and peed on the petrified stump.

Grandpa had to chuckle. "It's all the same to Buddy. A tree is a tree, whether it's millions of years old or not. It still has its uses." He smiled and leaned forward, elbows on his knees, eyes straight ahead, his hands fiddling with something. Out of the corner of his eye, Danny could see it was one of his stones.

He passed the rock to Danny. It was about the size and shape of a plum cut in half. Its white surface was worn smooth and the depression invited Danny's thumb to rub across it, back and forth, back and forth. His voice as steady and even as always, Grandpa said, "Mother Nature seems to have created these with us in mind. They're called worry stones. They fit beautifully between your fingers and your thumb. The ancient Greeks believed rubbing them would lessen tension and anxiety and bring a person peace. I think it works. They feel good in your hand and they can help you forget your troubles for a while."

Grandpa sighed. "Your mother's having a hard time right now."

Danny said nothing. *Rub, rub. Rub, rub.*

"She's doing the best she can."

*Rub, rub. Rub, rub.*

"She really loves you and Jen."

Nothing from Danny.

"She has to do what she thinks is right."

"Right?" exclaimed Danny, startling the dog. He turned

toward Grandpa, narrowing his eyes. "What do you mean, right?" he challenged. "What's *right* about getting drunk? How can it be *right* to burn my father's clothes?"

It was Grandpa's turn to be silent.

Danny shoved himself off the bench and threw the stone into the thorn bushes. He stalked through the back gate, oblivious to his dog who followed closely.

# Chapter 14

## Tuesday

After half an hour of aimless walking, Danny found himself back at his mother's old school. Wide gray-flecked granite steps led to the front doors. He sat and Buddy rested his muzzle across Danny's feet. Danny squinted into the indifferent sun and wished for his New York Yankees ball cap. A headache had smoldered to life behind his eyes.

A police cruiser pulled to a stop in front of the school. Since the last assault, Buddy had been wary of police cars if they came near. The dog rose, nose twitching, all senses on alert. Danny reached over to stroke Buddy's head without taking his eyes off the figure getting out of the car.

It was Sgt. Sandhu. He wore his summer uniform. The black leather belt at his waist held a baton, a radio, and a holstered gun. He stopped beside the open cruiser door to put on his cap, hesitated, and then threw the cap back.

Buddy relaxed and his tail started to wag as the police officer came near.

Danny said nothing as Sgt. Sandhu reached over to tousle Buddy's ears.

"Hi Buddy. How are ya', boy?" The officer sat beside Danny. "Hi. Your grandpa said you might be here."

Danny refused to meet the officer's eyes.

"We need to have that talk," Sgt. Sandhu said quietly.

"About what?" Danny replied, sounding surlier than he had intended.

"Some stuff about your family."

He snorted. "Family? What family? My dad's in jail and my mom's drunk. *That's* my family." The bitter words brought a sudden sting to his eyes.

"Try not to be too hard on her, Danny. She's having –"

"*Having a hard time?*" He looked squarely at the police officer. "Everyone's telling me that *she's* having a hard time! Well, what about me? Who cares about what *I* think? Last night she burned all Dad's clothes!"

"I know. She told me," Sgt. Sandhu replied, in the same even tone.

"She *told* you?"

Danny paused and grappled with this new information. It meant...Sgt. Sandhu had already spoken to his mom *and* his grandparents. He'd come, on duty and in uniform, to find him. He knew about the burning and still defended Mom...

"I know this is hard on you, too," he told the boy. "And on your sister." He paused, then wet his lips and looked away. "In fact, it's not easy for anybody."

Danny no longer had any idea what the facts, in fact, were. Now more confused than angry, he ground his palms into his eyes until little white fireworks exploded in the dark.

"It looks like you're hurting. First, let's go get you something for that headache," Sgt. Sandhu said, heading for his cruiser. "Then we've got some people to see."

It was a short drive back. "I'll take Buddy while you get a couple of aspirins, okay?" said Sgt. Sandhu. He took the dog around back as Danny shuffled up the steps. The screen door window was open, and his grandparents were in the living room, speaking in low tones. To ensure they knew he was there, he clumped to the basement bedroom in his shoes. His baseball cap hung in its usual place. He slipped it on, the smell of dust and sweat as familiar as the easy fit of the cap. He lingered and then went to the bathroom medicine cabinet for some aspirin. He shut the cabinet and looked away from his reflection in the mirror. He pulled his cap down over his forehead. The bill's shadow smudged his blue eyes.

Grandma and Grandpa had moved to the backyard where they were talking to Sgt. Sandhu. Danny hesitated, uncertain whether to join them or slip out the front. But Sgt. Sandhu noticed him and waved him over. Danny jabbed his hands into his pockets and shouldered open the screen door. Grandma and Grandpa looked at him, and turned quickly away, but not before he noticed that even Grandpa had been crying.

Twenty minutes later, the police car pulled up in front of a nondescript downtown office tower. Sgt. Sandhu parked directly in front of the revolving doors under the *No Parking* sign. Danny could see passersby peering suspiciously at him through the tinted glass. He glared back.

The doors opened into a typical office lobby. A uniformed

security guard, the kind Danny called a rent-a-cop, nodded at Sgt. Sandhu.

The elevator opened on the sixth floor and Danny followed Sgt. Sandhu to a heavy wooden door with an intercom beside it. They were buzzed into a furnished waiting area. Sgt. Sandhu motioned toward a chair. "Have a seat."

They were alone in a windowless room. The far wall held another door, except it was metal. Beside it was a full-length mirror. Danny knew from watching movies that it was a two-way mirror. A camera hung from its corner.

The inner door opened and one of the biggest men Danny had ever seen filled the doorway. The man shook Sgt. Sandhu's hand.

"Nice to see you, Rajiv."

Sgt. Sandhu gestured toward Danny. "This is Danny McMillan."

"Hello Danny," the stranger said. "I'm Phil." Danny replied with a grunt and didn't rise from his chair.

"Please come in, Danny. Your mom's already here." Phil turned and led the way.

Danny heard voices coming from a nearby office – his mother's and another woman's. "I can't believe I got that drunk," his mom said.

"Don't be too hard on yourself," the woman replied. "It's been a bad time. It could have happened to anybody."

"But Danny and Jen *saw* me like that; they're going to think they can't trust me to take care of them."

"It was just an error in judgment."

"I know that, but –"

Phil noticed Danny listening and hustled him into another office. He turned toward Danny. His muscular arms bulged from his golf shirt. He had a bristly buzz cut and a long, thin scar stretching from the side of his nose right across his cheek. He looked like a marine or a heavyweight boxer. Who *was* he?

"Danny, let me tell you a little bit about why you're here, and then you can ask questions, okay?" Phil said, taking a seat behind a desk.

Danny shrugged and dropped into a chair, trying to look unconcerned, even though his head throbbed. He pushed up the bill of his baseball cap and looked straight at Phil, then crossed his arms. Sgt. Sandhu took the chair beside him.

Framed diplomas hung behind the desk – a Bachelor of Criminology from McGill University, a Twenty Year Service Award from the Royal Canadian Mounted Police.

"I used to be an RCMP officer," Phil said. "I worked for twenty years in and around Montreal. I was involved mainly with fighting organized crime – biker gangs. They owned the drug, prostitution, and illegal gambling operations in Quebec. Sometimes, we'd get inside information from an informant who'd help us. These gangs were bad – powerful, violent, and cruel. If they found out who ratted on them, that person and his family were as good as dead."

Danny kept his arms crossed, but Phil had his attention.

"Sometimes…sometimes people need more protection than the normal justice system can give. We offered the informants witness protection. We'd hide them in safe houses 'till they'd testified in court, and then…well, then we'd give them new identities and relocate them."

The word *relocate* echoed in Danny's head – *we're going to have to move.*

"I worked with a psychologist – Dr. Sung – in the Witness

Protection Program. We'd help these people and their families start new lives."

"So what's all that got to do with me?"

"A couple of years ago we had a case where the informer was a hit man for one of the biker gangs – and he regularly beat his wife. Badly. Dr. Sung and I had two problems. We had to protect him and his family from the biker gang, *and* we had to protect her from her husband." Phil paused. "First we gave them all new identities and relocated the whole family. Then we gave the wife and children a second set of new identities, and moved them, so the husband couldn't find them.

"This made Dr. Sung and I realize that sometimes when things are really bad at home, the regular system can't fix the problems. So, when I retired from the RCMP, Dr. Sung and I moved here to start a program called NIVA – New Identities for Victims of Abuse." Phil clasped his hands and leaned forward. "There's no easy way to say this, so I'll just say it. In the next few days, your whole life is going to change. It's going to be a bigger change than you ever dreamed of – and you're not going to like it."

Danny uncrossed his arms. "My father's no mobster, he's not a – not some sort of *psycho* who's going to kill Mom," he replied through thin lips. "Even that doctor said so."

"Danny," Phil continued, "we rely on the police to tell us when there's a situation – a threat – that goes beyond the usual legal means for protecting the victim. These are the cases where divorces and restraining orders and short jail terms won't do the job."

Sgt. Sandhu leaned toward Danny. "I'm the one who referred your case here."

"*What?*" said Danny, his eyes going wide. He stabbed his index finger at the police officer. "You? I thought you were trying to *help* me! And now you're saying my dad's a criminal and we have to run away?"

"He *is* a criminal," Sgt. Sandhu said. "And you're not running away. You're saving your mother's life…and Jennifer's…and maybe your own."

"*No way.*"

The police officer kept his eyes locked on the thirteen-year-old boy. "You're going to have to move," he said.

# Chapter 15

## Tuesday

The broad river split the city in two. Danny dropped onto a vacant bench overlooking the steep-sided valley. His head throbbed, and he felt like he was going to throw up. He hung his head and massaged his temples. His thoughts were puzzle pieces that would never fit together again. *What had happened to his parents? What had happened to his family? What was going to happen to his life?*

Gradually he became aware of his surroundings. Rollerbladers swept past. Joggers puffed their way up the hill. He heard the clip of high heels approaching then receding, and smelled the faint scent of roses. A mother was reading nursery rhymes: *Humpty Dumpty sat on a wall...*

He breathed through his open mouth and pressed his back into the bench. The warm wood felt good. He stretched both arms out along the top, tilted his head back, and allowed the sun to loosen his face. Little by little, the knot in his stomach was replaced by the twist of hunger. He had no money. And no house key. Not that it made any difference. Apparently he didn't have a home, either.

But where do you go when you can't go home? Where do you go when you don't *have* a home? He knew some kids slept away their summers in the river valley under bridges, or in little nests they built out of branches and discarded cardboard. But he wanted to punish everybody else, not himself.

Stay with friends? He didn't have friends anymore. And he didn't have bus fare to get to his neighborhood, and even if he did, they'd be looking for him there.

*Where do you go when you can't go home?* The phrase sounded familiar. Then he remembered the black-and-white poster outside the school counselor's office: a girl, sitting on concrete steps, head down, hands hiding her face. *Where do you go when you can't go home? The Youth Emergency Shelter. Y.E.S.*

Yes, that's where he'd go. It was somewhere on Whitney Avenue. He'd passed the sign a hundred times, but hadn't paid attention. He'd have to go down into the valley, cross the river, and head up the ravine on the other side. It would take him a while, but there were lots of bike and footpaths and he should be able to make it in about an hour. It was a good plan, he decided, and it would keep him out of sight in case they'd started looking for him.

At first, the trails were busy with carefree couples strolling arm-in-arm and mothers pushing strollers. But now he was more and more alone, and between trees he began to see the small fires set by the homeless to keep them warm at night.

He picked up his pace to get out of the darkening valley. Mosquitoes had already descended by the time he reached the valley ridge.

Danny checked his bearings and crossed the bridge. There it

was, on the other side. Most of the shelter's narrow windows had their red-and-white checked curtains closed against the horizontal rays of sunset.

The door was unlocked. He hesitated and then pushed it open. A heavy, middle-aged woman sat typing at a computer behind a counter. She glanced over and Danny saw the plastic name tag pinned to her shirt: VOLUNTEER – Grace.

"Need a room for tonight?"

He nodded.

"You're in luck," she said. "There's one vacant. Follow me."

A set of keys clinked at her hip. She led him up a narrow staircase and scooped up some linen from a wheeled rack: two white sheets, one checked pillowcase, and a thin, graying towel.

The door to room 107 was slightly ajar. She pushed it open and dropped the bedding on the foot of the cot's plastic-wrapped mattress. "Blankets are in there," she said, pointing to a narrow closet, "along with a toothbrush and toothpaste. Bathroom's at the end of the hall, soap and shampoo in each shower stall."

Grace took a key off the ring and handed it to Danny. "There's a fridge on the main floor with sandwiches and drinks. Help yourself. Breakfast is downstairs at eight." Danny moved aside to let her pass. She turned around. "We like to keep a record of the people who stay here," she said. "What's your name?"

Danny looked her straight in the eye. He snorted. "I don't have a name."

She paused. "Okay," she said. "Have a good sleep." She turned around and closed the door softly behind her.

Back at her desk, she picked up the phone and dialed. "He's here," she whispered.

↙

The orange display on Danny's sport watch lit up his tired face each time he squinted at the time – 11:31, 1:10, 1:46, 3:37. He punched and flipped the chunky piece of yellowed foam inside the pillowcase and flipped it over. The blanket was scratchy. The plastic cot cover crackled each time he rolled over. The old building creaked and groaned. The hot room smelled of dirty socks, but when he opened the window, the traffic noise kept him awake.

Fragments of the psychiatrist's courtroom testimony started ringing in his ears. *He's a bully. He's a dangerous man. This is a high-risk relationship. He's like a spider. We're in the category of homicide prevention. My gut tells me Mr. McMillan is one of the most dangerous men I have ever met.* His thoughts swirled. By 4:30 a.m., tension had exhausted him, and he no longer had the strength to hold open his eyelids. He fell into a restless sleep.

↙

The room seemed vaguely familiar, but everything was distorted, out of proportion. His bedroom ceiling stretched upward and narrowed to a point that let in a shaft of weak light. The window was missing, but the bed and other furniture were mostly in the right places. He was sitting on his bed, flipping through an assortment of comic books, looking for the right one. But he wasn't quite sure which one it was, and the piles around him kept growing as if they were boiling up from the mattress.

A small crack of light showed under the closed door. Something small, perhaps the size of an eraser, crawled under it.

As it moved toward him it appeared to grow larger, until he could see that it was a spider.

He wasn't afraid of spiders. In fact, sometimes in the summers he'd catch daddy longlegs and let them stalk around his hands and arms. Grandma had told him not to kill spiders, even when they crawled into the basement, because they preyed on mosquitoes and other unwelcome insects.

Yes, that's what it was, a daddy longlegs, but a bigger one than he'd ever seen before. He idly wondered how big it would get as it advanced toward the bed.

The spider's movement started to look jerky. As each leg thrust forward, it got longer and the body tilted at a crazy angle. The hair on Danny's arms bristled as the spider grew bigger than a mouse, then bigger than a cat, and then bigger than a wolf. It kept on growing and kept on coming.

Now it was halfway across the room, and its melon-sized head was even with the mattress. The top joint of its legs was level with his eyes. The spider's pace slowed, but with each deliberate step it doubled in size.

Danny's heart began to pound as he scrambled backward across a sea of heaving comic books. He clutched at the blankets and pulled them around his throat.

But there was no hiding. The spider was very close now, and Danny stared up in horror at the feelers dangling above its eight lidless eyes. A pair of hanging jaws as long as his arm started clicking open and shut, open and shut. The spider's putrid breath smelled of burning rubber and hot tar.

Danny shoved off the wall and propelled himself between the spider's legs. The hair on its abdomen raked his skin. He could hear the spider's jaws snap shut on his pillow, sending feathers flying.

He ran for the door but it had disappeared. His eyes rolled wildly as he searched for a way out, but the room was a prison.

The spider spun around and stood, staring, its jaws clicking open and shut, open and shut. Danny backed up until he hit the wall, his palms splayed out at his sides.

The spider lifted two front and two back legs at the same time. Its head and four front legs moved to the left. Its abdomen and four back legs moved to the right. It had split in two.

The head stayed where it was, jaws clicking, as the abdomen began stalking him. Danny scrambled along the wall until he wedged himself into the corner and could go no further. Still, the abdomen came at him, its crusty black casing studded with spikes, its claws banging the floor with each step. It approached the wall and then drew up to the boy, trying to force him out of the corner. Its needle-sharp spikes pulsed closer and closer, threatening to impale him. When the abdomen lunged at him from the side, he shot forward, straight into the waiting jaws of the spider's head.

Danny bolted upright in the bed and screamed, his chest heaving and his hair soaked with sweat. He clawed his way through the blankets and streaked for the door, his eyes rolling as he looked for an escape route. He found the door handle and slapped it down, but it wouldn't open. Blood pounded in his ears. He sank to the floor and gasped for breath. Seconds ticked by. He didn't know how many. Nothing in the room was moving, and he gradually under-stood it was all a nightmare. He ached for Buddy. He longed to have the dog lick the tears off his face and rub his warm body into Danny's, to jingle the sweet music of his dog tags in Danny's ears.

# Chapter 16

## Wednesday

*Knock-knock-knock.* Pause. *Knock-knock-knock.* He rubbed his eyes, loosening crusty bits along the lashes and at the corners. Where was he? What time was it? He looked uneasily around the room and then remembered where he was and why he was there.

He glanced at his watch. 10:15.

*Knock-knock-knock.* "Open the door. It's me."

The voice was unmistakable. Sgt. Sandhu's.

Danny briefly considered not answering. But the only way out was through that door, so he might as well open it now.

He twisted the key and the bolt slid back. Sgt. Sandhu, wearing casual clothes, stood in the doorway. It was Wednesday, the day Danny's soccer team used to practice. Sgt. Sandhu's day off.

The police officer held a grocery bag in one hand and a paper bag full of doughnuts in the other. He stayed in the hall and offered the bags. "Fresh clothes. And some breakfast. I'll meet you downstairs in twenty minutes." His voice was purposeful, like his coaching voice at soccer practices. Danny took the bags and shut the door.

Thirty-five minutes later he appeared in the lobby. He'd pulled his cap down over wet hair.

Sgt. Sandhu was chatting with the new volunteer, Dave, a muscular young man now behind the counter. "Ah, here he is," said Sgt. Sandhu, rising from his chair. "We'll let you get back to work, Dave. Thanks."

He led Danny down the sidewalk. This time he'd come in his own vehicle, a candy-apple red pickup truck, starting to show rust around the wheel wells. The fenders had a couple of scratches and dents that he'd never repaired. At soccer practice, he had called it his bachelor buggy – the thing he'd spent all his time and money on before he got married and had twin daughters. "I used to think cars were important," he'd said.

Danny plopped onto the passenger seat and dropped the plastic bag on the floor. Before Sgt. Sandhu started the truck, he turned to the boy.

"Everyone was worried about you."

*Good.*

"We're all relieved you're safe."

*Right.*

"But we have to go back to the NIVA office."

Danny tugged down his cap even more, crossed his arms, and examined his runners. Sgt. Sandhu tuned the radio to a local pop station. He didn't nag Danny to fasten his seatbelt.

Same building, same elevator, same intercom. Inside Phil's office, Mom, Jen, Phil, and a woman Danny guessed was Dr. Sung were waiting.

Sgt. Sandhu greeted everyone and Catherine started to rise.

The police officer made a subtle hand motion and she sat again.

Danny took the farthest chair. He hadn't thought about his sister at all. Her shoulders were hunched forward as if she were in the principal's office, waiting for a punishment. He'd been so caught up in his own feelings, he hadn't considered how all of this was affecting her. Mother and daughter sat side by side, but it was as if an invisible wall of ice separated him from them.

"Welcome, everyone," Dr. Sung said. "Now that we're all here, I'd like to explain how everything is going to unfold. You'll be making a number of choices today. There are a lot of decisions to make before tomorrow."

Danny's eyebrows arched under his cap. *Tomorrow?* He hadn't even processed what happened yesterday; how could something be decided by tomorrow?

"Giving you new identities means making quite a few changes to your past," Dr. Sung continued, "but some things can stay the same. For example," she said, looking first at Jennifer and then at Danny, "your school marks won't change, but it'll look like you went to a different school. That goes for your medical records too – same details, different doctor."

She addressed Catherine. "Things are a little more complicated for you. You'll get a new social insurance number, but we can't duplicate your employment history. School and medical records are one thing – usually, nobody checks them. But if you apply for a job, a new employer will want to check your references, and we can't risk someone finding out your employment history is faked. What education do you have?"

"Two years of community college, in office management."

"And your job history – how old were you when you were married?"

"Twenty-three."

"Twenty-three." She pursed her lips. "Hmm, I think it would be better if you didn't finish high school. That way no one will expect to see a diploma. We'll say you didn't work after you got married, and before that you worked in retail sales – department stores, convenience stores, as a waitress. That kind of thing."

"But how will we support ourselves when we get there? I haven't worked since Christmas, and all our savings are gone."

"I've been working with your divorce lawyer on that. I know you don't have any savings left, but you do have a nice house full of furniture we can sell. You also have two cars, and Paul has the insurance business. Your lawyer's pretty sure she can convince a judge it would be fair that he keeps the business and the SUV and you keep the house, its contents, and the car. She thinks your share of the matrimonial property settlement will be worth about four hundred thousand dollars. We can sell your things and that'll give you enough money to start a small business in your new location. I can handle all of that for you, and until that happens, the NIVA program will give you enough money to get by."

Catherine's voice was flat. "You mean social assistance?"

Dr. Sung nodded. "Yes. But hopefully not for too long. You won't be as comfortable as you are now, but you won't need assistance for very long, either."

Catherine leaned back. "What about child support?"

"Well, that part's not so good. We have a Maintenance Enforcement program, but it can't guarantee your anonymity. Also, paying child support would mean that Paul would be entitled to some information about you, your income, the kids' education, whether they are even alive. It'd be a thread tying you to your past. We can't risk it."

Catherine pressed her lips together. "That's not something I'd thought about."

"I'm afraid there are going to be quite a few things you haven't thought about."

Dr. Sung made notes on her clipboard. "You need to understand you're not going to get any official papers about these things, like a job history." She pointed to the questionnaire. "This is just for your family's use, so when questions come up about your past you have an agreed-upon story. Now, what about locations? Is there any place that you've always wanted to live?"

"Well, Paul and I talked about moving to Victoria. We both like the climate."

"Then that's one place you can't go, because he'll look for you there. So we should be thinking about sending you in the other direction. We can relocate you to a small town, but it's easier to slip in unnoticed in a bigger community. How about Regina, or Winnipeg?"

Danny had never been to Regina or Winnipeg, but everyone said they were cold. Windy Winterpeg.

"Well…" said Catherine, looking around for help. "I don't know…"

"Okay," said Phil. "Then let's talk a bit about where you're going to be *from*. We usually pick a city similar in size and climate to the one you're in now. Saskatoon is like Edmonton. It's on a branch of the same river, and we've used it for relocations before. You'll have enough general information that you can bluff your way through basic questions – what the surroundings look like, and how the seasons are."

"Okay," said Catherine uncertainly.

"All right," said Phil. "If we agree that you'll be from Saskatoon we should move you farther away than Regina. Since they're both in the same province, too many people will know Saskatoon and that could get you into trouble. So, I suggest we relocate you to Winnipeg."

"Well, if that's what you think…" said Catherine.

"Okay," said Phil. "We'll start organizing our paperwork on the basis that your family is moving from Saskatoon to Winnipeg."

"I've never been to Winnipeg," Catherine said, massaging the scar on her hand. "How – how will I manage?"

"You'll manage fine," replied Sgt. Sandhu. "You'll manage just fine because you'll be alive."

# Chapter 17

## Wednesday

"Now, let's pick some new birthdays," the psychologist continued. "Jen, what's your birthday now?"

"September the first."

"Well, we don't want complications with the school year, so you need another birth date around then so you're still in the right grade."

"But I'd like to have it when school's on, so I can have parties with the class, like the other kids."

Dr. Sung smiled. "Sure thing." She turned to Catherine. "What day of the week was she born?"

"It was a Wednesday."

"Then we'll stick with Wednesday – it's one less detail to be confused about later." She consulted a notebook. "June, 1993. The Wednesdays are the 2nd, 9th, 16th, 23rd, and 30th."

"June 9th," said Jennifer.

"The 9th it is," Dr. Sung replied, writing the date on her clipboard. "Catherine?"

"I was born March 12, 1963. It was a Tuesday," she said rue-fully. "Mom always said I was full of grace."

"Another Tuesday nearby would be –" she flipped through her notebook. "How about February 26th?"

"Sure."

"And Danny?"

"June 13, 1989," replied Catherine. "Also a Tuesday."

"So maybe another Tuesday in June?"

"What about April Fool's Day?" Danny interjected. "Maybe that was a Tuesday."

All eyes looked at him.

"Let's go with June 20th," Dr. Sung said. "Okay?"

Danny shrugged. *All of this is about someone else,* he thought. *How can I have a different birthday?* Birthdays had always been so happy. His mom had told him and his sister how she'd loved birthday parties when she was growing up, and she wanted them to grow up with memories they could treasure too. And they *had* been good birthdays.

Now he was going to have two birthdays. And he wouldn't be celebrating either of them.

⚒

"The hardest part," Dr. Sung said, "is new names."

Danny looked at the others, seeking some clue as to how to act, how to react. Dr. Sung had on her professional face, and Phil looked sympathetic but firm. Jennifer seemed bewildered and grabbed her mother's hand. Catherine's face drooped. None of it was helpful to Danny, who was starting to feel like an orphan.

Phil cleared his throat. "We recommend you change all three

names – first, middle, and last. The middle name is negotiable. You can keep it, but it's better if there's a clean break. You might want to keep the same initials, though. So let's start with last names. We suggest something fairly simple. It makes it easier to blend in."

"Can I go back to my unmarried name?" Catherine asked.

"No," Phil replied. "Too obvious. Let's keep the same initial, *M*. What about Mayer?"

"Mayer," repeated Catherine, trying it on like a change of clothes. "It's okay with me."

Dr. Sung took over. "Most people find their first name is the most difficult. Usually, your nicknames or pet names are related to your first name. Catherine, what do you call your children?"

She looked at Jennifer. "I usually call her Jewel." She turned her gaze to her son. "And Danny is Danny-boy."

"Okay. Jennifer, you might be able to keep the same nickname if you choose a name with that *J* sound – maybe Julia, or Judy, or Juliet. Then your mom can still call you Jewel and neither of you will have to think to use your new name each time."

Phil turned to Danny. "Yours is a bit tougher because your nickname has your real name in it. Maybe you can think of something similar – David maybe, and your mom can call you Davey-boy."

Danny looked at Phil, his face blank. *I might as well be a character in a science fiction book. You pick out your new life the way you choose vegetables at the store: one bin labeled NAMES, another BIRTHDAYS, and a rack of FAMILY TREES. Squeeze them and weigh them and take your favorite ones to your new home. The price? Well, you pay with your past.*

Danny leaned back. "This," he said, "is nuts. There's no way I'm changing my name. *I won't.*"

"I'm sorry," Phil said, "but this is going to happen, even though you don't want it or like it. You'll be happier in the future if you take part in this decision. Otherwise, we'll have to pick for you, and that's just not a good idea."

"I want to keep my initials," Jennifer said. "I like them. Jennifer Elaine McMillan. I'll take Julia. And maybe Erin as a middle name."

"Those are…nice, Jewel," Mom said. She turned to Danny. "I don't want to keep my initials…I think it would be better for me that way…I've been thinking about Susan. Susan Louise. But I think you should keep your initials too, Danny. Okay?" Both Jen and Catherine looked at Danny.

"No problem," he replied. "I've already decided. My name is Daniel Paul McMillan."

Catherine closed her eyes and bowed her head. She looked up at him and half-whispered, "Please. I don't want to do all this and have to fight you, too."

"We could look in a phone book…" Jennifer suggested.

*Yeah, right,* thought Danny. *Now I'm going to pick my life out of a phone book.*

Dr. Sung smiled at Jennifer.

"I kind of like Perry as a middle name," Catherine suggested softly. "Would Perry be okay with you?"

"Fine."

"And I think David is a good choice, given what they've said about nicknames."

Everyone waited, but he didn't reply.

Phil changed the subject. "Let's talk about Paul," Phil said. "His full name is…"

"Paul Frederick McMillan."

"All right. For simplicity's sake, we'll drop the middle name. So it will be something Mayer."

Catherine snorted. "Let's call him Laurie. He always hated those 'girly' names for boys."

"Mom!" Danny yelled, staring at her as if she'd burned him.

Dr. Sung intervened. "Perhaps that's not the best choice."

"Okay," Catherine replied. "You pick."

"How's about William? William Mayer?"

"That'll be fine."

"Next we need a family history and a family tree. We have to strike a balance. On one hand, it must be different enough from your actual family historics that the information can't be used to identify you. On the other hand, it has to be close enough to your real life that you have a hope of remembering the details without getting mixed up. So, first with Paul. When a woman has two children, we recommend saying that you separated right before the first child was born. Paul was absent until you tried to reconcile briefly a couple of years later. You became pregnant again, and then Paul died. This history explains the lack of photos of dad and means the children don't have much to say about him."

Dr. Sung's pen scratched across the paper. "Paul, of course, was also an only child, and his parents are dead." She paused. "And your parents, Catherine? What are their names?"

"Mom's Patricia Lynn Wilson – well, she was born Smith."

"Good. We can leave her unmarried name as Smith. And your dad?"

"Samuel Brent Wilson."

"Okay, let's change his last name so that will change your birth name too. Any suggestions?"

"Buchanan?"

"Perfect." Dr. Sung made notes.

"The next choices are – well, they're more obvious. You'll be an only child – I guess you are anyway, right? And your parents died in a car accident a little while ago."

*Grandparents. Car accident. Death. They're pruning Grandma and Grandpa out of the family tree.* Danny squeezed his eyes shut. Grandma and Grandpa. They'd been crowded out of his mind since he'd left their house on Tuesday. *Was* it only yesterday? Time muddled itself and he couldn't seem to remember, but he would always remember the carefree summers he'd spent with them in earlier years.

Grandma called herself an avid "urban forester." She considered it her mission to plant a broad range of trees, shrubs, and flowering plants. She'd walked him around the yard to point out the various leaf shapes, the insects that ate the plants and those that ate other insects, and the power of sunlight to turn a sunflower's head. He, Grandma, and Mom had planted his Grade 2 Arbor Day tree – a scrawny spruce sapling – beside the one his mother had planted thirty years earlier. He'd scooped out the hole with an empty tin can as Grandma dissolved the fertilizer in a pail. He'd steadied the sapling as she'd patted the earth around it and soaked the soil with the pale blue water. Two years ago, Grandma wanted Jennifer's tree planted there too, to make a "family of trees," but Dad had said no. Instead, he planted it beside their garage where the shade stunted its growth.

# Chapter 18
## Wednesday

Catherine and Jennifer drove home in the car, and Sgt. Sandhu took Danny. Buddy was wriggling at the gate, and his tail slapped back and forth when he saw the boy. They tumbled around in the grass and for a moment, Danny's mind blocked out everything. He wanted "now" to go on forever.

He stayed outside until Mom called him for dinner. While Danny ate, Catherine pushed dishes around the cupboards and wiped the already clean sink. Finally, she turned and leaned against the counter, her palms beside her for support.

"I'm sorry, Danny. I'm so sorry." The corners of her mouth twitched downward as her lips trembled.

He wanted to yell. *Don't cry. Why are you crying! Why is all this happening to me?* But he could see the pain in her face and he knew it was the same pain he felt.

"Where's Jen?" he asked gruffly, scraping his chair back.

"She's…she's gone downstairs. She's watching a movie," she

replied, not resisting his attempt to keep her from making yet another sad, impossible apology.

Jennifer's plate sat on the downstairs table. She'd eaten her sandwich center and left the crusts. Smudged fingerprints and greasy crumbs clung to the side of the empty milk glass. The TV was playing a Disney movie. Her fingers were corkscrewing a lock of hair.

They needed to talk, but he didn't know how to start. Most of the time, they had nothing much to say to each other. They'd kept their distances, and since December, they'd drifted even further apart. At home he preferred his own company, and at Grandma and Grandpa's he immersed himself in comic books while Jen played hopscotch with the neighborhood kids. He was alternately ashamed of and furious with his parents – how could Dad do that? How could Mom let him? Soon, cold anger surged over shame and drove him into his room with the door slammed shut behind him.

But since the trial, the ground had shifted again. As often as he had been angry, he was also now worried – worried about his dad in jail, worried that his mom wasn't the strong, happy mother he'd always known, and worried about himself, his life and his future. Today in the NIVA conference room, his worry had included Jen. She was embroiled in this mess just as much as he was. And, if they moved, if this *thing* happened to them, what family would he have left?

He slung himself into the armchair. For the first five minutes or so, he said nothing, his eyes on the screen but his mind rehearsing what he was going to say.

"Jen."

"What?"

"This move...do you wanna move?"

She looked at him. He kept his eyes on the screen. *When you wish upon a star, makes no difference who you are...* Jen had the remote in her hand, but didn't mute the volume.

"No," she answered.

He paused. "We have to figure out a way to stop it."

*Like a bolt out of the blue, fate steps in and sees you through...*

"What're you gonna do?" she asked. "Run away again?"

The words stung and he felt his blood rise to his cheeks as he glared at his sister. "Isn't that what they're saying our whole family should do? What? D'you buy all that stuff they said? You really *believe* that Dad'll kill Mom?"

Jennifer looked at her brother, her face rigid. "Dad's been mean to me, too."

He jerked back. "Mean? What are you talking about, *mean?*"

"Like Mom said. He'd yell at me. He'd tell me I was an idiot. He never let me play on any teams. He...called me names."

"You've been talking to Mom."

"She didn't know. I didn't tell her until after Dad went to jail."

Danny's eyes narrowed. "So he was mean to you. So he called you names. I bet he never hit you. So what?"

It was her turn to get angry. "How would you know?! It was always *Danny-boy* this! *Danny-boy* that! Sports and fishing and all kinds of stuff, that's what *you* were doing." She jabbed a finger at her brother. "You didn't even *notice* me, I just got left behind!" Her eyes leaked tears, and she lashed out. "He was even mean to the dog! I saw him! He kicked Buddy for no reason – more than once!" Jennifer leapt from the couch and sobbed her way upstairs.

He sat, stunned and alone.

Danny turned off the TV and went up to his room. He was over-whelmed and had trouble accepting what he'd just heard and what it meant for him. He closed his eyes. Last night's fragmented sleep in the shelter felt like it had happened in a past life, and he hadn't had any rest since then. He flipped his pillow, searching for a comfortable spot, then shoved it over his head and tried to will himself to sleep.

It didn't work. He lay there, thoughts swirling around in the air, his mind gearing up again, trying to piece together these new bits of information. Jen said that Dad had been mean to her, but he'd never seen it and he hoped it hadn't happened. But now, as he thought back, he could see that maybe she *had* been discouraged, even excluded, while he was busy enjoying, but not sharing, his time with Dad. Dad and Jen weren't together often, but maybe during those times, Dad *had* been mean to her. And Buddy *had* shied away from Dad. Just because you don't see something, doesn't mean it didn't happen.

He stared up at the glow-in-the dark stars glued to his ceil-ing. They came from the gift shop in the Space Sciences Center. Grandma and Grandpa had taken him and Jen there to see the star show in the planetarium. Back home, they had spread out the star chart on Danny's bed and sticky-tacked the stars to the ceil-ing. Now that he thought about it, that was around the time they stopped visiting their grandparents so much. He'd wanted to see them more, but Dad always said it interfered with something he had planned. And Dad's promises to get together with Grandma and Grandpa "next weekend" had been easily made and easily forgotten. Somehow, those facts were the same, but their meanings now shifted from ordinary and regular to planned and deliberate, from innocent to sinister. If Dad could beat up Mom and be mean to Jen and kick Buddy, what else might he do?

The stars still clung to the ceiling above him, Polaris centered over his bed, Ursa Minor above and Ursa Major off to the left. And, farther off, his own astrological sign. "You're a Gemini, Danny-boy – the Heavenly Twins. They say it's a good sign for a boy – Pollux and Castor were heroes who went on daring adventures and had the power to calm the seas," Grandma had said, her fingers stroking under his chin.

And there was Perseus who killed the snake-headed Medusa and rescued Andromeda from the sea monster Cetus. "They're all above you in the night sky," Grandma said. "Family dramas, great stories of love and loss, honor and betrayal. And a thousand years from now, Orion will still be hunting with his two dogs."

Grandma and Grandpa. They'd been crying in the backyard. They *knew*. And they weren't crying about the past, they were crying about what was still to come. So they knew. They knew he was going to have a new identity. They knew his family was going to relocate.

And now *Danny* knew that he might never see them again.

# Chapter 19
## Thursday

A rare summer-morning thunderstorm startled him awake. The smooth sound of rain ceded to the drumming of hail. Danny was disoriented. He looked at his alarm clock – 8:00 a.m. He'd been asleep for hours, yet he still felt groggy, as if his head were wrapped in gauze. His sinuses were congested and the right side of his face was crusty with snot and salt. At some point, he must have cried himself to sleep last night. He grabbed a fistful of bedsheet and wiped his eyes.

His mom knocked on his door and he immediately stopped moving. She opened it a crack and called gently to her son. "It's time to get up." A little louder. "Danny."

She stepped inside. "I'm going to open the window, okay?"

He pretended to be asleep. She slid open the window and the fresh smell of ozone flooded the room. She gazed down at him. His entire blanket was tangled around him. The loose limbs of sleep had already tightened, and it was clear he was awake. "Come downstairs when you're dressed," she said. "We have company."

Phil was in the kitchen sipping coffee from Dad's favorite mug. His large frame spilled over the sides of the wooden kitchen chair and only one wide finger fit through the mug handle. Danny remained in the doorway even after Phil suggested he sit.

"I'm here to help you sort through some of your things," he said, as if it were just another routine task. "I'm going to bring the suitcases up from the basement, and then you have to...pack."

Danny stayed in the doorway.

Phil tilted his head and looked at him. "Would you like me to explain it now...or would you rather talk about it in your room?"

Danny spun on his heel and walked away. The neighbors could have heard his bedroom door slam.

He tumbled onto the bed, clenched his fists, and fixed his eyes on the stars. He was still rigid ten minutes later when Phil came up the stairs.

"Hey, Danny, can I come in?"

When the boy didn't reply, Phil gently turned the knob and entered. He held a suitcase in each hand and placed them beside the desk. "We could pop these on the bed and I could give you a hand."

Danny didn't move.

"Okay," Phil said after a pause. He moved a pile of clothes to the desk, and sat on the chair facing the boy.

"Let me tell you how this is going to work. You don't need to say anything, but you do need to listen."

*I wish I were deaf.*

"You need to take the things you want for the next few weeks – say, until the end of September. Clothes, books, shoes, your sports equipment, that sort of thing. And any of your personal stuff that doesn't identify you. So," he said, "you can take pictures, trophies, ribbons and your sports stuff as long as they don't have team names – or your name – on them.

"And – no pictures of your father. You have to leave anything that identifies you, and anything that doesn't fit in these two suitcases. No school books, birthday cards, letters – no diaries, if you ever kept them."

He cleared his throat. "Dr. Sung and I had a meeting with your grandparents. You're going to see them soon and you can ask questions, but I'll give you an idea about how they're going to help.

"In a week or so after you move out of this house, they're going to come in and sort through everything. They'll organize and box all the things you'll need later – winter clothes, toys, games, souvenirs, your stereo, and some kitchen things – as much as possible, as long as it doesn't identify you. We'll put it in storage, and in a couple of months we'll deliver it to your new house – the program has an untraceable way to get it to you. It's important that we prevent your grandparents from being too involved."

Danny sat up and narrowed his eyes. "And the stuff that *does* identify us? What's going to happen to it?"

"Your sports awards, family photos, scrapbooks, cards, letters, all those sorts of things – your grandma and grandpa will take them and keep them safe."

"For how long?" Danny challenged.

Phil looked at the floor for a moment. "We can't know the future, Danny." He stood and pushed the chair under the desk. "I'm going now. Take some time to pack your things. Don't leave it – it'll take longer than you think." He paused. "Sgt. Sandhu's coming by this afternoon. You've got one more thing to take care of."

The knock was firm.

"Go away," Danny said.

"It's me. Open the door," Sgt. Sandhu said.

"Leave me alone."

"We need to talk."

*How many times have I heard those words in the last week?*

"Danny, please. One of the things we need to talk about is...
Buddy."

*Buddy?*

"Danny. Open up."

Danny dislodged the chair from its place under the doorknob. When Danny didn't open the door, the police officer turned
the handle. Buddy nosed it open and wiggled into the room. He
smacked his nose against Danny's legs.

Automatically, the boy reached down to scratch the dog's
head. "Hi, Buddy-boy," he said tenderly.

"Can I come in?"

Danny said nothing. He returned to the bed, the dog content-
edly flopping at his feet.

Sgt. Sandhu straddled the chair. "Buddy can go with you to
the new place, but we need to take out his microchip. It can be
used to identify him and lead to you."

Danny had never even considered that Buddy was one of the
puzzle pieces that might not fit into the new picture. This was
getting more and more unreal.

"We've called the vet and she has one appointment open later
today. I think you should come."

"Buddy doesn't like the vet."

"That's why I said you should come."

"I don't understand what's happening!" He leapt up and startled the dog.

"It's our only option."

"But the judge said no one had *proved* that Dad would ever do anything to Mom. You never *proved* it!"

"In our legal system there's a difference between what *is* true and what can be *proven* to be true. We don't have enough hard evidence to satisfy a judge, and judges decide cases based on evidence, not just on the truth."

"*That's* justice?"

"Well, it may not seem fair to you or to your family, but yes, that's the way our justice system works. There have to be rules and we all have to follow them, even if we don't like them. I'm sorry Danny, I'm not a lawyer, and I can't explain it better. Domestic violence is a very difficult kind of crime, and the criminal law doesn't always deal with it very effectively."

Danny paced the room. Buddy watched him and whined.

Sgt. Sandhu rose. "It's time. We have to take Buddy to the vet."

"No."

"Danny, I'm sorry –"

"How many times am I going to hear 'I'm sorry'? Sorry doesn't *fix* anything!"

"You're right. It doesn't fix a thing. But it's honest." He paused. "This relocation has to go ahead. *That's* not a decision you get to make. But you do have a choice to make here, now, about Buddy. Either you come with me to the vet, or I take him on my own, or…he can't go with you."

Danny's jaw clenched as tight as his fists.

"Come on, Buddy," Sgt. Sandhu said. The police officer slapped his thigh and the dog's tail started to beat. "Let's go for a ride."

Buddy jumped into the truck, his tail slapping back and forth against the bench seat. Sgt. Sandhu left the passenger door open and then got in the driver's side. He sat quietly, looking out at the warming summer day. He waited.

A few minutes later Danny got in and shut the door. Sgt. Sandhu said nothing as he drove away.

Buddy's first experience with the vet hadn't been good. Before they'd had a chance to vaccinate him, he'd contracted parvovirus. When he started vomiting Mom had rushed him to the vet, where Dr. Kuskovski injected him with a sedative, shaved his leg, and started an intravenous drip of antibiotics and fluids. Buddy was at the clinic for days. Danny and his mom visited every day. Dr. Kuskovski told them Buddy had a fifty-fifty chance of living, and if he did survive, he might have permanent heart damage that would leave him unhealthy for life. Danny had cried every day, and at night he'd whisper promises to be good and keep his room clean and listen to his parents, if only Buddy would live.

Dad was disinterested. "Should've had him vaccinated earlier, Catherine," he said. On the fifth day, the dog was awake, and two days later Danny triumphantly led the skinny puppy into the house. Mom followed, carrying the package of antibiotics they'd picked up at the pharmacy. Dad just read his magazine.

Since then, two things were guaranteed to make Buddy

squirm – the smell of chlorine bleach they used to disinfect the cages and the green neon Emergency Animal Hospital sign on 34th Street. And there it was. Buddy dropped his Frisbee on the truck floor.

Inside, Sgt. Sandhu remained standing until the vet appeared. She wore her white lab coat unbuttoned. Dark-rimmed, rectangular glasses set off her high cheek bones. She reached across the counter to shake hands. "I'm Dr. Kuskovski."

"Rajiv Sandhu."

She looked at Danny and Buddy. "Hi, Danny. What can I do for you?"

"Can we speak with you privately?" asked the police officer. Sgt. Sandhu closed the examination room door. "The dog needs his microchip removed," he said.

"Is there something wrong with it?"

"No. It just needs to be removed."

Dr. Kuskovski looked at Danny, then back at Sgt. Sandhu. "And you are…"

"A family friend."

She looked at Danny. "Is this right, Danny?"

He shrugged his shoulders and avoided her eyes.

Well," said the vet, "I guess you can always have one reinserted later."

The procedure only took a few minutes. When it was done, Buddy shook himself and then raised his hind leg to scratch at the incision.

"You'll have to keep him from scratching until the freezing wears off, and then he won't notice it anymore. It shouldn't take more than an hour," the vet said.

Sgt. Sandhu pulled out his wallet and placed a few bills on

the counter. The assistant handed him a receipt. Then she offered Danny the dog's collar.

"Don't forget this," she said.

Danny reached for it, but his hand was intercepted by the police officer's. "I'll take it," he said quietly.

Danny jerked his hand back from the police officer's touch as if he'd been burned.

*Oh my God. It's really happening.*

# Chapter 20

## Thursday

"Why are you doing all of this?" Danny asked, abruptly breaking the silence.

Sgt. Sandhu stopped at a red light. "Because I have to. Because I care about you." He turned to face the boy. "Because I have a wife and two daughters. And because I hope someone would help them if they were in danger, like you are."

He turned off the ignition in front of the house. "Spend some time working on your room. Later this afternoon, my wife, Anita, and I will have your family over for a barbeque. You're going to practice meeting strangers."

Four o'clock came quickly. Catherine tapped on Danny's door. "We're leaving in twenty minutes. I thought maybe you'd like to get washed up and changed."

He was lying on the unmade bed, looking up at the stars. He hadn't washed or even brushed his teeth and was still wearing Wednesday's clothes. Reluctantly, he decided to take a shower.

On the way to the Sandhus, Catherine explained the visit. She sounded like she had a sore throat. "It's kind of like a rehearsal," she said. "The Sandhus are going to pretend they're our neighbors at the new place. We're going to speak with them as if…in our new identities."

So that's what Sgt. Sandhu meant by *practicing*. Danny felt light-headed. He began scratching Buddy's head mechanically, back and forth, back and forth.

Sgt. Sandhu was sitting on the front steps of the small white house. Perched beside him were his identical twin daughters, their short, black hair pulled into messy pigtails. They were wearing identical outfits – baggy, red shorts with flowers on the borders and white T-shirts with the same flowers trimming the sleeves. From a distance, there was no way to tell the girls apart. He'd seen them a couple of years ago when their dad brought them to soccer practice, but they were just toddlers then, and he hadn't paid them much attention.

As usual, Buddy bounded up ahead, tail wagging, muzzle thrust forward in greeting. Sgt. Sandhu stood and gave them a welcoming smile.

"Hello. I'm glad you could make it," he said, reaching out. "I'm Rajiv and these are my children, Amina and Amruta."

Catherine shook his hand. "I'm Susan Mayer, and these are my children, Julia and David," she said.

"Pleased to meet you, Julia, David," Sgt. Sandhu said, his face not betraying that this was anything but a neighborly visit. "Come around to the back. We've got some cold drinks waiting."

With a giggle, the twins jumped up and chased the dog through the gate. A chemical smell of lighter fluid lingered around the flaming charcoal briquettes. Danny started when he recognized Phil at the grill. He wore a small apron that barely reached around his waist. Several plastic deck chairs circled a patio table shaded by a green umbrella. Pitchers of lemonade and iced tea sweated on the table beside a stack of daisy-print plastic tumblers.

Two of the deck chairs were occupied – one by Sgt. Sandhu's wife, and the other, by Dr. Sung.

Sgt. Sandhu made the introductions. "Susan, this is my neighbor Phil, and over there is his wife, Connie," he said, pointing at Dr. Sung. "And, of course, my wife Anita." He gestured toward Danny and Jennifer. "And here are David and Julia."

Smiles, nods, hellos, and small talk. "Isn't it a beautiful day?" "Yes summer's been just great this year." "Even the mosquitoes aren't too bad…."

The twins grabbed Jennifer and yanked her to the corner of the yard. "Wanna see our sandbox? We could play house. I have a tea set," one of them said.

"It's my tea set too!" the other twin whined.

"Lemonade or iced tea?" asked Anita.

"Iced tea, please," Catherine replied.

Danny buried his hands in his pockets and looked away.

"I think David would like lemonade," Catherine answered for her son.

The refreshing drink splashed over the ice cubes. Anita walked over to Danny and handed him the glass. "Here you go, David."

"Homemade, David," Phil called from the barbeque. "I squeezed the lemons myself."

Buddy nosed every corner of the yard, then returned to brush against Danny's legs. When Danny reached down to pet him, Phil tried to restart the conversation.

"David, what's your dog's name?"

Danny turned his back. "Come on, Buddy," he said, leading the dog away from the patio to the shade of a leafy tree. He sat on the ground and leaned against the trunk, far enough away to remain uninvolved.

Disregarding his attitude, the others continued with questions and small talk in voices loud enough that he would hear them.

"So – where do you come from?"

"Saskatoon."

"And what made you move to Winnipeg?"

"Well, I…we…always thought it would be a nice place to live…" Catherine's voice thinned.

"Got any relatives here?"

"Ah, no."

"Well it's a great place to raise a family," Phil stated pleasantly. He arranged hot dogs and steaks on the grill. "Connie and I have lived here all our lives. Got to prepare yourselves for the winters, though. Downtown Winnipeg is the coldest place on earth, they say. What were the winters like in Saskatoon?"

"Well, they're…cold too.…"

"What kind of work do you do?" asked Dr. Sung.

Catherine took a long sip of iced tea. "I usually work in sales – retail sales."

"And are you looking for a job or have you already lined one up?"

"I'm still looking for a job.… I wanted to move first and get the children settled before school starts."

"Susan, how do you like your steak?" Phil asked.

"Medium, please."

Anita rose from the table. "Rajiv, come and help me bring plates and the food." She looked over her shoulder. "I hope Julia and David like potato salad and corn on the cob, because we've got plenty."

"Sounds wonderful," replied Catherine, sitting back.

Phil called over to the sandbox. "Julia, hot dogs or a steak?"

The twins were busily slapping wet sand between their palms to make mud pies, while Jennifer added dry sand to the yellow plastic water bucket.

"Julia?" he called, this time a little louder.

It was not the name, but the silence and the pressure of three sets of eyes that caught Jennifer's attention. She looked first at her mother, then at Phil who immediately held her gaze and said, "Julia – hot dog or steak?"

"Hot dog."

He nodded. "Comin' right up!" He smiled at Danny. "And you?" he asked, without using a name.

"Steak," Danny mumbled.

"Sure thing."

Anita brought out a casserole dish covered in plastic wrap, and a few more trips in and out produced a steaming pot of corn, French bread, hot dog buns, a green salad, and assorted condiments.

Phil slid the steaks and hot dogs onto a platter. On any other day, Danny would have been first in line.

"Girls!" Anita called. "Wash up for supper, please. Amina, Amruta, please show Julia where the bathroom is. And bring me your glasses; I've got more lemonade here."

Dr. Sung and Catherine started making their way around the table, filling their plates and topping up their drinks.

Jennifer and the twins reappeared, and Anita helped her daughters with their plates. The only ones still without food were Sgt. Sandhu and Danny.

Sgt. Sandhu walked over to the boy and crouched beside him. Instead of looking at him, he reached out to stroke the dog.

"Why don't you come over and eat," Sgt. Sandhu said gently. "I'm sure Buddy would like your steak bone when you're finished. I can only imagine – no, I can't even imagine – how hard this must be for you. But there is simply no way to make it easier. Please, come over to the table. You don't have to participate, but at least come and listen. You need to know what's still ahead of you."

Sgt. Sadhu reached to touch Danny's arm. The boy pulled away, but his actions were slower, more resigned. His anger was gradually ebbing away, like the dying coals on the barbeque. He no longer had the energy to keep it burning. He felt exhausted. He just wanted someone to take care of him.

Sgt. Sadhu returned to the patio. The boy followed, his lemonade glass ready for a refill.

A lull fell over the group as they sat with plates balanced in their laps. Only the twins chattered on, still absorbed in their world of play. When everyone started leaving their cutlery on their plates and lifting napkins to their lips, Sgt. Sandhu caught Danny's eye.

"Would you like to give a couple of these bones to Buddy? He's been so patient, waiting for us to finish." Sgt. Sandhu gave Danny permission to leave the table – allowing him to be a spectator for a while longer, instead of a participant. As soon as he moved away, Sgt. Sandhu resumed the rehearsal.

"So tell us a bit about yourself, Susan. Have you always lived in Saskatchewan?"

"No…," answered Catherine. "I was born in Edmonton, but my parents and I moved to Saskatoon when I started school. I'm an only child," she volunteered a bit too quickly. Self-consciously, she took a gulp of iced tea.

Dr. Sung spoke. "You must have gone to Lake Diefenbaker, just south of Saskatoon, for summer holidays. I hear the swimming and boating is great, and the fishing's not bad either."

"Well…yes," faltered Catherine, "of course we went there many times. Great place."

Anita turned to Jennifer. "Are you looking forward to school, Julia? What grade are you going into?"

"Four."

"What's your favorite subject?"

"Science."

"How old are you now?"

"I'm eight. I'll be nine in…" There was an awkward silence as she realized her mistake. "I guess I'm…" She turned to her mother. "I *missed* my new birthday?" she asked in a voice that was equal parts confusion and distress.

"Ah…." said Catherine. "Maybe we'll have to rethink that one."

Dr. Sung smiled reassuringly. "Just let us know."

Silence stretched over the group as if they were all holding their breath, waiting for someone to take the lead. *Where are they going with this charade?* Danny wondered. *Haven't they said enough, squirmed enough – suffered enough?*

Sgt. Sandhu spoke up. "I think this would be a good time for dessert. Rhubarb pie with ice cream." He cleared the dinner dishes as Anita set out the dessert plates.

Phil cleared his throat. "Remember, you can steer a conversation by asking questions, moving the focus away from you and onto others." He sighed. "Most people are only too happy to talk about themselves, and they'd rather talk than listen."

Catherine nodded.

"And try not to volunteer information. It's likely to just trip you up and cause you grief later on. You can also turn conversations to your advantage," he coached. "For example, take the Lake Diefenbaker comment. Instead of floundering around and wondering what to say about it, ask her if she's ever been there or knows someone who goes there. If she says no, you'll be safe in making up a few things. If she says yes, then ask her about it – how did you like it? Where did you stay? What did you do? – and you'll learn some things for the next time you're asked."

Catherine nodded again. Her face had taken on a gray, ashen look, as if she, too, were suddenly exhausted, overwhelmed by the rehearsal. She picked at her dessert while Anita reminded the twins it was bath time. The sun stretched their shadows and Catherine stood to say good-bye. Her shoulders sagged and she kept her distance from her hosts. The gap ensured there wouldn't be any embracing – only nods and concerned looks, thank-yous and take-care-of-yourselves, and good-byes.

But before they could leave, Sgt. Sandhu approached Danny. The next words fell from his lips like a verdict.

"You leave tomorrow."

# Chapter 21
## Friday

Not a single thing in Danny's room had moved when his mom knocked on the door the next morning and said it was time to go to his grandparents'. As he rubbed the sleep from his eyes, his thoughts tumbled together and he developed a plan.

*I'll stay with Grandma and Grandpa. Mom can move away for a while – and Jen too, if she wants. Then Dad'll get out of jail and he won't go after Mom. In a couple of months Dad will have had time to prove he can keep his promise and Mom will realize he isn't a threat. Then Mom and Jen can move back – and I'll still be Daniel Paul McMillan.*

The new plan nudged him forward. He opened the door and went downstairs.

Three suitcases were lined up at the door. Four family photo albums lay in a pile beside a pillar of CDs and DVDs. Jennifer sat on the floor beside a pillowcase bulging with stuffed animals, twiddling her hair around and around her finger.

Danny called Buddy and quickly maneuvered out the door.

It was a beautiful summer morning on Grandma and Grandpa's street. The neighbors paused from weeding gardens to give them a cheery wave. Danny pulled his mouth tight, dropped his eyes, and headed inside.

The table was set for brunch. Grandma was at the stove, flipping pancakes.

"Hi Danny. Grandpa's out back, would you tell him we'll be ready in ten minutes?"

"Hi Grandma," he replied. He took a breath and his new plan helped him settle his stomach butterflies.

Grandpa stood out back. He clenched a red spool the size of a basketball hoop in one hand, and with the other he was teasing apart the strings tethering the wings of his freestyle kite.

"Danny!" Grandpa said. "Don't let the dog over here or I'll never get these strings straightened out!" Buddy was just brushing past Danny's legs.

"Buddy!" Danny called as he reached to grab the dog's collar. No collar.

Buddy loped up to Grandpa. He rubbed his body against Grandpa's legs, his tail slapping at the kite strings.

"Buddy! Sit! Lie down!" Grandpa commanded. Buddy did his best and eventually sat, but not before hopelessly tangling the strings.

Grandpa gazed at Buddy and then over at Danny. "I was hoping we could go together and fly the kite until brunch is ready, but it seems Buddy had other plans for us."

"Buddy, get over here," Danny scolded. Kite-flying would have been the perfect time to talk to Grandpa about his new scheme.

"It's okay," Grandpa said, untangling the dog and shifting the disabled kite onto the picnic table. "There probably wouldn't be enough time, anyway." He smiled thinly. "Why don't you put some food and water out for Buddy while I wash up."

Danny retrieved dog food from the garage, filled the dishes, and made sure both gates were securely closed before he went in. He didn't need Buddy deciding to chase down a squirrel, especially when the dog had no collar or ID tags.

They took their usual places at the table. Danny inhaled deeply and tried to set aside his worry about his planned talk with Grandpa.

For the first few minutes, the warm food was comforting. Light conversation centered on the meal. "Please pass the eggs." "Is there more toast?" "Anyone for more pancakes?" But lifting his eyes from the plate was like popping the cap off a bottle of soda water – the calm water wasn't calm anymore.

Mom's eye twitched.

Jennifer twirled her hair.

Grandma and Grandpa pushed cold food around their plates.

The butterflies started again.

Grandpa coughed into his napkin and dropped it on his nearly-full plate. "Let's just leave the dishes for later," he said. "Maybe we could go to the living room."

One by one, the others quit the table and moved toward the doorway. Danny remained seated. The butterflies swooped.

"Wait!" he called. "Grandpa, can I talk to you outside?"

Grandpa stopped and turned around. "Sure. Let's go out back."

Grandpa left room on the park bench for Danny. Buddy picked up his Frisbee and charged over, but Grandpa said, "Not now, Buddy-boy, come lie down."

Danny sat beside Grandpa. He leaned forward to scratch Buddy's head as he laid out his new plan.

Grandpa didn't interrupt. When Danny had finished, Grandpa looked away and was silent for a long while. When he finally turned to face his grandson, Danny saw the dark circles below his eyes.

Looking directly into his grandson's eyes, Grandpa said, "I'm sorry. It — it can't be that way." He paused, swallowed, and strained to say the next words. "You wouldn't be safe."

Danny pressed himself into the bench, anger narrowing his eyes, his voice flatly defiant. "I don't believe you."

"If there were any way to change the past, I would. Your mother would. Sgt. Sandhu would. Everyone would. We'd go back to when — to the time when your dad started cutting us off from your family. I'd…I'd insist, I'd persist, I'd find out what was wrong and I'd stop it." He blinked rapidly. "But I didn't do that and now, I can't."

He turned away and made a show of scratching his eyebrows, but Danny could see he was wiping away tears.

"Your family slid away from us years ago, when your dad — did what he did. Since Christmas, Grandma and I have had you back in our lives. Having you with us has filled a hole in our hearts. Do you think we'd tear that hole open again if we believed there was any other way?" He swallowed.

"Then why can't she just go alone?" Danny demanded. "Why do I — why do I have to change *my* identity? What have *I* done wrong?"

Grandpa reached to hold Danny's arms, but the boy pulled back. "It's *because* of you – you and your sister – that your mom has to do this. If it were only her, she could stay and take her chances." He took a breath and gathered himself. "But she can't risk leaving you kids without a mother. And she can't risk *your* lives along with hers."

Danny's heartbeat throbbed at the back of his throat. "But – but – he said he loved her! I was there! You weren't! I heard him say it! The judge said he should have counseling!"

Grandpa no longer tried to stop his tears.

"Your dad doesn't love your mom the way…the way your mom loves you. He loves her like – like a miser loves money. He loves to control her, to possess her, to have power over her. And if he thinks he's going to lose that power and control…well, he'd rather kill her than let her go free. And that's not love."

Danny felt like he was plunging down a cliff in freefall. He lurched up and bolted blindly for the back gate. Buddy followed closely.

He sleepwalked through streets he'd walked a hundred times before, but today they had shifted orientation, their names had vanished, and the map lines rearranged to go nowhere. He lifted his arm and wiped his shirtsleeve across his face, forced his fists back into his pockets, and put one foot in front of the other. Buddy stayed close.

He wasn't sure how much time had passed before he found himself back at his grandparents' gate. He hadn't thought about where he was going, but Buddy's gentle nudging had returned him to the house. The dog sat patiently and waited for him to lift the latch. Danny hesitated before walking through.

Rather than entering the back, he walked around to the front.

Staying out of sight, he peered through the picture window. All four were sitting in the living room, Mom beside Grandma, and Jennifer on Grandpa's knee. They were talking, but Danny couldn't make out the words.

He went around back, took a deep breath, and entered.

The conversation stopped. He stood in the doorway. On closer view, the scene from the street – a family chatting on a Friday morning – had shifted focus, and he now saw discarded tissues and faces as raw as if frostbitten. Grandma stood up quickly and whispered, "I'll call the taxi."

The grandfather clock made the only sound in the room with its relentless *ticktock, ticktock* – each swing of the pendulum sweeping the present into the past.

Grandma returned. "It'll only be a couple of minutes. They have a cab in the neighborhood. They know about Buddy...."

*Ticktock...ticktock...ticktock...ticktock...*

Grandpa stood and strode over to Catherine, his arms wide, enveloping his daughter. She stood to sink her head into his shoulder, sobs pouring out freely, a lifetime of grief threatening to drown them all. Tears pulsed down Jennifer's face and Grandma held her tightly, stroking her granddaughter's hair, wetting it with her own tears, murmuring sounds that weren't words, because there were no words left.

"No long good-byes, Catherine," Grandpa said as he kissed her forehead and gently pushed her shoulders away. "You have to be strong, and take care of your children." He held her at arm's length, his grip on her shoulders firm. "Promise me you'll take care of your children."

Danny watched hollowly as Grandma and Grandpa switched places. Grandma embraced her daughter while Grandpa absorbed his granddaughter's anguish into his own. Danny felt like his feet had come to the end of the world. His legs, his arms, his head – everything was too heavy to move. He watched Grandma, Mom, Jennifer, and Grandpa mesh together in a tangle of grief.

The clock stopped ticking. Grandma left Catherine and approached him. She pulled his numb body into her own and urged his arms around her.

"Danny," she whispered into his ear, "when things are tough, look up to the stars and remember those same stars shine down on all of us, and we'll love you for as long as those stars shine in the sky. Although you can't touch *them*, their light can touch *you* and remind you there is no end to our love for you, no end to your mother's love for you. Tomorrow it may seem that all the world has changed, but love endures like the stars. Be strong. And live the best life you can live."

He blinked unseeing eyes. Grandpa touched Grandma on the shoulder, and said softly, "Patricia, the cab is here, can you help them out?"

Grandma gave Danny a last, close squeeze and kissed him softly on the cheek. "Good-bye, Danny," she said, pulling away.

Grandpa stood in front of Danny and reached one hand to touch his grandson's shoulder while the other searched for something in his pocket. He pulled out the small white stone Danny had thrown into the thorn bushes. He offered it on an open palm.

"Take this with you, Danny-boy. Keep it with you, and hold it when you need help. Stones are strong, and they can help you be strong too. Use it when you need to, and when you're ready, you can let it go."

Danny reached out. Grandpa put the stone into Danny's palm, curling the boy's fingers around it. He held Danny's fist tightly in both hands and then pulled his grandson to him and hugged him close. "No long good-byes, Danny, no long good-byes."

Grandpa let him go. "It's time," he said softly.

# PART TWO

# The Second Trial

# Chapter 1

"It's number twenty-one," said Sgt. Sandhu, handing Catherine two keys. Danny's face fell when he saw the place they were going to call home – a line of sad-looking row houses on the border of a strip mall parking lot. Peeling window trim outlined mismatched curtains and draped bed sheets. A patch of lawn too small to park a car separated one sidewalk from the next. A few adults lounged on steps and in webbed lawn chairs, smoking or watching children tear around on bicycles and skateboards. They stared at the new family moving in.

Number twenty-one was squeezed into the middle of the row. Someone had torn out a strip of grass under the window for a flower bed, but only crab grass and thorns grew there. A tabby cat, missing one ear, squatted under the steps.

Catherine walked hesitantly up the sidewalk. Someone had used knotted fishing line to try to repair a ragged L-shaped tear at elbow height in the screen door. She unlocked the water-stained inner door. Before she stepped over the scuffed threshold, she turned, a brave smile on her face.

"C'mon, kids, we're home," she said.

"I'll bring the suitcases," said Sgt. Sandhu. "I think we'd best leave Buddy in the van for now. You three go in and look around."

Danny straggled in behind Jennifer. They entered a short hallway with a shallow closet along one wall and a set of metal coat hooks screwed into the other. The hall opened into a living room and a set of stairs to the second floor. He walked across the cement-gray carpet. He barely glanced at the furniture as he marched to the bare window above the kitchen sink. It overlooked a common area surrounded by identical units.

Danny turned to his mother. "There's no place for Buddy."

"Don't worry, it's not for very long. We'll manage."

He brushed by his mother and headed up the stairs.

The second floor had three rooms and a bathroom. The master bedroom was half the size of his parents' old one. The bathroom faced the street. Two cramped bedrooms looked down on the common area. Jennifer had already checked out the rooms and chosen the one farther from the stairs.

"Doesn't matter to me," he muttered, and punched his hands into the pockets of the shorts he'd been wearing for days. He turned on his heel and strode out.

Their six suitcases lay on the living room floor. Sgt. Sandhu asked Danny to take them upstairs while he spoke with his mom.

Danny scowled, but picked up two bags. "Jen can carry her own," he announced. He halted at the stairs and eavesdropped on Sgt. Sandhu and his mom.

"The telephone will be installed in a couple of days," he said.

"Once you have it, call this number," he said. "They'll put you in touch with the NIVA reps here."

"Okay."

"It's critical you don't contact anyone in Edmonton. Not now…not ever."

Silence.

"Paul's being released – today's Sunday – so in the next couple of days. When he finds out you and the kids are gone…well, that's the most dangerous time. He'll do anything he can to find you or flush you out."

"I understand, but I'm worried about Danny."

"I know. I am too."

"If only there were some way to make him *believe*…to get him to trust me, accept that this is the only way…" she stammered, "…to save us all."

"He's a bright boy. He'll figure it out. Until then, you'll have to have faith that he'd never knowingly put all of you in danger. I don't believe he'd deliberately do it, but he might make a mistake, an error in judgment, and endanger you that way. It's just another one of the risks you're going to have to guard against."

Danny grabbed his mother's suitcases and trudged up the stairs. He dropped them in her room and went to get Buddy. He grasped the dog by the scruff of his neck and led him from the van. Buddy's nose twitched and he made a lunge for the cat. The neighborhood children abandoned their play and crowded around the border collie.

"What's his name?" "Can I pet him?" "Are you coming to live here in the condos?" "Does he bite?"

Danny struggled to keep his dog in check as Buddy tried to sniff every hand. The children smiled and giggled. Danny smiled too.

"His name's Buddy, and he doesn't bite," he said, crouching to hold the dog's neck while the children fussed over him.

"Oh, he licked me!" cried a young girl who stuck out her hand to be licked again.

"C'mon, Buddy-boy, it's time to go in," Danny said, pushing past the children.

"What's your name?" asked a boy about Jennifer's age.

Danny's smile faded. He led the dog up the front steps without a word.

Buddy raced around the condo and checked out every smell, his nose twitching like jelly shaking in a bowl. It didn't take him long to zip up the stairs.

Sgt. Sandhu was still talking. "I'll go and pick up some fried chicken while you get settled a bit. I'll have to be off pretty soon after dinner."

"Thank you. How can I ever thank you…"

"Stay alive. Just stay alive, and it will all be worth it."

Danny took the stairs two at a time and was out of sight before Sgt. Sandhu had left the kitchen. Buddy followed close on the boy's heels.

The police officer returned with a splotchy cardboard box and a small plastic bag. Danny had opened his suitcases, but had tugged out only a toothbrush and a fresh T-shirt. He'd had a shower, but he hadn't even shampooed his hair before the water ran cold. He wiped a wide arc across the green-edged mirror and gazed at his foggy reflection. His eyebrows were thickening and a few more hairs had appeared on his upper lip. He was beginning to look more like his father. Until now, everyone had said he looked like his mother.

He could smell the food even before he was half-way down the stairs. Lunch had been quite a while ago. Even though his gut was sometimes knotted with worry, he was hungry. Both Sgt. Sandhu and his mom looked relieved when he appeared at the table in a fresh shirt. Mom had laid out the chunky green plates she'd found in the cupboard. Cloudy glasses sat beside each plate. Some of the cutlery matched. Sgt. Sandhu opened the box of chicken and dumped fries out of a bag. Danny grabbed his favorite pieces. There wasn't much conversation. It didn't take them long to finish. There was no dessert.

"Could you help clear the table?" Mom asked Danny.

He picked up his plate and looked around.

"There's no dishwasher," he said.

She scanned the pressed-wood cupboards. "Yes, I see that now," she said with a thin smile. "Please just stack them by the sink." She used a dingy dishcloth to wipe the arborite table.

"Let's go into the living room for a bit," suggested Sgt. Sandhu.

They sat around the artificial oak coffee table. Mom and Jennifer took the sagging couch. Sgt. Sandhu and Danny were left with the armchairs. The red seat cushion went *whaa* as Danny sat, releasing the musty smell of old cigarettes and spilled beer. He stroked the arms, made oily and sticky by many hands.

As he spoke, Sgt. Sandhu looked back and forth between Danny and Jennifer. "I know this isn't much compared with what you're used to, but it's the best we can do for now. Don't worry, you know about your mom's plan, and it will all work out in the end. Remember, it isn't safe for anyone to know your old names.

It's a secret, one you must always keep. This is the most important secret of your lives, because your lives depend upon keeping it."

Danny fidgeted. He had a better idea, one that would give him back the life he wanted. Mom's plan didn't amount to a *secret* at all, did it? It was nothing but a lie – names and dates and a made-up past. And she'd said she'd never lie again. *I'll give it 'till Christmas,* he said to himself. *Then I'll contact Dad, he'll forgive Mom, we'll move back, and this 'between' time will all just be a bad dream.* He'd be right and they'd all be wrong. A Christmas to look forward to.

Sgt. Sandhu stood. "I – I have to go now. Remember to call NIVA when you get your phone. They'll help you…adjust." He moved to the couch. Jennifer and Catherine rose. The police officer reached for Jennifer and hugged her to his chest.

"Good-bye, Julia," he said. "Take care of yourself, and your brother, and your mother." He kissed her gently on the top of her head, and let her go.

He brushed away a tear. He picked up a bag from the coffee table. "This is for you, David." Danny sat stiff-necked as he took it. He reached inside and pulled out a new braided dog collar, much like the old one. It had two round brass tags that jingled as the collar moved. He turned them over. Each one was blank.

Sgt. Sandhu offered his hand. Danny rose awkwardly and reached out. The officer grasped Danny's hand, and placed his other palm over the top.

"Good luck, David. Take care." Their eyes locked briefly, but Danny broke the contact and looked down.

"Thanks for the collar," he mumbled, steeling himself against showing any emotion. He fiddled with the collar.

The police officer looked at Catherine. She moved around the table and took his hands in hers.

"You're a brave woman, Susan. You're doing the right thing."

"Thank you," she choked. "No long good-byes."

"No long good-byes," the police officer repeated as he started toward the door. He paused in the entryway.

"This is for you and the kids," he said, holding out a white envelope he'd pulled from his back pocket. "From Anita and me."

She took the envelope. "Thank you," she stammered.

Sgt. Sandhu took a deep breath, collected himself, and said, "Don't leave anything to chance. Those notes you've made – keep them only until you have them memorized – then burn them."

She nodded.

"Good-bye, Susan. Good-bye and good luck."

# Chapter 2

Danny buckled the collar on the impatient dog. The last couple of days had been hard. As they had driven away from their Edmonton home in the unmarked police van, he'd hung onto the worry stone. Jennifer had clutched her love-worn teddy, Shakesbear, and wiped away tears with her favorite blanket. They'd spent that night in a motel that resembled the YES. He'd never been to a motel, and it had never occurred to him that air conditioning could be optional. He pretended he didn't care, but he was too nervous about getting lost or losing collarless Buddy to do anything but stay in the dingy room.

Now he hoped he could find an off-leash park somewhere near the condo. Buddy needed it. Danny put the new collar on Buddy and when he saw the leash, the border collie dashed to the door.

His mom glanced at her watch. "Can you be back by nine?"

Danny looked at his wrist. No watch. He'd forgotten it at home.

He left without a word.

"See you later, Davey-boy," his mom whispered at the closed door.

All eyes followed the new kid as the dog led him down the sidewalk. He turned abruptly and aimed for the mall.

A few featureless shops hung off the end of the parking lot. Abandoned grocery carts littered the parking spaces. A group of teens shared a smoke in front of the video store. There were two ways he could avoid them: go behind the mall onto a scruffy field, or angle toward a cluster of duplexes down the street. Although he wanted to let Buddy run, the dark was gathering and he opted for the street.

The day after they'd left Edmonton, Sgt. Sandhu had driven them around Saskatoon in the afternoon heat to show them the places they were supposed to be 'from.' They'd cruised bumpy streets. Single-storey houses older than Grandma and Grandpa's huddled unevenly, back from the sidewalks. They were almost all the same. Steep-pitched roofs ended in wobbly gutters added like an afterthought.

"This district's called Greenview," Sgt. Sandhu said. "These houses were built in wartime. You can see some of them have been nicely kept up, and some of them haven't. The original owners usually live in the nice-looking ones. The others tend to be rented by lower-income people with young children and immigrants on their way to something better. We picked this neighborhood because there aren't many families like yours, so it's unlikely you'll bump into someone who actually lived here. All the street names start with *Green* – Greenhill, Greenway, Greentree – easy to remember."

Mom wrote it down.

A stumble over a frost-heave on the Winnipeg sidewalk jolted Danny back to the present. Dusk was falling. He ran his fingers through his hair. Part of him wanted to get off this road and back into the condo. Another part of him didn't want to ever return to the place he already despised. He chewed his lower lip and then steered Buddy back to the complex. As they rounded the far side, he saw a sign he hadn't noticed before. It announced the condo complex's name: New Haven.

*New Haven!*

His mom and sister were cuddling on the couch when Danny returned. His mom looked tense and she rose to greet him.

He shuffled his feet. "Do we – should we take off our shoes at the door?"

"I think it's okay to keep them on. We won't worry about it."

He bent to unsnap the leash and spoke without looking up. "Where should we keep Buddy's dishes?"

"I've put them in the basement. The front entrance is too small, and in the kitchen he'd just be underfoot." She paused. "And it's only for a while, a few weeks…"

"Okay," he replied. Buddy's nose had already led him to the bottom of the stairs. Mom had moistened the food just the way he liked it. His muzzle dove into the water dish.

Danny scanned the basement. Someone had laid thin linoleum tiles over the concrete floor. A metal stand supported an old portable TV made before there were remote controls. A ratty couch and chair faced the dusty screen. Someone had tacked old tablecloths over two narrow windows, making the room gloomy. He sighed, turned his back, and went up to his bedroom.

He threw his suitcases on the bed and began to unpack. He tried to organize his things in the drawers and closet the same way he'd had them at home, but a week's worth of clothes ate up all the space. He had to hang his hoodies in the closet. He dumped his sports gear on the closet floor. *It's a good thing the rest of my stuff won't arrive until we move to a bigger place*, he thought. There was no desk. He'd have to do his homework at the kitchen table. He was tired, but he'd forgotten his watch so he didn't know what time it was. But it didn't really matter anymore, did it? The only time he cared about was the time this would all be over. Until then, he'd coast.

Mom had settled on the living room couch in a shaft of morning sunlight. She was studying the newspapers Sgt. Sandhu had bought in Saskatoon so she would know a little more about the place. She lifted her head. "Good morning. I was hoping you'd come with me to the grocery store so we can buy some food. We need breakfast."

Danny rarely went for groceries. Mom and Jennifer shopped. He spent time with Dad.

Dad. He swallowed and then focused on his mom's request. But – no car. They'd left it at Grandma and Grandpa's. They'd have to walk and carry back their groceries.

"I have some money from Grandma and Grandpa, and Sgt. Sandhu gave us some too. You can pick out some things you like," she said lightly.

Danny squinted. "When're we gonna get a car?"

"It'll have to wait until we get the money from the house sale."

He didn't *want* the house sold. But they needed the money, and after all, he didn't want to live this way, not all the way 'till Christmas.

"I'm sorry, I know this isn't what you want, but I need your help. And we need to work together." They locked eyes. Her lined face looked tired but her gaze was strong, and her eyes tugged him into today's reality. Monday, August 12th: the day of his father's release.

Mom and Jennifer held hands while Danny dragged behind. Someone had set a grass fire on the field behind the mall. The ground was scorched as black as asphalt. An old school was perched on the field's far edge. It was in even worse shape than the one Sgt. Sandhu had shown them – Greenview Elementary – the one he was supposed to have 'attended' in Saskatoon.

They filled six grocery bags in short order. Mom scooped up their favorite treats: microwave popcorn for Jennifer and ketchup potato chips for him. As they trudged back she said, "Since we can't carry too much at a time, we'll have to shop again tomorrow. But this way we won't buy too much, seeing as we're moving soon anyway."

They loaded the groceries into the empty cupboards. The few bags of food left them looking bare.

"Let's have lunch," Mom said.

Danny got out the dishes. There were exactly four of everything: bowls, plates, mugs, knives, forks, and spoons. They'd have to do dishes by hand three times a day. No stacking them into the dishwasher to run once a day.

"After lunch," Mom said, "we'll take the bus and get you registered in your new schools."

"Why can't we take a taxi?" Danny whined.

Catherine took a breath before answering. "Well, two reasons.
First, even though Grandma and Grandpa gave us some money,
I need to be careful with it, because it's going to be a while before
our first payment comes from the government. Second, you'll
know which bus to take when you go to school."

"Why do we have to take a bus at all?" challenged Danny. "I
saw a school across from the mall."

"Well, the schools you're registering in are in the district we'll
be moving to when we buy our house. That way you won't have
to change schools after just a month. And they're better schools
than the ones here." She paused. "You must believe we've thought
this through and have a plan to make this as painless as possible.
I'm taking charge now, and I'm going to take care of you. Things
will all work out, you'll see."

Danny got up to leave.

"I'll do the dishes," she said. "Why don't you two go outside
for a bit, and maybe meet some of the neighbors?"

"What's the point?" Danny retorted. "You just said we're moving soon anyway."

# Chapter 3

Catherine unfolded bus schedules and a city map. "The bus goes from here at 1:10 p.m. Today we have to make a transfer, but don't worry. On school days, the bus is direct. Okay?" She tucked the family history into her purse.

The bus came late, which meant the connecting bus had left the transit station before they arrived. There wouldn't be another for twenty minutes. Catherine gave them coins for the vending machine. Danny idly kicked a stone around the pavement. Not many people waited at the station, mainly elderly ladies and young-looking mothers pushing baby strollers with wheels as big as Danny's bike's. He leaned against the bus shelter's outside wall, even though the wind had picked up and it was cool for a mid-August day.

On the bus, he sat alone at the back. Mom guided Jennifer onto a seat nearby. Fifteen minutes later they turned into a residential district. Well-tended lawns surrounded trim houses in orderly rows. Mature maple trees alternated with hedges. Generous green fields opened on each side of the road. He could see a school – no, two schools – ahead. Jennifer pulled the cord to ring the bell. "Later, the whole ride will take you twenty minutes at most," Mom reassured them as they waited for the back doors to open. "Don't worry."

The schools faced each other – École Westlawn Elementary School, and Queen Elizabeth Junior High.

"Let's register you first…David," Mom said. "We'll do Julia after that."

He dragged behind her.

A woman about Mom's age gazed at a computer. "I'll be with you in a sec," she said from her desk.

"Jewel, do you want to go outside and look around while we register?" Mom asked.

"No," the girl replied, slipping her hand into her mother's.

Danny sat in one of the chairs along the opposite wall. Sunlight spread through a large window.

"I'm Theresa Helpan. How can I help you?"

"I'd like to register my son for school."

"Are you new to the neighborhood?"

"Yes, we've just moved here from…Saskatoon."

"Okay," she said, reaching into a filing cabinet for some papers. "Since you're new, you'll have to fill out this form." She handed Catherine a pen and a sheaf of papers. "Did you bring his school records from Saskatoon?"

"Nooo," Mom hesitated. "We…couldn't get them in time."

"All right," Ms. Helpan smiled. "But we'll need them as soon as possible."

"No problem," Catherine replied. She moved toward one of the chairs.

"You can fill them out here at the counter," the secretary volunteered. "It's easier to write."

"That's okay," Catherine mumbled as she took a seat. Once the secretary was back at her desk, she pulled the family's new history from her purse. She pretended to use it as a writing surface while furtively checking the information. When she finished, she placed the form on the counter.

The secretary frowned at the form. "This is a closed boundary school. You live outside our boundaries. I'm afraid you can't register here."

"But the place we're at is just...temporary. We're buying a house in this neighborhood. We plan to move on the first of October – and I don't want to register my son at another school and then transfer here after just a month. And I have my daughter," she lied, pointing at Jennifer, "already registered at the school across the street."

The secretary looked dubious. "For sure by the first of October? Our cut-off date is September thirteenth."

"Would you please extend it for us? I need just a little more time. My parents passed away and I'm using my inheritance to buy the house, but I won't have the money for another month or so," she said, looking directly into the secretary's eyes.

"Oh, I'm sorry." Ms. Helpan's voice softened. "I'll talk with the principal and see if he'll make an exception."

"Thank you very much."

"You're welcome. Now, I still need to make a copy of your son's

–" she scanned the paper for Danny's name.

"It's David. His name is David," repeated his mother. "I'm sorry, he's been a little distant, what with his grandparents dying and all. He hasn't adjusted to things – yet."

"Of course. It must be difficult." She smiled at Danny but he remained stone-faced. "May I have his birth certificate?"

"I'm sorry," Mom faltered. "I left that in Saskatoon by mistake. With some of the papers I left with the lawyer," she finished lamely.

"Well," she replied. "I'll have the principal call and let you know whether he can enroll here. You can give us a copy of the birth certificate and his school records then." She looked at the form and furrowed her brows. "You haven't filled in your phone number," she said.

"Our phone isn't connected yet. We just moved in yesterday. They said it would be about a week. I'll call you just as soon as we have it."

"Ah. Very well. And you should know we can't pay for the bussing since you're out of the district." The secretary seemed uncomfortable with all the uncertainties. She reached under the counter for another form and offered it to Danny. "Here, take this. It's a list of options. As soon as your spot's confirmed, I'll need to know your choices so we can schedule your timetable. And this is the school supply list."

Danny didn't budge. His mom reached for the papers. "I'll take that," she said, "and I'll be sure he fills it out."

"That's fine. Well, good-bye…" the secretary looked at the form again "…Ms. Mayer. We'll be in touch."

"Susan," replied Catherine. "Please call me Susan."

Once outside, Catherine spoke to Danny through gritted

teeth. "You're not making this any easier. Would you *please* cooperate?"

"Didn't you teach me, if you can't say anything nice, don't say anything at all?"

She kept her eyes on her son. "Please?" she asked again.

He looked at the ground.

"Jennifer – Julia – let's go register at your school. David – you can wait outside, look around."

Jennifer took her mom's hand as they crossed the street. Once they'd disappeared into the elementary school, Danny gazed around. Soccer pitches, baseball diamonds, playgrounds, and bicycle paths stretched behind both schools. Farther back, behind the junior high, it looked like there was still another school with a green belt all around it. In spite of himself, he was impressed. It'll do until Christmas, and it'll be great for Buddy, too.

Soon Jennifer and Mom came out, holding hands and laughing.

"That didn't take long," Danny grumbled.

"The school didn't seem as hung up on details and I was better prepared," his mom said. She stopped laughing and stared at Danny.

*She sees I look like my dad, now that we're away from him. That's why she never laughs with me,* he thought.

"Let's go," Catherine said. "It's three-thirty and we can catch the bus straight home." She smiled, but only with her lips.

⚒

"Why don't you take Buddy for a walk?" Mom suggested as she unlocked the door. She didn't have to suggest it – Buddy insisted.

This time, the late-afternoon sun encouraged them to roam farther along the residential streets and bike paths separating one condo complex from another. People swung their cars into the mall parking lot to make last-minute dinner purchases. Instead of staying on the road, Danny turned right, toward the mall and the field. Sure enough, there was that school. Brown brick, single storey, with a flat tar and gravel roof. A tarmac skirt led to half a dozen portables strung along the sides. A few children took turns bouncing a striped rubber ball against the wall, careful to avoid the windblown paper cups and Styrofoam boxes at its base. Buddy was a kid magnet, so Danny detoured around them toward the portables.

Metal grates covered windows set high into the walls. Four wooden steps led to each padlocked, steel door. A tattered flag hung at the top of a steel pole that had once been painted white.

Danny crossed the dusty lawn. *Harry Smith Junior High*, he read. He circled the building, walking to the empty oil-stained parking lot. Beyond it lay a weedy field with a ball diamond back-stop and a soccer pitch. He tilted his head to the side. How could the small field fit two playing areas? Dry grass crunched underfoot as he scanned the area. The two fields actually overlapped one another. Home plate was off to the side of the far goalposts. First base was scuffed into one half of the soccer field, and second base was on its touch line. Only third base lay outside the soccer field. A pitcher's mound, unevenly covered in red shale, sat right on the center line of the soccer field.

Queen Elizabeth Junior High was starting to look even better. "Tomorrow we'll come back with your Frisbee, okay Bud?" he said to his impatient dog. They headed home for supper. Danny ignored the kids' pleas to play with the dog, and two sharp tugs got Buddy through the door.

"Oh good, you're home," his mom said when the screen door slammed. "Your sister's out back playing with some kids. Would you please call her in?"

Peering through the back door he saw Jennifer off to the side, turning a skipping rope for some girls who looked a couple of years younger than she was. They giggled as each slap of the rope tore out a few more blades of grass.

Danny opened his mouth to call her and then caught his breath. What was he going to call her? He couldn't say Jennifer. He wouldn't say Julia. He turned and started for the stairs. "You call her. I'm feeding Buddy," he snapped.

He grabbed the water dish and opened the basement door. A furnace and a stubby water heater took up one wall and empty storage shelves climbed another. The bag of dog food leaned against bare concrete between exposed wood studs. Copper pipes trailed down into a deep laundry tub. Someone had replaced one tub leg with a length of two-by-four. Yellowish-brown rust stains covered the bottom and crept up the sides of the once-white plastic sink. He quickly rinsed and filled the dog dish.

He heard his mother. "Jewel, come in, it's time to eat."

*Okay*, he thought. *Nicknames.* He'd never used his sister's nickname, but it kind of made it like it was before. *I can do nicknames*, he decided.

Jennifer chattered at the table. "They're mostly younger than me, Mom, but lots of 'em are girls, and it's almost like they're competing to play with me. It's kinda fun, they wanna show me everything. I mean, they're young and all, but I'll have lots of company 'till we move to the new house."

"That's sounds great, Jewel," Mom replied, stroking her daughter's arm. She turned to Danny. "What about you? Maybe you should get out and meet some of the kids...." Her voice hung in the air.

"No."

"It'll give you some time to practice for school. They're young, they won't ask so many questions about you."

Danny scooped the last of the macaroni and cheese into his mouth and pushed himself away from the table. Downstairs, he flipped on the TV and jerked back when the knob made a grinding sound like microphone feedback. He spun the channel knob through all the stations. All five of them. And one of them was French.

*Great*, he thought, flopping onto the couch. *Welcome to the five-channel universe.*

# Chapter 4

Tuesday and Wednesday were reruns of Monday. He resented the morning shopping trips, but they passed the time. Afternoons dragged by in front of the TV. Eat, walk the dog, TV, bedtime. When no one was looking, he picked up the receiver of the chunky telephone. A scratched plastic tag covered a smeared number. Still no dial tone.

On Thursday morning, the warm weather surrendered to solid rain.

"We've got enough groceries for now," Mom announced. "Let's shop for school supplies. And," she smiled, "we'll buy an umbrella."

Danny used to love his annual school shopping trip almost as much as picking out Hallowe'en treats. Happy memories lightened his mood and he was the first one into the mall. He browsed through a forest of *Back to School* signs. He kneaded neoprene ballpoint pens and pungent markers between his fingers. He bent the cellophane-wrapped packages of lined paper until they squeaked. He ran his fingers along the spines of vinyl three-ring binders that snapped open and shut and smelled like blow-up pool toys. Mom helped Jen with her list, and soon only one item remained.

"Mom, what's a graphing calculator?" Danny asked. "I don't see anything like that here."

Catherine flipped through the selection of calculators hanging from metal pegs. "You're right, I don't either. We'll have to ask."

The clerk told her they were a specialty item she could buy only at an office supply store. In an upbeat voice, Catherine said "Good. I'd planned a trip downtown tomorrow, anyway. We'll get your calculator and buy each of you some new clothes for school."

They divided the bags and carried them home. Danny spent most of the rainy afternoon in his room, sorting through his supplies, testing each pen before laying it in a neat pile. He realized he was going to need a few more things: a pencil case and a backpack for the bus. And he'd forgotten to buy a new eraser. Every year, his mom bought him a new one, even if he hadn't used up last year's. He loved the velvety feel of the pink rubber, its baby-powdery smell, and the way it flexed between his fingers. He decided to make a list.

When Danny took it to the kitchen to show his mom, he found her writing some figures on a pad of graph paper. She looked up and moved her arm to cover the receipts. But when her eyes met his, she dropped her elbow.

"Don't worry, Davey-boy, I've got enough money to get us through. I just have to keep track of it. Grandma and Grandpa will send us some cash when they sell our furniture and the other belongings, and after that, of course we'll be getting the money from the house sale. The court application to divide the property is today. I have a good feeling about it, Davey."

Thinking about the court application gave him stomach butterflies. He dropped his list on the table and strode to the basement.

He must have fallen asleep in front of the TV, because the next thing he heard was his mother calling them for dinner. In the kitchen he looked again at the telephone mounted on the wall. He picked up the receiver. Still dead air.

He stayed quiet at dinner. Jen chatted more than she chewed. "The kids want to come over, Mom, and see my room."

Catherine had kept a low profile for the five days they'd been here. Except for the trips to the store and the school, she'd stayed inside too. When she poked out her head to empty junk mail from the mailbox, some of the neighbors had tried to catch her eye or start conversations. She had smiled and waved and looked busy, and closed the door as quickly as possible. Now, Jennifer was ready to open the door and let the world in. Danny was not. Catherine hesitated and then gave her daughter a candid answer.

"Well, Jewel, I think that'd be okay, but your brother isn't ready for visitors yet, so you may bring your friends in, but leave your brother alone – deal?"

Jennifer didn't hesitate. "Deal!" she said, trotting for the door.

Catherine turned to Danny. "Even though it's still raining, I think you'd better get Buddy out for a walk. It doesn't look like it's going to clear up anytime soon." The words 'Buddy' and 'walk' sent the border collie scrambling for his leash. Danny's mom smiled at him. "Don't forget your umbrella."

The umbrella stayed propped in the corner. A boy pedaled a bicycle up the walk. He was six or seven years old, and didn't seem to notice his clothes were soaked through. "Can I walk your dog?" he asked, flicking his eyes back and forth between Buddy and Danny.

"Tell you what," answered Danny. "You can hold his leash while I get my hat."

"Sure," he replied, thrusting out his hand. "Hi, boy," he said. The boy abandoned his bike to wrestle with the dog. Buddy jumped back and forth across the boy's thin body, delighted to have a new plaything. "Can I come with you? Please?"

Danny surprised himself with how quickly he agreed. The boy hopped on his bike and eagerly asked, "Which way d'we go?"

"This way," said Danny, as he started toward the *New Haven* sign.

The boy pedaled along in the gutter, keeping up a steady patter. Danny half listened. He wanted a dog, but his stepdad was allergic; he'd had a goldfish named Bubbles, wasn't that a stupid name but his sister had picked it, but Bubbles had died after a month and his mom wouldn't buy another one; he was going to start Grade 1 this year and Mom was going to make him walk with all the dorky girls…

As the boy droned on, Danny felt a tug of happiness. He was enjoying the company. No one had talked to him about normal things in months and months. He was lonely. He'd lost his old friends and hadn't made any new ones.

"…will you go to?"

The question caught Danny off guard.

"Which school will you go to?" repeated the boy.

"Um…, I can't remember the name. It's a ways from here."

"Why don't you go to Harry Smith School?"

"'Cause we're not gonna live here long. Next month we're moving."

"Oh." The boy kept pedaling. "How come?"

"Just…because."

The boy paused, considering Danny's answer. "Before you go, can I walk your dog?"

"Maybe," he replied. "Maybe."

It felt good to be wanted.

They squelched into the entry. He made sure the dog went downstairs before shaking the water from his coat. Danny jogged upstairs. As he was rummaging through the few remaining clean clothes, he could hear girls' voices through the bedroom wall. They seemed to be playing house, each one taking a different role.

Today's clothes were too wet to stash under the bed with the rest of his dirty laundry. They had to go into the laundry room. As he bent to scoop up the pile, a smell like moldy mushrooms wafted up. He carried the armload downstairs, losing a couple of socks along the way. He dropped the laundry and flicked on the light.

No washer.

No dryer.

Just the stained plastic laundry tub.

He left his clothes where they'd fallen, smacked the light switch, and kicked the door shut.

# Chapter 5

A high-pitched ring woke Danny on Friday morning. It took him a few groggy moments to figure out it was the phone. Mom answered. Danny crept to the top step, not wanting his mother to know he was listening.

"Yes…that's a relief…How – how did he act?…No….What's her best guess?…and the ID?…All right, well, Danny's really struggling. I think he still doesn't believe all this is necessary… Yes, the move should help. This place is a dive…Yes, what number can I call you at? Okay. Thank you. Good-bye."

Danny slipped back into bed and lay there. It wasn't hard to figure out what they'd been talking about. Yesterday's application. He finally rose and went downstairs. The table was already set.

"Oh good, you're up," his mom said. "I wanted to speak with you before your sister gets down."

He sat and gulped his orange juice. He didn't put down the glass. Instead, he spun it around and around between his two hands, watching the liquid slosh up the sides. "Our phone works now. Did you hear it ring?"

He grunted.

"It was a man from NIVA. He was letting me know what happened in court yesterday. I want to tell you. I'm keeping my promise to you, not to hide anything anymore." She took a breath and continued. "The hearing went as we expected. Your dad came to court and asked to know where we are. He said he wanted to see you – and your sister.

"The judge refused. But she did say he could come back to court in a year and ask again."

Danny stared into the glass.

"The judge divided the property the way we asked. Your father got the insurance business, and I got the house. Because he doesn't get to see you, he doesn't have to pay any child support." She licked her lips. "Paul will go into the house today to take some of his things. Then tomorrow, Grandma and Grandpa can start collecting our stuff. It'll only take them the weekend to sort through it. My lawyer has already arranged to list the house for sale on Monday."

He tipped back the juice glass for another drink, but it was already empty.

"Danny," she said earnestly, "things are going as planned. It's working out, and it'll keep working out – you'll see."

He looked at his empty plate, then plunked down the glass and shoved his palms against the table until his chair balanced on two back legs.

"But," he said, "if the judge said Dad could apply again in a year, then…" He stopped as he saw the tears gathering along her lower eyelids.

"Danny. You must believe me," she said, her voice firm. "It'll *never* be safe to have contact with your dad. Not now. Not a year from now. Not ever."

Danny dropped the chair's front legs to the floor and went upstairs without breakfast.

He lay on his bed and stared at the ceiling. He struggled to sort out his thoughts.

Maybe the whole mess had become too big for him to stop. It had seemed to have its own momentum, like a boulder rolling down a hill. Even Grandma and Grandpa seemed to think this was the right thing to do, and even Grandma and Grandpa didn't know his new name. *But I could run away again, back to Edmonton, and live with Dad.* The Youth Emergency Shelter popped into his mind. *Where can you go when you can't go home?* What did it matter? By Monday, his home would be gone.

But if he went back to Edmonton he wouldn't see his mother. Or his sister. He and his dad would have to live in a different place.

*I can never go home again.*

*I love my mother.*

*I want to love my father again.*

*I want to be Danny McMillan.*

*My plan is still the best one.*

He massaged the taut muscles in his neck. *I'll go along with things, wait a few months, then contact Dad, and make things right. We'll move back, I'll live with Mom and see lots of Dad, Mom'll be safe, and all of this will be just a bad dream.*

He relaxed. His plan would work. In the meantime, he'd go along with his mother. He'd be nicer to her; he didn't want to see her cry anymore. He knew she'd already cried enough for a lifetime, and she was doing her best. A few months of this – he could do it. It wouldn't kill him.

He returned to the kitchen. "Is there any toast left? When do we go shopping? I thought of another thing – I need a new watch."

He watched his mother's posture soften. "Toast coming up," she said as she turned to the counter and smiled.

Shopping went well. They bought the rest of the school supplies, and Mom didn't blink an eye when the graphing calculator cost a hundred and twenty-five dollars. Danny picked up a copy of *Sports Illustrated* and a new CD. Jennifer chose a book on making paper dolls, while Mom treated herself to scented candles, a lighter, and the newspaper. They picked through a couple of department stores for their back-to-school clothes. He chose the latest digital sports watch – even better than the one he'd left at home – and a sturdy backpack.

They went beyond their six-bag limit and lugged their purchases onto the bus. When they got home, a manila envelope was sticking out of the mailbox. It was addressed to *Susan Mayer*, and the return address was a box number in Saskatoon.

Their new identities had arrived.

Catherine called both schools. She gave them the phone number, confirmed she had the papers, and said everything was going well and she expected to receive her inheritance soon. She hung up and went to Danny's room.

"They said they'd hold your place until September thirteenth. As long as we can show them a contract to buy a house before then, there's no problem." She handed him a paper. "It's time to pick your options."

He scanned the course descriptions: Outdoor Phys Ed, Choral Music, Band, Woodworking, Cooking and Baking, Art,

French, Ukrainian, Chinese, German, Yearbook, Sewing, and Community Service. While he tried to make up his mind, he could hear his mother on the phone. "Yes, I'd like to see some houses in the Westlawn neighborhood…No, I don't….Yes, that would be fine. See you tomorrow at one."

Downstairs, he found her looking at the newspaper's real estate section. "There's a realtor coming tomorrow to take us house shopping," she said brightly. She turned to another section of the paper. "What kind of car do you think we should get?"

Danny took Buddy and Buddy took his Frisbee out to the school grounds. After a happy hour, they returned to find Catherine in the living room, drinking coffee with one of the neighbors.

"This is my son, David," she said. "David, meet Ms. Watson. She's Katie's mom – you know, Katie, who's playing upstairs with Jewel?"

"Hi," he replied, but kept moving. "I've gotta get Buddy some water." He overheard Jennifer talking with a girl about making paper dolls.

To anyone visiting, it was a normal household.

The visitors left, and Jennifer modeled her new clothes. She challenged Danny to a game of Snakes and Ladders. "And I brought my Disneyland cards," she said.

"Okay," he replied. "Get ready to lose."

While the spaghetti sauce heated, Catherine slipped upstairs and opened her inlaid wood jewelry box. She pulled out a heart-shaped crystal the size of a quarter, a gift from the kids for Mother's Day. It dangled from a fine string of nylon fishing line, as thin as spider silk. She carried it to the kitchen and gently hung it in the window, where it caught the summer sun and radiated all the colors of the rainbow. She smiled.

After supper Danny and Jennifer played several hands of cards, and Jennifer announced she was the winner.

"I let her win," Danny replied.

"Sore loser!" Jennifer called as she headed for bed.

Danny decided to get to bed early too. He wanted to listen to his CD and read the magazine. He stretched out on the bed, Buddy sprawled at his feet. He popped on his headphones and started flipping the pages.

Buddy's sudden bark startled him. The dog jumped to the floor, his nose twitching back and forth as if he were on the trail of a squirrel. He barked again, and now Danny could smell it too – something was burning. Buddy zipped downstairs with Danny after him. The smell was rolling out the kitchen door.

His mom was standing at the sink. She'd placed the candle in it and seemed to be burning some papers. As he approached he recognized the family history questionnaire.

"What're you doing?" he asked in alarm, moving closer.

"Hey, Davey-boy," she answered. "I'm getting rid of these because we don't need them anymore. We have our new papers now." She smiled at him. "No fireplace, so I decided the safest spot was here." She turned back to the flame, feeding the papers one at a time, the blackened edges shriveling and crumbling into the sink, the smoke braiding around the crystal heart. "Even though we're only going to be here a while, we don't want to burn down the place, do we?" she joked."

# Chapter 6

The phone call came very early the next morning. It was still dark outside. Danny saw the hall light turn on and heard his mother hurry by. He pushed the light button on his new watch. Four twenty-three a.m.

His heart started to pound.

His mom picked up the receiver.

For a few moments, nothing.

And then it started. A howl like an animal caught in a leg-hold trap. Buddy jumped to the floor and raked the door with his claws. When Danny opened it, the dog shot downstairs.

He moved slowly, one deliberate footstep after another, both drawn and repulsed by the sobs he heard coming from the kitchen. Mom was jackknifed, as if she had taken a blow to her stomach. Her breath came in gasps. The abandoned receiver bounced up and down on its coiled cord as she pushed blindly past her son. She tripped over the bottom stair and collapsed onto the carpet like a puppet with its strings cut. Buddy jumped back and forth over her body, nuzzling her gently and making deep-throated sounds that blended in with her moans.

Danny could hear a man's voice calling distantly from the dangling phone.

"Susan? Susan?"

Danny moved forward as if in a trance. He stared at the receiver, still swaying up and down. He lifted it and held it to his ear.

"Susan?" asked an urgent voice. "Are you there?"

"It's me," he replied, his voice sounding flat and mechanical.

A pause. "David?" Another pause. "David?"

Danny felt like the world had gone out of focus. "Yes," he said.

"David, I'm Scott, from NIVA. Is – is your mom okay?"

"No."

"David, listen to me. I'm coming straight over. I'll be about ten minutes. Do you understand?"

Danny closed his eyes.

"Listen. Stay by your mom. I'll be there as soon as I can."

The line went dead. He held the receiver, the dial tone buzzing in his ear. Stiff-armed, he replaced the receiver and took a few slow steps toward his mom.

Jennifer had appeared and was crouching on the top step. She'd pulled her nightgown over her bent knees and clasped her arms around her shins. She rocked back and forth as she pressed her lips into her kneecaps, her fingers twirling a strand of hair. Mom still lay on the carpet with her arms folded over her head as if warding off a blow. Her moans gave way to a repetitive chant.

"Ohmygod. Ohmygod. Ohmygod. It's – all – gone –"

Soon, she didn't even cry anymore. She lay motionless, her eyes staring. Jennifer still rocked back and forth, back and forth. Danny perched on the edge of the couch. The border collie ran to each of them in turn, thrusting his muzzle into hands, licking faces, trying to rescue them all.

A sharp rap at the door. Danny looked at his watch. Four thirty-five a.m. Twelve minutes since the phone call. He opened the door.

"David, where's your mother?" asked a short, stocky man wearing a windbreaker over a T-shirt and sweat pants.

Danny moved aside, clearing Scott's view. Catherine lay on her side with her eyes closed.

Buddy growled as Scott moved toward her. "David, can you call the dog?"

"Come, Bud," Danny called in a thin monotone.

Buddy didn't move, his warning growl unchanged.

"David, I need your help – your mom needs your help. *Please.*"

Danny finally moved and grasped the dog's collar. "C'mere, Buddy," he repeated. "It's okay, boy. He won't hurt her."

The dog sat, but his head remained lowered and his eyes never left the stranger.

Scott crouched and touched Catherine on the shoulder.

"Susan. Susan. It's Scott. It's okay, Susan. You need to sit up."

For a long minute, no one moved. Then Catherine jerked up to a sitting position.

Danny looked at his mother's face, then at Scott. It was like looking from one stranger to another.

"Susan," Scott said, "let's get you to bed. I'll tell the kids." He helped support her up the stairs and into her room. "Just rest now. We'll talk later." Jennifer squished her body against the wall to let them pass. After settling Catherine, Scott returned to the girl. He squeezed her shoulder.

"You must be Julia," he said in a soothing voice. "Come downstairs with me, and we'll talk about what happened."

Scott guided her to the couch beside her brother. Danny still had a firm grip on the vigilant dog.

"It's – it's your house in Edmonton," Scott started. "There's been...an accident." He paused. Both children stared at him. "There's been a fire. An explosion and a fire."

Danny tilted his head and blinked. "A fire?"

"Yes."

"Bad?"

Scott looked from one face to another. "Bad. It's burned to the ground." Scott paused. "I'm sorry."

Blood pounded in Danny's ears, each throb repeating his mother's words.

*It's – all – gone –*

Saturday, August 17th, 2002. His parents' sixteenth wedding anniversary.

They didn't open the curtains that day. No one answered the door when the realtor rang. Danny and Jennifer drifted about the condo, picking up snacks when they felt hungry and even when they didn't.

Catherine remained shut in her room. Danny heard a few bouts of sobbing but mostly it was quiet. Jennifer tiptoed past her mother's door and shut herself in her room.

Danny didn't cry that day because he didn't know what to cry

for. Or maybe it was that he'd already cried for his past and if he
started again he'd be caught in a revolving door, going around and
around and around, never able to exit. He zoned out in front of the
TV. It was too much trouble to get up and switch from the French
channel. Buddy patrolled the house, sometimes lying at Danny's
feet, other times sitting in front of the closed bedroom doors.

Finally, Danny heard doors opening and closing and water
running. Mom must have let the water run completely cold before
leaving the shower. About an hour later, she plodded downstairs.
She looked wrung-out, her face strained, shoulders slumped, a
shadow in a housecoat. He was sitting at the kitchen table thumb-
ing through *Sports Illustrated*.

"Did you get something to eat?" she asked flatly, shuffling to
the stove to fill the kettle. When he didn't reply, she said, "I'm not
hungry either." She spooned some instant coffee into a chipped
mug and stood vacantly beside the stove, waiting for the water to
boil. Without turning around, her voice a monotone, she said, "I
think we all need a quiet day today. That would be best." She didn't
say anything else as she poured the water and trudged upstairs
to dress.

Danny's evening drifted by on the couch, the living room
chair, and eventually, his bed. He didn't fit anywhere, and his plans
had unraveled again.

He woke the next morning to the sound of his mother on the
telephone. This time he waited until she hung up before going
downstairs. Mom sat at the table, yesterday's mug refilled with
instant coffee, a bottle of aspirin at its side. She'd dressed and

combed her hair, but her pale skin seemed to hang from her face and her eyes were hollow.

"We don't have many groceries left," she said. "Would you come to the store with me and help carry bags?"

*How could groceries be important now?*

"Okay," he replied uncertainly. "I'll dress and get Jennifer."

"No, we won't have much to carry, don't wake Jennifer."

He hesitated and then said, "Okay, Mom." When he returned a couple of minutes later, she had opened the drapes and stood blinking into the warm yellow sun.

"I've left Jen a note," she said as she put on sunglasses. "Let's go." He tugged on his baseball cap and softly shut the door behind him.

The neighborhood kids were already hard at play. He kept his eyes down to deflect any curiosity or conversation.

They didn't talk on the way to the mall. Catherine rifled through a rack of newspapers and picked out the *Edmonton Journal*. She sent Danny to the cooler for two cans of pop. They took their purchases to an empty table in the far corner of the concourse. Catherine removed and folded her sunglasses with exaggerated care. She kneaded her eyes with her fingertips before looking at her son.

"I spoke with Scott this morning. He told me there's an article about it in today's paper."

Danny glanced at the folded paper. He'd never paid much attention to newspapers. The news had always been about somebody else – up to now. "Grandma and Grandpa will fill out the insurance claim for us. It'll probably take a while. It's going to be complicated. Grandma and Grandpa didn't have a chance to get any of our things out. The only thing left is the land. So, we'll have to be more careful with our money." She reached under the table and put her hand on her son's jiggling knee. Awkwardly, Danny reached for his drink and took a long swallow.

"So, now we just…keep on…keep going. We follow our plan. Almost the same as before. We've come too far to let him win now. Soon, he'll never be able to hurt us again."

She slipped on her sunglasses. "I need to go into the bathroom for a minute," she said, rising and leaving Danny alone.

He pulled the newspaper toward him and started flipping the pages.

It was like looking for your own obituary.

Not dead on this page.

Flip. Not dead on this page.

Flip.


### Spectacular Blaze Destroys One House, Damages Two Others

Sunday, August 18, 2002. Edmonton—An explosion and fire ripped through a west-end home in the early hours of Saturday morning, completely destroying one home and damaging two others. Six fire trucks responded to the three-alarm blaze, but it was already raging out of control when firefighters arrived. "I've never seen anything like it," said Captain Rogers. "It was like a bomb went off inside. It's a miracle no one was hurt." Both neighboring houses caught fire when burning debris exploded onto their roofs. Everyone was safely evacuated, but the fire did extensive damage to three houses before fire-fighters could contain the blaze.

The blast shook neighborhood houses and onlookers wearing pyjamas and housecoats poured into the fire-lit streets. Many were holding each other and crying. "The noise was deafening," said one elderly gentleman. "I thought someone had started a war."

Captain Rogers told reporters the explosion may have been caused by a natural gas leak in the basement. "But it's rare to see an explosion of this magnitude caused by just a gas leak," he said.

Firefighters say the house was unoccupied at the time of the blast. "I think the woman and her two children are on vacation," said a neighbor. Officials estimate the blaze caused $500,000 to $600,000 in damage to the three houses.

The cause remains under investigation.

# Chapter 7

Danny avoided his sister when they got home. He grabbed Buddy's leash and vanished out the door. Buddy led the way to the school grounds. Danny hurled the Frisbee and the dog raced after it, sometimes leaping up and catching it mid-air. After fifteen minutes Danny's arm ached and the dog flagged.

Danny walked to the crest of a gentle slope, far away from everyone. He sat on the grass, removed his cap, and closed his eyes. Buddy lay close beside him, and he ran his fingers along the dog's head.

"Well, Buddy, did he do it?" he said aloud. "Was it really Dad?" He hadn't let himself think much about his father since the phone call. He was worried about his mom, his sister, his grandparents, and himself. He couldn't let himself worry about his dad too. Like Mom, he'd made *his* plan – contact Dad in a few months – so he'd leave his thoughts about Dad in the future rather than think about him now.

He plucked a blade of grass and began shredding it with his fingernails. *So, did he do it?* Since yesterday, the question had slowly seeped into his brain like slow rain. *Mom said he'd burned her. Jen said he'd kicked Buddy. Mom said he'd threatened to hurt Grandma and Grandpa. Grandma and Grandpa…*

Where was the stone? Had he lost it? His breath caught. The last time he'd had it was in the shorts he'd been wearing when they left Edmonton, the same ones he was still wearing when they got to Winnipeg. He'd shoved his clothes under the bed and later had dumped them all in the basement.

He jumped up. "Come on, Buddy, we've gotta go."

Jennifer sat with her legs tucked under the coffee table, her new pencil crayons arranged in a rainbow. One hand was up at her face twirling her hair around and around, while she colored a picture with the other, the pencil gliding back and forth across the page in a rhythmical arc, always carefully staying in the lines.

"Where's Mom?" Danny demanded.

"She took the laundry to the laundry room."

"What laundry room?"

"Out back across the common area – at the end, where the door is different than the others."

His heart drummed. Mom always checked pockets. Had she found the stone?

The air in the laundry room was muggy and warm, a tangled mix of smells: detergent, fabric softeners, and unwashed clothes. His mom leaned across a dryer, fumbling with change. She looked up.

"Hi. I thought we'd all feel better if we had some clean clothes."

His voice was urgent. "Did you find a stone in one of my pockets?"

"No," she answered, her eyebrows raised.

"Well, did you check *all* my pockets? Did you?"

She paused. "I always check the pockets."

*Under the bed,* he thought. *I had the clothes under the bed.*

Danny spun about and rushed to his room. Buddy followed closely and crouched beside him as he dropped to his knees and peered under the bed. He thrust his arm underneath and swept his hand back and forth.

Nothing. Danny's heart pounded. *Where was it? Did I lose it? How could I have lost it?* He continued swinging his arm back and forth like a windshield wiper but felt nothing but dust balls. He turned and sat heavily on the floor. He stared straight ahead at the open closet. There were his blue shorts, draped across his catcher's mitt and tennis racket. He scrambled over and pulled them out, and shook them frantically upside down.

Nothing. He flung the glove and racket behind him. Then he saw it. There it was, white on the brown carpet. He picked it up, locked it in his fist, and closed his eyes.

"Found it, Buddy. I found it."

Buddy wagged his tail.

Catherine spent the rest of the day cleaning house. She dragged the old kettle-shaped vacuum across the scratchy carpet. She aired out the place, changed the beds, and cleaned the bathroom. She washed the kitchen floor and swept the front steps. She didn't ask Jennifer or Danny for help, not even to take out the garbage. By supper, the laundry was neatly folded and back in the drawers.

"I've been wondering about the flower bed in the front," she said matter-of-factly. "We could borrow some garden tools and clean it up. It's late in the season, but there are probably still some flowers on sale. What do you think?"

He didn't know what to say. He was grateful his mom seemed to have returned to normal. She was taking care of things. She was taking care of him.

He didn't know why he watched the news that night, but he did.

There it was. Black smoke boiled out of the hole where the roof used to be. Crimson flames licked up the outside walls and pushed the foul smoke higher and higher, warping the night sky. The windows blew out in a volcanic blast of glass and debris. A man stood silhouetted against the flames, a microphone at his lips, shouting words that couldn't be heard above the roaring fire. Firefighters in sooty yellow gear hauled hoses from fire trucks pulsing with red and blue lights. Then, the camera panned across a group of people huddled on the streets. Danny recognized Mr. and Mrs. Butler, their faces showing fear and horror in the firelight, and the Hoopers' children, their arms around their mother's legs and their faces buried in her housecoat. The neighbors watched the shingles on their own houses blister and curl. Danny saw the remaining walls of his house collapse in on themselves as the fire plowed through the backyard trees to the fence and garage.

He knew the greasy black smoke smelled of burning rubber and hot tar. And it didn't stop until it was all gone.

# Chapter 8

"I've called the realtor again," Catherine announced Monday at breakfast. "She's coming later. We'll go look at some houses."

When the door bell rang, Catherine made the introductions and they headed for the agent's car. Alice Wu drove a sleek, black Mercedes. Danny slid into the cool leather seats and breathed in the new car smell.

Catherine and Alice chatted back and forth about location, price, and features. Catherine said it had to be by Westlawn School because she'd already registered the children there.

"What was your house in Saskatoon like?"

"Oh…smallish, older."

"Are you looking for the same type of thing?"

"No…a little newer, a little bigger."

They drove up and down the streets to get a feel for the area. "A nice choice of neighborhoods," Alice remarked, "and a good high school, too."

The car swung to the curb and Alice consulted her papers. She checked addresses and showed them some houses. The first ones were roomy, but too expensive, and Alice asked if they'd consider a condo.

"We *need* a big yard for our dog," Danny answered non-negotiably from the back seat.

"Yes, we do," agreed Catherine.

"All right, let's go this way," Alice said, swinging the car south. The new district was called Forest Lawn. The houses had more variety, some smaller ones tucked in amongst larger neighbors. "Let's start looking inside, shall we?" Alice asked brightly.

Danny shuffled through the tour. He wouldn't have wanted anyone poking through his bedroom at home, looking at *his* things, opening *his* closet doors.

After a few hours, everyone was tired. They hadn't seen anything suitable. Alice suggested they get together again together on Friday. "That's when the new listings come out," she said.

One day trailed into the next. Everyone pretended life was normal and no more complicated than usual. They lugged groceries, and Jen played with the other kids. Catherine made small talk with some of the neighbors. Danny took Buddy for long walks, kept his distance, and watched a lot of TV.

Alice called on Friday. "Looks like we might have a match. The area you wanted, the right size, in your price range – possession October first."

Catherine's smile spread from her lips to her eyes.

The house was more humble than the others on the block, but the grass was a fresh green and a red honeysuckle bloomed around the window.

The inside was clean and orderly and the kitchen had been renovated.

"There's a washer and dryer in the basement," Alice said, "and there's a one-car garage."

"I want to see the back yard," said Danny.

"Right this way," Alice replied.

Six bird feeders hung from the box elder tree. *Those'll have to go*, thought Danny, picturing Buddy frantically trying to bark the birds off their perches. But a chin-high fence completely enclosed the yard. Patio bricks circled a cinder-block fire pit and a stack of split birch rested against the garage wall. It looked okay to Danny. He and Jennifer continued to poke around as Alice and Catherine talked price.

"I'll be paying cash," said Catherine. "I won't need a mortgage."

"That's great, because it means we can move on it quickly, and this house isn't going to last on the market for long."

Alice directed them to her car. Catherine's eyes swept across the yard. "Yes," she said, "we could be comfortable here for a long time. I'll call my lawyer as soon as I get home, to find out how soon I'll get my inheritance."

Alice smiled. "It sounds promising, Susan."

Catherine telephoned Scott right away. Danny heard her ask about the insurance money and the talk went back and forth. After a long silence, she said, "I understand. I'll wait for your call. Good-bye, Scott."

Catherine joined her children in the living room where they were playing another game of Snakes and Ladders. "Scott will try to find out about our insurance claim," she said, "but the office might be closed for the weekend and he probably won't get through 'till Monday. So, we'll just have to be patient and keep our fingers crossed." The corners of her mouth turned up and made little crow's feet around her eyes.

It was good to see Mom smile again.

⚒

Danny hadn't paid much attention to the old man who lived alone at the far end of the complex. The stairs had been converted to a wheelchair ramp. Danny saw him occasionally while walking Buddy. The old man took short, careful steps, and leaned heavily on two canes. Danny usually saw only the top of his head as the man concentrated on his feet. No matter how warm it was, he always wore his beret and a long-sleeved shirt tucked into trousers held up by a leather belt.

"Nice dog yuh got there," he'd remarked as Danny walked Buddy past him one day.

"Thanks," Danny replied quickly, unwilling to pause and be drawn into conversation. After that, he'd gone out of his way to avoid him.

But Danny and Buddy were out early one Sunday, before the neighborhood kids took over. The old man seemed stronger, his steps more sure, his chin up, looking ahead instead of down. This time, he caught Danny's eye.

"Sure is a nice dog yuh got there. What's his name?"

"Buddy."

The old man braced himself on one cane and dropped his liver-spotted hand to the dog's twitching nose. He stroked Buddy's head. "Hello, Buddy. I used to have a dog," he said. "A black lab. Called him Ranger. Best dog a man could want."

Danny watched Buddy lean into the old man's hand.

"But he got old, 'n' so did I, 'n' now I'm here 'n' he's gone. I sure do miss that dog." He straightened. "I'd like another one, but I got these brand-new hips 'n' those doctors have me in 'n' out of hospital more often than a man can sneeze. I just couldn't manage to take care of one." The old man now leaned both hands on the cane.

"What's your name, son?"

Danny paused. A choice.

No, not a choice. A dilemma.

*Danny or David?*

*The house burned down. Nothing left of Danny.*

*No proof it was arson.*

The old man cocked his head to the side, waiting for an answer.

*No future for David, though. David was just a stopgap in Danny McMillan's life.*

*Birth certificates. School records.*

*Mom or Dad.*

"David," Danny replied. "But we're moving next month," he added quickly, hoping the old man wouldn't bother remembering his name if he wasn't going to be there long.

"David." He nodded, but his face tensed. "I had a son named David –"

Danny's fist clenched Buddy's leash.

"But he's gone too…" His face crumbled like sandstone. "Gone a long time now, since that senseless war, sent by a president who thought it was fine for other people's sons to die for his ideas. But it was a long time ago, and you can't cry forever."

The old man straightened. "The kids here call me Papa Joe."

"Papa Joe," Danny repeated flatly.

"Well, see yuh 'round, David," Papa Joe said, lifting his cane in front of him. "You take good care of that dog." Papa Joe stepped away.

The realtor rang again on Monday morning. "No, I haven't heard yet," Catherine said. "It's a bit out of my hands. We have to wait for the lawyers to finish, and you know how lawyers are…Yes, lots of paperwork. I'll call you as soon as I know."

Catherine dialed Scott's number. Had he been in touch with Phil? What had her parents said? Was the claim in? Why was the investigation taking so long? Sorry, sorry, it's so hard to wait.

Danny didn't want to hear any more sorries. He didn't want to wait. He wanted to know. Either Mom was right, or Dad didn't do it. Would it change anything if he knew?

Of course it would. Either Mom's right or Dad's right.

But maybe Mom could be right 'till Christmas, and then Dad could be right for the rest of their lives.

He rubbed the worry stone, which he'd kept with him like a secret since the fire. He'd call his grandparents. They were making the insurance claim and were in touch with the police. They'd know. He'd memorized their number last Christmas when he had started seeing them again. He'd take some change and use the mall pay phone. He'd never called long distance from a pay phone, but it couldn't be that hard, could it?

He scooped some coins from his mother's wallet, put Buddy on the leash, and made a beeline for the mall. He left the dog tied to the bicycle rack and shouldered through the revolving doors. A bank of phones hung just inside.

His fingers trembled so much he nearly dropped the coins. He didn't know much it cost, so he just kept jamming money into the slot until his palm was empty. He listened for the dial tone and then pressed the numbers.

One ring. Two rings.

*I am sorry. The number you have dialed is no longer in service. Please consult your directory.*

Danny hung up.

His grandparents had lived in that house for forty years and always had the same phone number. Why would they change it? Had they done it before or after the fire? Maybe it didn't mean anything. Maybe it was something the NIVA people routinely recommended.

But he remembered Grandpa's words…. *Having you with us has filled a hole in our hearts. Do you think we'd tear that hole open again if we believed there was any other way?*

# Chapter 9

This time, it was a knock at the door, not a phone call. Scott stood there, his face ashen, shifting his car keys nervously from one hand to the other.

"Is your mother home?" he asked. His eyes didn't meet Danny's.

Catherine had been in the kitchen, going through the newspaper, circling *Used Cars*, *Help Wanted* and *Businesses for Sale* ads. She came to the doorway.

"Scott?" she asked.

"May I come in?"

Danny slowly stepped back. He sat on the bottom stair.

Catherine motioned Scott into the living room.

"Where's Julia?" he asked.

"Outside, playing."

"Please sit down."

The two sat facing each other across the coffee table. Scott stopped juggling his keys and set them on the table. "We've heard from the police and the fire department. The explosion and fire are highly suspicious, and the detective suspects arson. But there's not enough hard evidence to take anyone to court. They've closed their investigation."

Danny welcomed the words. Not arson. Good for his plan.

"But..." Scott hesitated. His words sounded rehearsed. "There's a problem with the insurance."

Catherine grabbed the edge of the table with both hands.

Danny swallowed.

"The gas company records confirmed the explosion happened at 1:07 a.m. on Saturday morning."

Catherine didn't move.

"Paul's agency held the policy. He cancelled the insurance. It expired at midnight on Friday."

Catherine blinked once, twice, three times.

"I'm so sorry," said Scott.

Catherine stayed in her room for the afternoon, so Danny took Jen to the store to buy macaroni and cheese and dog treats. On the way back, Jen said, "I thought it'd turn out better than this. I guess we're not moving for a long time."

He stopped and looked at the condo complex. It looked different, now. It was supposed to have been a temporary stop, but now its camouflage had melted away and he could see it was his final destination, no different than the neighboring units, shabby and shapeless as houses on an old Monopoly board.

*Go to jail. Go directly to jail. Do not pass Go. Do not collect $200.*

Danny's shoulders sagged as if the grocery bags had suddenly filled with heavy weights.

That evening they heard their mother up and around, but she didn't leave her bedroom. Jennifer suggested they play cards, and when Danny said no, she started to cry. Tears poured out of her as if from a thunderhead that had billowed up and could no longer contain its load. Danny squeezed her like Grandma and Grandpa had just two weeks ago, a grip full of pain, shared misery, and of deep, deep fear of being forever alone.

⚒

Catherine was out of bed early the next morning, making breakfast. Danny hesitated before going down. He was glad she was up again, but nervous about what he'd see.

He tried not to look surprised. The circles under her eyes were deep purple. Her clothes hung off her like a roll of paper towels left out in the rain. The coffee cup shook as she lifted it. A pill bottle sat beside the empty coffee pot.

"Good morning," she said wearily, "would you mind waking your sister so we can have breakfast together?"

"Okay."

He returned a minute later and busied himself with juice and cereal until Jen appeared. They talked like machines. "Pass the milk." "More toast?" "Strawberry or raspberry jam?" The food was tasteless and they all ate as if they had to.

Jennifer cleared the table and washed dishes without being asked. Danny and Catherine dried and put them away. When they'd draped the wet dishtowels over the backs of the chairs, she said, "Can we go into the living room." It wasn't a question.

She sat on the couch with Jennifer close beside her. When Danny moved to sit in the armchair, she said, "No. Come, sit here. On the coffee table where I can see you." He perched in front of them. She turned slightly so she could see both her children. Then she reached out and took Danny's hand in her left and Jen's in her right.

"Danny. Jennifer. I – I can only say this once. This is the last time I'll ever speak of Paul. It doesn't matter what the fire department or the police decided about the fire. I know he did it. When he found out we were gone, he realized he couldn't hit me again, at least not physically. So he used another weapon against me – against us. He used fire to destroy all our things. And he didn't care how reckless it was, whether our neighbors were hurt or even killed. I was his target and because I love you, you were his targets too. And he didn't care if anything or anyone else was hurt along the way.

"He's done it again. He took away our past by burning the house. He cancelled the insurance to force us into poverty and take away our future. But – poverty – this was his final assault. He may think he's won and gloat over what he's done to us, but he has *not* won.

"We won because I'm still alive." She squeezed both their hands and held them fast. "And you're both still alive. And the rest doesn't matter. He's never going to find us, and he's never going to hurt us again.

"Susan, Julia, and David. We are winning the war."

# Chapter 10

Alice Wu telephoned that afternoon. Danny overheard her urgent voice. Another buyer was interested in that perfect house.

"There's been a problem with my inheritance," Susan replied. "It went up in flames."

The realtor never called again.

Danny heard water run into the bathroom sink and a few minutes later his mother came downstairs with her chin up and back straight. She fried chicken and potatoes and whipped up chocolate pudding. Danny stole glances at her, and although she looked thin, her movements showed the confidence he'd always seen when she cooked. After their plates were cleared, she explained the next day's plan.

"We'll get you both registered at the schools here. This is just a temporary set-back. Everything will work out. You'll see," she said.

*Right,* thought Danny. But he didn't have a plan anymore, either.

⚖

Friday, August thirtieth. Danny's new school was within walking distance, but Julia would have to take the bus. The yellow bus stopped right in front of New Haven. Neighbors suggested Susan just take the bus with Julia and the other kids on the first day of school and get her registered then. When Susan mentioned it to Julia her daughter's shoulders relaxed.

"I didn't want to tell you before," Julia said. "Katie said there'd been a strange man driving around the complex. He was looking into her window. Her mom called the police and they arrested him. I was scared to go on the bus by myself."

Danny stiffened. *If Mr. McMillan were released today, this would be the most dangerous time for his wife – the time he is most likely to seek her out and hurt her again.*

Susan went straight to the Watsons'. She returned a half-hour later and called Julia down. She gave her daughter a long hug. "It's okay, sweetie," she said. "It was just a Peeping Tom."

⚖

Susan gathered Danny's birth certificate and school records and they headed for Harry Smith Junior High. An older woman with a pinched face and severe black-rimmed glasses was sorting papers behind the office counter. They completed the same forms and the secretary handed Danny an option sheet.

"School starts Tuesday. Best make your choice now."

The sheet listed only four options – French, Art, Choir, and something called *English Skills*.

"What's *English Skills*?" asked Danny.

"Oh, you can't choose that one," the secretary answered. "It's only for English as a Second Language students." She frowned over her glasses, as if he were born yesterday.

*How am I supposed to know that,* Danny thought. "We didn't need that option at my old school," he replied sourly.

There was nothing to sing about, and Danny figured he would be useless in French, so that left Art. Danny put an *X* beside Art and tossed the form back. Things were not off to a promising start.

"Is there a supply list?" Susan asked.

"No." The secretary turned her back and flipped through a filing cabinet. She returned with another form. "Do you want your son in the hot lunch program?" Susan swallowed and stared at the sheet. Her eyes scanned the paper.

"How – how much –?" she started to ask.

"It's free if you're on social assistance," the secretary interrupted.

Susan signed the form.

Danny's face went hot and he bolted from the office. He walked home without waiting for his mother.

⚖

Labor Day weekend, the last weekend of summer. The condo complex buzzed. Julia had met a couple of kids in her grade. She quizzed them about the school. What were the teachers like? Was the principal mean? How long did they have for recess? But she stopped twiddling her hair when her mom reminded her she'd be with her on the bus. Julia scooted outside for a final fling at summer.

Danny's face was dark. He wanted to go to that school about as much as he wanted a vaccination. But there was nothing to do at the condo, at least nothing he was willing to do. He had no bike and no hope for one, no money for the bus. He'd walked Buddy two, three, four times a day, but he'd not made any friends.

He shut himself in the basement and turned on the TV.

Sunday was torture. Julia's tears turned her face into a swollen mask. Her mom stroked her hair, hugged her, and offered to play cards, but Julia cried her way through the pages of a photo album. She hauled out the manila envelope, plucked out her birth certificate, and flung it against the wall.

September first. Her ninth birthday. Danny had completely forgotten. And now he had no idea what to do. Recognize it? Ignore it?

Consider it Remembrance Day?

Fridge magnets pinned up a calendar, the bus schedule, grocery coupons, and bills. The used car ads were gone. Susan calculated expenses in a dollar-store ledger and propped the book against the cloudy plastic flour and sugar canisters. She'd made lists of things they needed: a clock radio for each bedroom, a CD player, some houseplants, a second set of towels.

"Next weekend, we'll hit some garage sales and see what we can knock off the list. It's a good time to shop. Lots of people are getting rid of their clutter before winter."

Danny snorted. *Well*, we *won't need a garage sale any time soon*, he thought.

$$\wedge$$

He was already awake Tuesday morning when his wristwatch alarm started beeping. He heard his mother setting out the break-fast things. As he turned off the alarm, dread began to creep into his gut.

He'd pretended he wasn't, but he was. Afraid. Afraid to go to school, afraid to be David Mayer, afraid of giving the wrong answer, afraid of embarrassing himself or giving them all away. So afraid that he didn't think he could breathe.

"David! Julia! It's time to get up!"

Some minutes passed. Danny heard the toilet flush and his sister's footsteps going down the stairs.

"David! Get up!"

He curled himself into a ball and punched his fists into his stomach. He thought he was going to vomit. Buddy nosed through the door and leapt on the bed, licking Danny's face. The dog wouldn't stop and Danny shoved away his wet muzzle. But today the dog kept at him.

"Okay, okay, Buddy-boy. I'll get up."

He rose and dressed. His new first-day-of-school clothes stayed in the drawer.

His mom wore her burgundy short-sleeved blouse and pressed linen pants, but they were too big, as if her body didn't belong in them anymore. Julia sat in her new clothes, an untouched piece of toast cooling in front of her, twirling her hair around and around her finger.

"But what if I forget, Mom? What if I make a mistake and say the wrong thing?"

"It's okay, Jewel," her mother replied, reaching across to cover Julia's hand with her own. "Everyone's going to be excited, and they won't remember everything you say today. Remember what Phil and Dr. Sung said. Give short answers and ask a question back. It'll turn the conversation away from you – and most people are more than happy to talk about themselves."

"Will you help me today, Mom?" Julia pleaded.

"Of course I will," she said, pulling her daughter over to sit on her lap. "We're all going to be fine." She consulted the bus schedule and reviewed it with Julia. "And you'll be taking your lunch every day, too, Jewel – you'll have to remember it. I've made your favorite – cheese and pickles."

She turned to Danny. "We have to be on the bus at 8:05, but your school doesn't start until 8:30. Today, let's all leave together. That'll give you some extra time to get there and find your way. I'm sorry I can't be with you…" She bit her lip.

"I know everything already," Danny snapped.

"I just want to make sure it all goes smoothly, if that's possible." She paused. "I haven't made lunch for you because I'm assuming you'll get it there."

"Why can't I just come home? It's only five minutes away."

"Because we have to take advantage of every program we qualify for. And if I don't have to send lunch, that frees up some of our money for other things." She paused and looked directly in his eyes. "Please."

"What about Buddy? Who's going to let him out at noon?"

"Today I have to register Julia and I'm not sure when I'll be back home, but tomorrow I'll be here and I'll take care of Buddy. I promise."

# Chapter 11

Danny ducked through the doors of the junior high. Students and parents looking for names bunched around lists posted on the walls. Shrieks and groans played up the excitement.

He scanned the banners above the lists: *Grade 7, Grade 8* and *Grade 9*.

He stroked the worry stone in his pocket and hovered on the edge of the crowd gathered in front of the Grade 8 list. Students discussed their room assignments.

"I'm in Mr. Thompson's class!" "Oh my God, who's Ms. Nguyen?" "Why did I end up with Mr. Sota?!" "We're together!" "We're *not* together!" "This sucks!"

The bell rang. Eight-thirty. The kids scattered like startled birds. A short, slight man stood in the middle of the hall, directing students to various rooms.

Now alone in front of the lists of names, Danny couldn't put off looking for his.

"Can I help you?" Danny turned around. "I'm Mr. Ishii," the man said, "the school counselor. You must be new here. What's your name?"

"Uh, David...Mayer."

"And what grade are you in, David?"

"Eight."

"All right. Let's see where you are." Mr. Ishii ran his fingers down the list until he found Danny's name. "Here you are. Ms. Nguyen's class. Room nine. You're in the portable outside." He paused. "Why don't I walk you there?"

"Don't need to," Danny said as he brushed by.

Portable nine was on the tarmac right outside the door. Shouts and laughter drifted from the open windows. The second bell rang as he mounted the steps. When the classroom door creaked open, all heads turned. He slid into the nearest empty seat.

A petite Asian woman stood at the front. She'd bleached her short black hair to an uneven orange and gelled it to stick straight out from her head. She looked so young Danny wondered if she could really be the teacher. She smiled at him.

"Welcome to my class. My name is Ms. Nguyen –" she pointed to her name written in green marker on the whiteboard. She pronounced it 'noi-yen.' "I know my name looks hard to pronounce. I'm going to do my best to say all of your names correctly, and if I don't, please tell me. And I want to know what you like to be called – Beth instead of Elizabeth, or whatever."

She walked back and forth. "I am *so* excited to be here," she said, her smile showing a straight line of white teeth. "This is my first year as a teacher, and you're my first home room class.

"So it's a special day. And it's even more special because –" she pointed to the ground "– this was my elementary school. I grew up here, just like you. So, even if I don't know any of you, I might know your older brothers or sisters, or maybe even your parents." Several students turned and whispered among themselves.

"And we're going to have a great year." She made eye contact with each student as she handed out papers. Danny rubbed his palms across his thighs when she approached.

"Looks like you're new here too," she said. "Welcome." He took the pencil and papers without meeting her eyes.

"Please fill in these sheets and I'll take attendance."

He looked down. Every school year started with names, but Danny had never seen this type of question sheet before.

My name is _____ and I like to be called

_____.

I am _____ years old.

Last year I went to _____ school.

I live with _____.

My favorite subject is _____.

My least favorite subject is _____.

Is there something special about you I should know?

_____.

☺  Ms. Nguyen.

Danny stared at the page as the teacher called names and each hand went up in turn.

"Aaron Abrams. I bet you're always at the front of your class. Belinda Bischoff. Linda? Okay, Linda." She made a note. "William Chin? Bill? Sure thing, Bill." Another note. "Natalie Franco… Andrew Johnston…Su-Min Kim…David Mayer…" Ms. Nguyen looked up. "David Mayer? Not here? Anyone know David Mayer?"

Her eyes scanned the room and came to rest on Danny, who was staring vacantly at the paper.

"David? Are you David Mayer?"

Danny looked up. Several students had turned to stare.

"Yeah. I guess so."

"Okay," she replied with a smile, as if there were nothing unusual in his answer. "Darlene Morningstar..."

Danny dropped his chin. He took the pencil, scribbled a few answers, flipped the paper face down, and slapped his pencil on top. He leaned back and crossed his arms.

"Chad Zane," Ms. Nguyen finished. "Well, that's everyone, from *A* to *Z*," she said, her smile making her eyes crinkle.

"Everyone please pass your paper to the person in front."

The heavy-set boy seated in front of him made a point of reading Danny's. He turned all the way around and snickered. He stuck his feet into the aisle and looked down his nose at Danny. His small eyes puckered into a chubby face.

"Great," he sneered. "Competition." He turned back.

Danny looked down. *Chad Zane,* Danny thought. *He's going to be fun.*

"All right," the teacher said, "we've got a lot to cover before the mid-morning break. Let's check timetables."

He half-listened as Ms. Nguyen made announcements about classes, options, teachers' names. By mid-morning, the warm room already smelled of nervous students and scented deodorant. The school bell startled Danny.

"Okay!" Ms. Nguyen called over the sudden clatter of students charging from their desks. "Ten minute mid-morning break! Everybody outside! Bathrooms and water fountains are inside!"

Danny was the first one out, but then had no idea what to

do. He jabbed his hand into his pocket for the worry stone. He refused to make eye contact with anyone. He drifted around and tried not to be noticed.

Inside, Ms. Nguyen sipped from her water bottle and started alphabetizing the papers. She paused when she came to Danny's.

My name is __Mud__ and I like to be called

_____.

I am _105_ years old.

Last year I went to __I don't remember__ school.

I live with _____My dog_____.

My favorite subject is ____TV____.

My least favorite subject is __School__.

Is there something special I should know about you?

I think life sucks_____.

He'd crossed out the happy face and replaced it with a skull and cross bones.

Ah, sighed Ms. Nguyen. *David. A challenge.*

The bell rang and students trickled in. The boys cuffed each other as they found their seats. Danny trailed behind. The rest of the morning dragged while papers pooled on Danny's desk. Textbook sign-out sheets, subject outlines, curriculum guidelines. Handouts like *Plan for Success!* and *Successful Study Strategies.* An assignment for Wednesday – *What I did on my Summer Vacation.* Finally, lunchtime.

"Just leave your stuff on your desks for now," Ms. Nguyen said. "Who from last year would like to lead the tour? How about… you," she pointed at a girl. "Linda, isn't it? And Andrew. Here's the list."

Linda and Andrew grabbed the papers and hustled out their classmates.

Classrooms, bathrooms, offices, gym, library, staff room, snack machines, photocopy room, cafeteria. Returning students clustered to discuss holidays, boyfriends and girlfriends, clothes, and teenage life.

"Hot lunch program in here," Linda announced. "Just give your name to the lunch ladies – but they get to know you pretty quick – and sometimes the food is even good." She spoke casually, as if a hot lunch program were part of every school.

"Hey David!" It was Andrew. "You in the program?"

Danny nodded.

"Me too. Come on, let's go in. You play soccer? Hockey? The basketball coach is great but don't bother with football, man, the team sucks." Andrew led him into the cafeteria. He slid a tray from a stack and ambled down the line. Danny followed closely.

"You get kinda tired of the food after a while, but every second Friday it's McDonald's," he said. "And in the winter there's hot soup. You'll like it after being in the portable. We can take our trays out, as long as we bring 'em back."

Andrew used his bum to push open the door and they sat on the tarmac. "You like sports?" Andrew asked again.

"Yeah," Danny replied. He thought of the ribbons and trophies he'd left behind in his bedroom, then speared a piece of chicken with his fork.

"Live round here?"

"Yeah. Across the hill."

"Been there long?"

"Couple a weeks."

"Watch out for the guys that hang out at the mall. They like to have a go at new guys. Chad's one of 'em. Likes to get other people into trouble, push 'em around. Gets 'em to lift stuff from the store for him. 'Specially the girls."

"Yeah?"

They finished their meal in silence and returned the trays. A couple of boys angled over when they saw Andrew.

"Hey, Andy? How's it goin'?"

"Hey, Rico! Where's Tom?" Andrew turned to Danny. "See ya 'round, David," he said, and then joined his buddies.

"Sure," mumbled Danny. He spent the rest of lunch sitting on the portable's steps. The warning bell rang, and he pretended to clean his fingernails while classmates climbed the steps beside him.

A foot bumped Danny's leg. Startled, he looked up.

"*Sorry, loser,*" Chad smirked. "Didn't see ya there." Chad loomed over him for a moment. Danny glared back, but Chad had already brushed by.

They squeezed five classes into three periods. The gym had once been a decent size, but it had been divided in half with a cinder block wall, and neither side was big enough for a proper game of floor hockey. A bored photographer snapped school ID pictures underneath drooping basketball hoops.

At the end of the day, Ms. Nguyen handed each student an agenda book. It reminded him of the day planners his dad used to have. But the cheap cardboard cover on his copy had already been bent back.

"Bring it to class every day," Ms. Nguyen said. "When we meet in home room, I'll check that you've written up your homework and kept track of assignments and tests."

On his way home from school, Danny threw his in the trash.

# Chapter 12

Danny dumped his stuff on his bed and scooped up Buddy's leash. Mom and Julia were already home. Danny ducked his mother's questions. He felt burned out. He ate in front of the TV and then trudged to his room for the rest of the evening.

Three dull days passed before Ms. Nguyen asked for his agenda. He shrugged and said he'd lost it. When she asked for his summer vacation assignment, he said the dog ate it. Other teachers started assigning homework, but he abandoned it on his desk or left it in his unopened backpack. Andy had asked him to play dodge ball a couple of times and although he wanted to, he felt himself stiffen up and found excuses not to. After that, he avoided Andy. Ignoring others was one thing he was already good at. Soon everyone avoided him.

On Friday, when Danny arrived home, his mother was wearing shorts and a T-shirt despite a cold north wind that raised goose bumps on her arms and legs. She was the gardener in the family. At home, she'd put out bedding plants and kept the yard tidy. She'd planted the short, fat carrots that Danny preferred, and snow peas, butter lettuce and red potatoes.

His mom pointed at their new 'garden.' "I've planted tulip, daffodil, and narcissus bulbs," she said. "They'll look beautiful when they come up in the spring."

"I thought we didn't have money," he snapped.

She hesitated. "David, I need this bit of earth…and so do you. I'm very careful with our money. But planting this garden is an investment in our future – Julia's, mine, and yours. We have to plan for our future or we won't have one."

"Plans! Look where all your plans have got us *so* far!" He swept his arm around. "This! *This* is where it got us! This piece of *crap!*"

She straightened and thrust out her chin. "You're right, David!" she snapped back. "*Nothing's* turned out the way I planned. So should I just give up? Stop living? Is that what you'd have me do?" She planted her fists on her hips. "Well, I *won't.* I *enjoyed* planting the garden today. And I'm going to *enjoy* those flowers when they come up. Sure, I could do nothing and be miserable –" she pointed at Danny "– just like you – but I won't! It's time to move on! Nothing's going to fall from the sky and fix our lives! *This* is it! And it's up to each of us to do something with it!"

Danny pressed his lips together until they were just a narrow red line. At that moment, he hated her.

The next day, Susan reattached the dog's engraved tags – 'Buddy. 21 New Haven, Winnipeg. 204-623-1961.'

By the end of the second week, Danny's teachers started asking him to stay after class. Each time it was the same. "You haven't been handing in your homework." "I don't see you making much of an effort." "I've looked at your marks from your last school, so I know what you're capable of." "What's wrong?" "You seem to be having some problems."

By the first day of fall, he was in the principal's office.

"By all reports," Mr. Kindermann said, interlacing his fingers, "you aren't doing very well in this school. But your records from Saskatoon show you can do quite well – when you want to."

Danny slouched.

"Is there anything you'd like to tell me?"

Danny stared. "I guess I'm not who you think I am."

"Well then," he replied, his tone conversational. "Who are you?"

"I'm a 'mere shadow of my former self.' How's that sound?"

The principal arched his brows. "Many of our students struggle with difficult issues, and we like to give them a little slack, time to settle in. But you've been here almost a month, and it's time to work. So, if you don't want to tell *me* anything, then let me *ask* you – what can I do to help? What can the school do?"

"Help? I've had nothing *but* help. And where's it gotten me? Right here. I used to be something. And now I'm *nothing*."

Mr. Kindermann leaned back. "That seems harsh."

"You have *no idea*," Danny growled. He stalked out without another word.

Mr. Kindermann saw Susan shortly after his meeting with Danny. He outlined the concerns.

Susan nodded. "Yes, we've had…family problems…Severe family problems."

"Yes." He paused, but Susan didn't elaborate. "Perhaps, we should move away from academics, and look at the broader picture. Have you considered counseling? We have a school psychologist.

He's very good and experienced. Would David see him?"

"I'll speak to him about it, but it's…complicated."

He smiled. "Let me know what you decide."

Susan broached the topic at dinner. "It would probably be better if you talk to someone."

"Forget it."

"David –"

"I'm not David!"

"If you're not David," Susan shouted back, "then we're all dead! Don't you see? It *can't* be any other way!"

"Well maybe we should just test that out, *Catherine*! Let's see who's right!"

Julia leapt up from the table. "You leave her alone! You're no better than Dad!" She rushed to her mother's side and circled her arms around her. Danny felt his sister's burning hatred. He turned and ran up the stairs two at a time, threw himself face down on the bed, and wished he could cry himself blind.

Danny didn't go to school the next day, or the next. Every morning he'd leave with his backpack and head toward the school. But as soon as he was out of sight, he'd detour to the mall. His four-dollar weekly allowance bought him return bus fare to downtown. He'd bum around the streets, going in and out of shops, eyeing merchandise he used to be able to buy.

*Just because I can't afford it,* he thought, *doesn't mean I shouldn't have it….*

He starting lifting small things – the pink eraser he always got at the beginning of term, a chocolate bar, some batteries. He'd smile as he shifted the five-finger bargains into his backpack on the bus ride home.

⚖

Susan received the call on the fourth morning.

"We need a note from the doctor if your child misses more than three days of school," the secretary announced curtly.

"He hasn't missed any school so far," she replied.

"Tuesday October first. Wednesday October second. Thursday October third."

"I...see," Susan said. "Perhaps you could make an appointment for him with your school counselor? As soon as possible?"

"Fine. Make sure he comes to the office on Tuesday. The counselor's a busy man."

⚖

Danny heard his mother climbing the stairs. She didn't even knock. He turned his music to maximum volume. She confronted him, hand on hips. She didn't look away until he glowered at her.

"What?" he said. He'd already prepared himself. A lecture. And then a fight.

She gathered herself and then slowly let her hands slide down her hips. She waited until Danny eventually removed one earphone. "I love you, David. The school counselor's going to meet with you next week," she said simply. "It's Thanksgiving, and I'm going to give thanks for the wonderful things I have in my life – you and Julia." She paused. "Don't give up on me now. And don't give up on yourself."

# Chapter 13

Danny threw off his headphones and couldn't get out of the house fast enough, but he and Buddy had hardly made it to the sidewalk when he heard Papa Joe.

"David! Buddy!" he called, his smile like a crease across his face. Buddy tugged at the leash to see the old man.

Papa Joe seemed surer on his feet and leaned less heavily on his canes as he reached to pet the border collie.

"I thought you two'd be gone by now. I thought ya were moving."

"Didn't work out," Danny mumbled.

"I was kinda thinkin' that, when I saw your momma planting them tulips. I said to myself, maybe they're gonna stick around."

"Yeah."

Papa Joe straightened. "Well, if you and Buddy here ever wanna come by 'n' visit, you know an old man'd like company."

"Sure," replied Danny. "See ya around."

"Bye, David," Papa Joe said, straightening his cap.

When they returned, his mom and Julia were on the floor beside the coffee table, playing cards. His mom's voice had softened. "Join us for some gin rummy?" she asked.

"Nah. I'm gonna watch TV."

"Okay. Maybe we'll come down later with pop and chips."

"Sure," he said. He paused to take in the scene. They looked at ease in the peaceful living room. He was tempted to stay, but it felt too awkward to change his mind now. Buddy padded downstairs with him. Danny sat on the couch, and the dog dropped his head in the boy's lap. Danny stroked Buddy's head and said, "Hey Buddy-boy, I'm gonna be nicer to Mom and Jewel. It's not their fault we're stuck here." But he didn't know how to start.

⚖

Bargain hunters packed Value Mart. The signs advertised *Thanksgiving Holiday Sale! Everything Reduced!*

"We all need clothes," Mom said. "David, your size is over there – see what you can find."

He moved along racks jammed past capacity. Stray garments and hangers littered the floor. He knew he'd grown – his old clothes were short in the sleeves and legs now – but he hadn't a clue what size to look for. While rummaging around, Danny spotted a familiar face. It was a girl from his art class – the very pretty girl whom he'd noticed, even though most of the time he was busy being invisible.

To his surprise, he liked art because he could keep his mind and his hands busy at the same time. Sometimes he forgot to be angry. The teacher, Mr. Thompson, was a reservoir of energy and ideas and praised students when the results were good and even when the results weren't so good.

And Danny had heard him encouraging this girl. "You have talent – talent and inspiration," he'd said. Danny had tried to peek at her work, but she sat three rows over.

Now here she was, her long hair, sleek and black, hanging loose over her shoulders. Her skin was the color of coffee, unmarred except for a scar running diagonally across the corner of her left eyebrow.

She stopped flipping hangers and caught his eye.

"Hey," she said.

"Hey," he replied.

She smiled, her eyes as deep as dark chocolate. "Art class, right?"

"Yeah. Art class." He blushed, suddenly embarrassed at being in a thrift store, looking at other people's abandoned clothes.

"Great store, huh? I come here all the time," she said. "You?"

"Ah…my first time," he replied, his tongue thick.

"You're new here."

"Yeah."

"Where ya from?"

"Saskatoon."

"Really? I have loads of relatives there." She paused. "But you probably never went to the Flying Dust First Nation Reserve," she said.

"No," replied Danny. He rubbed his damp palms against his thighs.

Silence hung between them, and the girl started searching through the racks again. Danny noticed his mom approaching. He started to move away.

The girl looked up and smiled. "See ya."

"Yeah," he mumbled.

⚖

By the next day's art class, Danny had decided he didn't want to avoid her anymore. He watched out of the corner of his eye, and paid special attention when Mr. Thompson bent to look at her work.

"Nixxie, blending colors with oil pastels just creates mud. You have to layer your image – like this." Mr. Thompson picked out some pastels and made a few marks on some scrap paper. "It just takes a little practice."

"It looks so easy when you do it," she replied.

"It's just practice, Nixxie." Mr. Thompson moved on.

*Her name is Nixxie,* thought Danny.

For the rest of the class, his eyes were on her almost as much as they were on his project. He copied her hand movements, but all he got was a brown smear.

"David, try layering the color. Don't stir it around like a pot of soup," the teacher suggested.

Across the room, Nixxie was listening.

⚖

Danny brought home two pieces of paper. One confirmed the appointment with Mr. Ishii – Wednesday, after lunch. The same time as art class.

The other was his report card.

Mom looked at it and then went upstairs to take a shower.

⟨⟩

Danny's mouth turned down as he entered the counselor's office. He slouched, his baseball cap adjusted to shield his eyes.

"Cap off, please," Mr. Ishii said mildly from behind the desk. "Please be on time in the future."

Danny hesitated, then removed his cap, but didn't look at the counselor.

"A few people have asked me to see you, but it looks like you don't want to be here."

"Damn right."

Silence.

Mr. Ishii said, "You are entitled to your opinions, and in this room you are entitled to express those opinions freely, but not in objectionable language." The counselor's calm, even tone didn't falter.

Danny counted off the seconds in his head.

"You don't seem happy here. Would you like to tell me about it?"

"No."

"All right." Mr. Ishii stood. "You can go now."

Danny blinked and looked up.

"I'll book another appointment in two weeks, but I'd prefer you come only if you want to. Otherwise, we're both wasting our time."

Danny left, still surprised at the meeting. *He's actually going to give me a choice?* he wondered, as he walked to art class.

⟨⟩

At supper, his mom said she'd been thinking a lot about a job. "So here's what I came up with," she said. "I'm going to start volunteering at Julia's school. They always need volunteers – in the library, as teachers' aides, organizing activities." Her tone became more confident. "I am skilled and good at my work."

"But how will that earn any money?" Julia asked.

"I noticed the school secretary is pregnant. She'll start maternity leave at Christmas, and they'll need a new secretary in January. I'm going to work, and smile, and be polite and reliable, and prove myself – and I'm going to get them to offer me the position without needing references."

"And we'll get off social assistance?"

"Yes. The pay will be reasonable, and we'd have benefits. Better than social assistance."

Danny's thoughts shot to all the things that could go wrong. "What if they don't hire you? What if they've already got somebody?"

Mom looked hard at Danny. "So, what am I supposed to do? Sit around and wait for a job to land in my lap?" Her voice had an edge to it. "Do nothing? Just coast through the rest of my life?"

She didn't need to add the words, *"Like you?"*

Danny slapped down his uneaten burger. His cutlery clattered to the floor, but he didn't stop to pick it up. He stomped up each stair and slammed the door behind him. He dropped onto the bed, flung his forearm across his closed eyes, and willed the tears away. After some minutes, he lifted his arm and looked at his watch.

Wednesday, October ninth. They hadn't even been here two months, and it felt like two lifetimes.

October ninth. His dad's forty-first birthday.

Susan had found some nicer clothes at the thrift shop, and now she looked good in slacks and a sweater that weren't too big. While Danny was making toast, she said, "I'll be taking the bus with Julia to and from the school every day now. Don't forget to lock the door on your way out."

*Like we have anything to steal.* He shrugged and said, "Okay."

Julia flipped her hair into a ponytail and tugged playfully on her mother's sleeve as they left.

Danny made sure there was food and water for the dog. "Sorry I can't be home at lunch to let you out, Bud, but I'll be as quick as I can after school. See ya later, Buddy-boy."

He stepped outside into icy wind and rain. Autumn had passed, and the first sting of winter was in the air. Leaves lay in scattered piles and decayed in the gutters. By the time he got home from school, the weather had shifted to freezing rain. He took Buddy for a quick run around the condos, but they were both drenched and shivering by the time they got back. His wet second-hand jacket smelled of its last owner. Danny used it to towel off Buddy before abandoning it. Just then, his mom and Julia burst in, laughing as they shrugged off their dripping coats and fingered back their wet hair.

Danny was startled to see how much Julia looked like their mom. She was growing tall and willowy and had Mom's hazel eyes.

"Hi," Mom said cheerfully. "How was school?"

Danny glowered. "Cold and wet."

Susan walked up to her son and rested her hands on his shoulders. Her eyes were shining, and her voice was strong. "Davey-boy, it feels *so good* to be back working. Doing things for – and with

– other people. Getting ahead. Come along with us, David. Let's be a family again."

Danny's eyes narrowed. "Family! Family! What kind of family are we?! Families have a past – and a future – what do we have? We've got *nothing. Nothing but lies!* We're all just frauds, right, *Susan?*"

"David! I am your *mother.* You have a *sister,*" she said, pointing at Julia. "It doesn't matter what the rest of the world calls us. We're not frauds. We're your *family!*"

He glared. "Yeah, and so is my dad!" He whirled away and took the stairs two at a time.

He shut himself in the bathroom. His bedroom door wouldn't lock, and he needed privacy. He needed to know the world would stay out and leave him alone. He looked in the mirror. Over the past couple of months his shoulders had widened. There was more hair growing on his body and shadowing his upper lip. He examined his reflection. He had his mother's hair color – but that was it. The shape of his face, his jaw line, the slant of his eyebrows – those were all his dad's.

He was his father's son.

He'd *be* his father's son.

# Chapter 14

The spider was back. Grandma stood beside Danny, calmly explaining that spiders were fascinating, no need to be afraid, almost all of them were harmless, in fact they were good to have around the house because they trapped flies. The spider swelled step by step, but Grandma didn't seem to notice. She was chatting on about the uses for spider silk. As she talked, it advanced. He tried to yell but his mouth was spun shut with spider silk. He watched, wide-eyed and paralyzed, as the spider crept up behind her, lifted two of its legs, and started drawing silk threads out of its spinets. The spider began spinning the silk around and around her, starting at her feet, circling her legs, and pinning her arms at her sides. Grandma was still talking. "Spiders just have to do what nature programs them to do, no point in getting upset about it." The spider lifted its spinets higher and higher, now encasing her shoulders, her neck, crushing her voice box. Danny shot up in the bed, clawing at his mouth, tearing his lips apart, trying to rip out the spider silk so he could warn her —

"Grandma! Grandma! Grandma!"

The door flew open and his mom dashed into the room. She grabbed Danny and hugged him fiercely, cradling his sweaty head against her shoulder, absorbing his sobs, stroking his matted hair, rocking him back and forth, back and forth. And he squeezed her back as if holding on for his life.

⚖

Now that his mother was working, more of the household chores fell to Danny. He resented each bag of groceries he carried home. Every trudge through the wind and pelting snow made him angry. He refused to use the laundry basket to carry clothes to the laundry room, and stray socks stayed where they dropped in the common area.

He didn't notice when the worry stone slipped out of his pocket and rolled under the washing machine.

⚖

Mr. Ishii tilted his head and gave Danny a courteous smile. "How are things today?" he asked, as he motioned Danny to sit.

"Fine."

Mr. Ishii opened a file folder and placed a pad of paper and a pen in front of him.

"You still don't seem very happy. Perhaps it would help if I asked you some questions."

"So ask."

"You did quite well at your old school, at least until Christmas, but your marks went down after that. You also stopped participating in sports. Did something happen at Christmas that you'd like to tell me about?"

Danny looked the counselor in the eye. "I can't."

Mr. Ishii met his gaze. "Is it the reason you've moved here?"

"Isn't it obvious?"

"All right then. I'll assume something disrupted your life and it wasn't pleasant. Let's move forward. What about this school? Do you like it?"

"It sucks."

"And why do you think that?"

"Everything's too small," he said, waving his arm. "The gym is a joke, the classrooms are crowded, there's no equipment in the science rooms, the portables stink with the doors closed and freeze with the doors open – what kind of school is this, anyway?" he finished petulantly.

"It's a converted elementary school," Mr. Ishii answered matter-of-factly.

"So why are we here?"

"Well, it's mainly financial issues that put us here. Demographics – you know what those are – how many children of what age are in the neighborhood, predicted future trends, money available to build new schools. Things out of your control."

"So you mean, now that we're poor, I get a second-rate education?"

Mr. Ishii steepled his fingers. "Do you think the teachers here are less competent or less dedicated than at your old school?"

Danny paused. He hadn't really thought about his teachers. Were they that different? But even his mom had said this wasn't as good a school.

"So," said Mr. Ishii. "Everything here is an obstacle to your success?"

"Yeah."

"Ah," replied the counselor. Again he paused. "But in your old school your marks were already going down after Christmas."

Danny pursed his lips.

"Perhaps then," Mr. Ishii continued, "you'll agree the way you feel now has more to do with what happened at Christmas, than the situation here at the school?"

No reply.

"Moving on, then. Have you made any friends?"

"No."

Mr. Ishii slowly flexed his fingers. "I assume you had friends in your old school?"

"Yeah."

"Are the students different here?"

Danny snorted. "Yeah."

"Can you tell me how?"

"They don't do the things I used to do with my friends."

"Such as?"

"They don't go bike riding. We never go to each other's houses. There's no money to go to movies. It's a pain to go anywhere on the bus."

"Oh. So, it's actually because they're poor?"

Danny rubbed his thumbnail along the seam of his jeans.

"Also something that's not in your control, David."

Danny squirmed.

"So," said the counselor, "if I can summarize. Something last Christmas changed your circumstances, and you're resentful and angry about it. Would you agree?"

"You don't know *the half* of it."

"Well, I can see that's true. But, we're here now, and where do we go from here?"

"I dunno."

A long pause. "Would you like to meet again?"

Danny didn't say yes, but he didn't say no.

"I'll book another appointment."

Danny left without saying good-bye. Mr. Ishii bent over his desk to make some notes.

⚖

The next day in art class, Danny asked to be moved closer to the window. "The light over here isn't very good," he told Mr. Thompson. "I think I'd do better over there."

"Certainly, if you think it would help," the teacher replied.

The move put him beside Nixxie.

He caught her looking at him, and she noticed him looking at her. A dropped pastel was an excuse to move closer.

"Hey," she said.

"Hey. You really do have talent," he said, looking at her paper.

"Thanks," she replied with a smile.

"What're you doing after school?"

"Nuthin' much."

"Wanna go over to the mall for ice cream?"

"Yeah, sure."

"Okay," he said, and they passed the rest of the class in nervous silence.

The day dragged, but when the bell rang, he hustled to Nixxie's home room, where he tried to look relaxed and casual as he leaned against the wall and waited.

"What would you like?" he asked as they entered the store.

"An ice-cream sandwich."

"Wanna stay inside or go outside?" he asked.

"Let's go out."

Even though it was cold, they sat on the concrete wall around the raised flower bed. The flowers were long gone, replaced by windblown garbage and lipstick-smudged cigarette butts.

Nixxie peeled back the paper wrapper. "Live around here?"

"Over in the condos," he replied, pointing vaguely in the direction of New Haven. "You?"

"Down the other side of the school, a couple of blocks."

They each took a few bites, using their ice cream to avoid looking at each other.

"Did you say you were from Saskatoon?" she asked.

"Uh…yeah," he replied, quickly recalling Phil's advice. "Where're you from?"

"I was born here in Winnipeg," she replied. She licked her sticky finger tips. "Hey, do you know Frank?" she asked. "He's having a Hallowe'en party at his place on Saturday night. Wanna go? Some people dress up, some don't. He won't mind if you show up. Just bring your own drinks."

"Okay," he said uncertainly, not at all sure Frank wouldn't mind.

She slid off the wall. "Thank you for the ice cream." She smiled. "See you at school tomorrow."

"See ya," he said. Then he added, "Nixxie."

# Chapter 15

Danny had always loved Hallowe'en. Over the years, his mom's needle and thread had transformed him into a cave man, a vampire, a robot, a ghost, and a head-hunting cannibal. When his sister was little, his mom would have Hallowe'en parties for them at home, but once Jennifer started school, they concentrated on going out door to door.

He poked around his room, wondering what he should do this year. He had no idea what to expect, really. How many would be dressed up? Fancy costumes or simple ones? How many kids were going to be there? Nixxie said he didn't have to dress up at all, and maybe that was the safest route.

On Saturday morning Julia was awash in a sea of construction paper, scissors, tape, and felt markers. She'd already cut out wavy-bottomed ghosts, full moons, and gap-toothed jack-o-lanterns and pasted them to the front window. She looked up from tracing the outline of a hissing cat on black paper.

"What'll you be for Hallowe'en?" she asked.

"Nuthin'," he replied.

"Then it's your own fault," she said. "*I'm* going to be a pirate."

He shrugged and moved toward the kitchen. His mom was washing up breakfast dishes. He leaned against the door jamb and mentioned he was invited out to a party that night.

"Where is it?" she asked.

"One of the kids from school – Frank."

"Far from here?"

"Close enough to walk."

"It sounds good. Are you dressing up?"

"Nah, they said we'd mainly sit around and listen to music and stuff."

"Any girls going?"

"Nah," he said. He looked down. The lie came easily, and he wasn't sure why he had said it at all.

"Just some boys from the school?"

"Yeah," he mumbled.

"Okay. What time?"

"Seven thirty."

"And you'll be home by…?"

"I dunno."

She pursed her lips and thought a moment. "Ten thirty?" she suggested.

"Sure. Whatever."

That afternoon, he went to the mall. Hallowe'en merchandise spilled from shelves. Impulsively, he decided to look for something for himself. He settled on a tube of white face paint and a six-pack of Coke. Then he went down to the hardware section of the dollar store and stole a lock for his bedroom door.

⚒

He thought face paint was the safest. He didn't want to go without anything, and if he felt like an idiot he could just wash it off – say it itched, or something.

He went to the bathroom mirror.

His father's features stared back.

He started smearing on the face paint.

⚒

Even though the sun had been down for over an hour, Danny glanced about to see if anyone was looking at him. He turned up his collar, but there wasn't any way to hide his skull bones outlined in white. He'd memorized Nixxie's address, but just to be sure, he'd written it in pen on his wrist where his watch would hide it from view. He carried the Coke cans in a plastic bag, which he switched from hand to hand as he made his way toward Nixxie's house. He was careful not to smudge the paint outlining the bones on the back of his hands.

The front curtains of Nixxie's boxy house were drawn but the outside light was on. He hesitated before striding up the sidewalk at a pace he hoped looked confident.

He tried to hide his surprise when the doorbell was answered by a white woman, who looked a bit like an older version of his own mother.

He swallowed and asked, "Is Nixxie home?"

She smiled. "Yes, of course," she said. "You must be David."

He stepped into the narrow entranceway.

"Nixxie! There's a skeleton here to see you!"

"Okay, Mom," came Nixxie's voice.

*Mom?* Danny looked around the modest living room. A thick quilt hung diagonally across the couch. He could see half of the hand-stitched eight-point star. It was indigo at its center, then radiated into royal purple followed by a ring of white. Its points were tipped in blue. A woven basket stored newspapers and magazines. A framed mosaic of drawings – feathers, buffalos, tipis, a drum, a rattle – hung over the loveseat. He looked at it curiously.

Nixxie swept into the room. An ebony leather strap cinched a calf-length black dress. Blood-red nail polish matched her lipstick. She reached up to finger a black studded dog collar buckled at her throat. She'd smudged what looked like soot under her eyes. A streak ran down each cheek. She'd used mascara to blacken her eyebrows into thick mats and angle them down toward her nose.

Her eyes twinkled. "See, I told you I love shopping at Value Mart!"

"Great costume," he said, putting his hands in his pockets. He pulled them out quickly when he remembered the paint. "I didn't know you liked Goth."

"Actually I don't, but it's cheap and easy. So – you're a skeleton?"

"Yeah," Danny mumbled, now feeling underdressed.

"And you'll be at Frank's?" Nixxie's mom interrupted.

"Uh-huh," Nixxie replied.

"Well, don't stay out past ten thirty, and if you need a ride home, just call and Dad'll pick you up."

"Okay Mom," Nixxie said as she shrugged into a man's large, black overcoat.

"See you later."

He turned to the door. A dinner plate-sized hoop strung with a spiderweb-like mesh hung from the back of the door. Clear glass beads scattered along the mesh caught and reflected the light. A bundle of feathers dangled from one side and a braided leather thong hung from the other. It was pretty, but why would people bring spider-web things into their house? He was careful not to touch it when he opened the door.

"Good-bye, David. Bye, Nixxie. Have fun."

Nixxie led the way down the walk. "This way," she directed, pointing to the left.

"Are you sure Frank won't mind me coming?" Danny asked, his voice rising.

"Nah, he'll be good with it. So what'd you bring to drink?" she asked, pointing at the bag.

"Coke."

"Share?"

"Sure."

Frank had taped a note to his front door. The shaky handwriting was meant to look spooky: *Use Back Door*. A bone white plastic skull replaced the back porch light cover. Nixxie rang the doorbell. Danny heard a wolf howl. Captain Hook's hat and eye patch appeared in the window. The pirate opened the door with his hook.

"Hi Nixxie," he said and then looked down the steps at Danny.

"This is David. He's in my art class. I said you wouldn't mind if he came."

"OK, yeah, I think I seen ya around the school." He held open the door. "Come in. We're in the basement, same as last year."

Danny knew a few names and recognized some faces, but he'd kept to himself so much he'd never talked to any of them. He dropped his drinks on the table and slipped off his jacket. A boy without a costume scanned him head to foot. Danny stuck out his chin and looked him in the eye. He knew he must look weird. He was wearing his first-day-of-school clothes – the stone-washed jeans and black T-shirt that had sat untouched in the bottom drawer ever since his mom bought them.

The boy squinted. "So what're you supposed to be?"

Danny flared his nostrils. "I'm Danny McMillan."

The boy's brows knitted. "Who's Danny McMillan?" he asked.

"Some dead guy," he replied, turning his back.

They had chips and pop and listened to some heavy metal. Half the kids were in costume: the Statue of Liberty, a hockey player, a tramp, a black cat. Part way through the evening, a kid named Ian put a movie in the DVD player.

"*Doppelganger*," Ian said. "It's great. It's about a teenager who has a shadow-double of himself who follows him everywhere and the shadow-double kills people, but he's the only one who can see it, and everyone else thinks he's the murderer."

"Ecccewww," said one of the girls, wrinkling her nose. "I don't like horror movies."

"Don't watch," Ian said, carting his popcorn bowl to the couch.

"Do you like horror movies?" Nixxie asked Danny.

"They're okay…sometimes," he added, not sure what the best answer would be, wanting to please her.

"I hate them," she replied. "I like action movies – fast cars and things that blow up. And westerns."

"Me too," he said quickly. They chatted about movies, actors, music. A few kids danced. He watched them and his palms began to sweat. Before he could ask Nixxie, the Statue of Liberty jumped up.

"Nixxie, let's dance!"

Nixxie kicked off her black boots and twirled in her bare feet. Her hips swiveled to the music. The flared sleeves of her dress momentarily revealed her long, brown fingers. Her hair fell across her face. When she threw her head back, the smooth, clean lines of her jaw and neck drew his eyes down across the soft swell of her breasts to her tight belt.

He wanted to be the one dancing with Nixxie.

The song ended, and Nixxie pulled on her boots. "I've gotta go or I'll be late," she said.

Danny jumped up. They said their good-byes and walked through the frosty October night. The stars twinkled – suns too far away to give heat, but close enough to light up the sky, the constellations timeless and unchanging. They always made him think about his grandparents.

Nixxie hugged the sides of her oversized coat close to her body. "What time do you have to be home?"

"Eleven o'clock," he lied.

"My parents don't want me out late. They worry. Sometimes I get mad at them, but I guess I can understand why they feel that way." She paused. "What about your parents?"

The answer wasn't something he'd thought out. "Sort of strict," he replied. "My mom worries, but she mostly treats me like an adult."

"What about your dad?"

"I don't have a dad."

"Hey, neither do I. I mean I don't have a biological dad – well I must've had one, or I wouldn't be here – but my real mom and dad are my grandma and grandpa. They adopted me. And they adopted my mom."

"Oh."

"It's complicated. My grandma's my A-mom, because she adopted me. Denise is my B-mom, my birth mom. But my A-mom is the same person as Denise's A-mom. Sometimes I think I should call Denise 'Mom,' too. Like I said, it's complicated."

He looked past the Goth makeup and glimpsed someone who was perhaps not what she seemed to be.

# Chapter 16

It snowed all Sunday morning. Then the sun appeared and spread its light as if it had never hidden its smile. Buddy clamped his Frisbee in his mouth and pawed at Danny's hand until the boy went for the leash.

Danny saw Papa Joe taking short careful steps along the unshovelled walk. The sight of the old man reminded Danny that he had a lock, but he didn't have the tools to install it. He asked Papa Joe if he had some he could borrow.

"Sure, I've got a tool box, what'd ya need?"

"I'm…not sure. A screwdriver. Maybe a hammer."

"What're ya doin'?"

"Putting a lock on a door."

"What kinda lock? One with a key?"

"No, just a sort of latch type," he replied, making a back and forth motion with his hand.

"As long as it ain't too big," Papa Joe replied. "The management don't like tenants changing things like locks."

It had never occurred to Danny he'd need anyone's permission to secure some privacy.

Papa Joe bent to scratch Buddy's ears. "They're in the basement, in a red box, beside the furnace."

Danny carted up the toolbox and set it on the towel Papa Joe had spread on the table. Papa Joe started sorting through his tools.

Danny looked around. Although the fixtures matched theirs – the same appliances, cupboards, counters – it looked homey. Enough keepsakes to fill a gift shop lined the walls. Gold-framed mountain scenes and seascapes elbowed for room with porcelain collector's plates, fancy mirrors, a barometer, and pictures of black labs cut from a calendar. But mostly there were photos that looked like they'd been taken a hundred years ago. Christmas, wedding, and school photos in cardboard frames, candid shots of summer holidays, family dinners and chubby babies: all sticky-tacked to the cupboards.

"I don't see your momma 'round in the days no more. She get a job?"

"Yeah. At my sister's school."

He nodded. "Working in schools. Pays good."

"Yep," said Danny. *Lie.*

"And yuh can't get home from school at lunch now, can yuh?"

"No."

He picked up the tools one by one, inspecting each as if he were worried it had changed since the last time he'd seen it. He sorted them either onto the towel beside his half-full ash tray, or back into the tool box.

"Must be hard on Buddy, bein' in all day."

"Yeah," Danny said, glancing at the dog. At the sound of his name, Buddy swished his tail back and forth across the floor. It had been two weeks since Mom started volunteering, and two weeks since the dog had been out at noon.

Papa Joe handed the boy a screwdriver and a hammer.

Danny took the tools. "Thanks."

Papa Joe scratched Buddy's ears. "So, I been thinkin'," he said. "Buddy here needs a walk during the day. And the doc says I need to have a walk every day so's the new hips keep workin'. But with the ice 'n' snow, sometimes it's hard for me ta get out, 'cause I worry 'bout fallin'. But if I had me a fine dog like Buddy, he could kinda watch out for me, and bark a lot if I fell down or somethin'."

Danny looked at Papa Joe, then at the dog. It actually sounded like a good idea. "I'll – I'll ask my mom," he said.

"That'd be right nice," Papa Joe replied.

His mom drummed her fingertips across her lips. "I'd have to give him a key. I don't really want to do that," she said.

Danny rolled his eyes. "Like, he might steal something? Like, we've got something *to* steal?"

She pursed her lips. "It's not a question of stealing. It's a question of privacy."

He crossed his arms. "It'd be good for Buddy."

She gazed back at him. "I'll think about it," she finally said.

The portable's steam radiators hissed and ticked but couldn't put out enough heat to keep the room warm. Ms. Nguyen was reading announcements when Chad swiveled to face Danny.

"How come you an' your mom always walk to the mall?" he asked, leaning forward. "Too poor to have a car? Your mom a drunk and lose her license?"

Danny's face flushed. Chad kept eyeing Danny's clothes. "So where'd a poor boy like you get such a pretty watch?" he sneered, pointing at Danny's wrist.

Danny's hands sweated and his heart thumped. For a moment he was lost for words. Then he remembered Andy telling him that Chad liked to push people around, get them into trouble, and even to steal for him. *He's not going to push me around.* "I stole it."

"Yeah? So, how'd ya like to steal me one?" he dared, narrowing his eyes.

Danny clenched his jaw and held his face taut. "No problem, Chad," he said.

They met behind the mall. Most of the boys Chad hung with were older. They seemed to have easy access to cigarettes. Chad was smoking, perched on the top rail of a metal fence, his feet propped up on the bottom rail and his shoulders hunched forward. His head was tilted downward so the smoke drifted up across his face and in front of his eyes.

Chad didn't say a word. He just stared at Danny, not moving, except to bring a cigarette lazily to his mouth. Danny didn't say anything either. He was still wearing his shapeless anorak, much too thin for the zero-degree weather and brisk prairie wind. He clenched his bare hands, refusing to shiver.

The mood was as tense as a drawn bow, and neither of them wanted to loose the string. It was an older boy who spoke first.

"So this is *Dav-id*," he said, pronouncing the name as if it were exotic. He fingered the silver studs along the bottom of his black leather jacket and spit into the snow. "So, ya wanna piss with the big dogs?" he asked, his upper lip curling.

Danny said nothing. Stay focused on Chad, he thought. Don't shiver.

"I guess we'll see if he's a rottweiler or a poodle-boy, hey?" Chad said in an oily voice. The boys snorted and laughed.

Danny struggled to breathe naturally, sure they could hear his racing heartbeat. He had started to sweat and his palms were slick with moisture, chilling them to ice. His head told him to run, but fear of humiliation clamped his gut and sucked up the adrenaline rushing through his body.

"David is a poodle-boy! David is a poodle-boy! *Loser!*" a pimply-faced youth sang in a falsetto voice.

"Shut up," said Chad. He took another drag on his cigarette and stared Danny down. "So, what's it gonna be?"

"By the end of the week," he replied, hoping they couldn't hear his voice tremble.

"What's wrong with now?"

"End of the week," he repeated, keeping his voice flat. He squared his shoulders, flicked up his collar, turned his back, and sauntered away.

By the time he got to the condo, he was shaking. Buddy circled Danny, rubbing his ribs across the boy's legs. Danny knelt to stroke the dog, and Buddy licked his frigid fingers. "Hey, Buddy-boy," he said, drawing comfort from the dog. Buddy's tail started its familiar beat against the floor – happy to be with Danny, to be where he belonged.

# Chapter 17

He decided it would be easiest to return to the store where he'd bought his own watch. He knew where they were, and he figured if he got there just as the store was opening, there wouldn't be many clerks or store detectives working yet. He settled on Thursday. That would give him enough time to lift bus fare from his mom's purse. And an extra ten just in case.

On Thursday, he pretended to get ready for school, but as soon as his mom and Julia left, he went to his room and turned on his music full blast. The downtown stores didn't open until ten. Plenty of time to install the lock.

The phone rang as he was leaving. He didn't answer it; he knew it was the school calling to see where he was. Once you'd been marked as a "skipper," the office red-flagged your file and followed up every absence.

He sat at the back of the bus, planning his strategy. He'd never tried to lift anything bigger than the lock, or as expensive as the watch. He knew the case would have an electronic tag glued to the back, and it would be too hard to pry open without someone noticing. He'd have to deactivate the tag. He closed his eyes and pictured the store – the floor plan, the exits, the exact location of the jewelry department. Jewelry counters were always monitored by security cameras, so he'd have to be careful.

He strolled into the store, his heartbeat speeding up with every step. He browsed through the magazine racks. Casually holding up a copy of *Sports Illustrated*, he angled himself to face the nearby jewelry department. He scanned the ceiling for the telltale darkened glass bulbs.

There they were – two – both behind the counter. One was probably trained on the cash register. The other was on the far side, near the diamond rings. Good news. Anything happening below the level of the counter was out of sight.

He shelved the magazine and began roaming the sale aisles. He looked for store personnel. Two sales clerks were transferring boxes from rolling trolleys onto shelves. Danny veered toward the jewelry.

The watches hung in a free-standing, swiveling glass stand. He remembered last time, for some reason, the stand hadn't been locked. Maybe the lock was still broken. He rubbed his palms across his jeans. What if it was locked now? He'd never get in. He'd have to ask a clerk to open it and then it would be impossible.

He stopped to scoop up some jewelry from a sale rack. He took about six pairs of earrings, all dangling from plastic tags. He rested them on the counter beside the watch stand.

There it was. The Pentathlete model, green with a brown strap. Danny made a show of neatly lining up the earrings. He leaned forward, examining them and shifting them about with his right hand. Carefully, without turning the stand his left hand tugged at the glass door.

It was still unlocked.

He kept inspecting the earrings. At the same time, he watched his progress in the wavy glass reflection. He slid open the glass door, swiftly lifted the watch off its hook, and palmed it up the sleeve of his anorak. Then he gently jostled the display stand with his shoulder as if it were an accident, and stealthily shut the glass door. Below counter level, he put his left hand into his pocket and felt the watch slide in.

He kept his head up as he returned to the earring rack where he re-hung the earrings. But one pair caught his eye: a string of three pea-sized jade beads hung from a gold-colored hook. They looked good, not tawdry like the other ones. He'd buy them for Nixxie. And they'd help him get out of the store.

He headed for the cashier. The clerk rang in the purchase. As he pulled out his wallet, he said, "They're a gift. Do you have a small box?"

The clerk smiled as if the gift were for her. "Sure," she said. When she bent to check beneath the counter, he put his left hand into his coat pocket and swiftly brushed his entire pocket across the desensitizing pad. When the clerk straightened, he casually stepped back.

"For your mom?" the clerk asked as she inserted the earrings.

"Yeah," he said, opening his wallet and handing her the ten-dollar bill. The clerk handed him his change and his purchase. He dropped the bag into the same pocket as the watch. Then he flashed a grin at the cashier and strolled past the security sensors.

*Success.*

Danny wormed his hands into his armpits as he waited for the bus. But once he was in the back seat, the warmth of the engine relaxed him. The bus reached the mall sooner than he expected. If he went to school now, he could catch the last morning class. Or, he could stay home until noon and practice forging his mother's signature.

It wasn't hard. Her signature wasn't always the same – sometimes she wrote the *S* as a separate letter, and sometimes she joined it to the rest of the word. Usually, it looked more like an *L* and the letters after the *y* trailed off into a scribble. *The biggest advantage*, he thought, *was that the school would never know the difference.*

After practicing about five minutes, he was satisfied. He wrote a note:

> Please excuse David from class this morning as we had a family emergency and I needed him here.
>
> Sincerely,
> Susan Mayer

*There. That ought to keep them from asking questions.*

He burned the paper with the practice signatures in the kitchen sink. He took Buddy for a quick walk and ate a peanut butter and jelly sandwich. He didn't bother to clear the dishes. He often had a snack when he got home, and his mom wouldn't notice today as different from any other.

He tucked the watch under the clothes in his dresser, scratched Buddy under the chin, and went to school. He stopped at the office to hand in the note. The secretary unfolded it, looked at it, looked at him as if he'd stolen something, and looked at the note again. "What kind of family emergency?" she snapped.

Danny had to stop himself from looking startled. But that now-familiar surge of adrenaline boosted his confidence, and the lie came easily. "My sister broke her leg. I had to help."

The secretary stared. "Right," she said. "Let me just make a note of that." She took a red pen and wrote across the bottom of the note: 'Sister broke leg.' She glanced back at him. "You forgot to put in the date. I'll just write that in too, shall I?" she said sarcastically.

He spun on his heel and walked away. *Screw you.*

Danny avoided eye contact with Chad all afternoon. He wanted it to happen in *his* time, under *his* control. At the end of the day, he sauntered into the portable. It didn't take long for Chad to turn around and cross his arms.

"So?" Chad said.

"So what?" he replied, drawing out the words.

Chad's eyes bore into Danny's. They were like two young rams with their heads down, ready to butt horns.

Danny leaned back, flipped up his sleeve, and checked the time on his watch. He was enjoying this. "After school tomorrow, Chad," he said. Smugly. In control.

It wasn't until he got home from school he realized he'd missed his appointment with Mr. Ishii. The thought pricked his conscience – but only for a moment.

# Chapter 18

Two items warmed Danny's pocket when he left for school on Friday – the gift-wrapped earring box, and the watch, still in its plastic case with the eighty-dollar price tag firmly attached.

Today was going to be a good day.

⚒

"What's with this?" Nixxie asked when he presented the package.

"Just open it."

She used her nails to peel back the tape. She pinched the sides, forced the top open, and peered in. Still not knowing what to make of it, she shook the box. The earrings landed in her palm.

"They're cool," she said.

He pulled out a five-dollar bill. "Let's get something for lunch at the mall."

She hesitated. "Sorry," she said. "Mom expects me home for

lunch every day except when I have volleyball or something. But I could go after school."

He remembered his appointment with Chad. Should he ask her along? Or go it alone? He didn't know how she'd react. He'd never seen her talk to Chad or any of the people Chad hung out with. She didn't seem to like that group. He decided he'd better do one thing at a time.

"Nah, I have to do some things with my mom right after school," he said. "So what about next week?"

"Yeah, okay," she replied. "Thanks for the earrings." In a heartbeat, the moment grew uncomfortable and she stammered, "I've gotta go."

He stroked the watch in his pocket. "See you next week," he said.

*

He walked to the mall with deliberate slowness. Although he felt confident, he still had that flicker of anxiety. He kept his hands in his pockets, running his fingers up and down the watch case, which now felt like a key that would open doors. He kept his face expressionless as he swaggered up to Chad. Cigarette smoke wreathed Chad's head. Danny stopped and draped his arm over a railing.

Without looking at Danny, Chad said, "Todd. Get David a cigarette."

Danny blinked. His dad's voice sprang into his head. *You wanna be an athlete, Danny? Don't smoke. They're coffin nails. Only idiots smoke.*

Todd pulled out a pack and casually flipped up the top. The

crumpled silver foil showed the tips of three cigarettes. He stepped toward Danny, offering the pack. Danny reached with two fingers and pulled one out.

He'd never smoked. And until now, he'd never wanted to.

Todd thumbed aside the foil, revealing the end of a lighter. He flicked it once, twice, three times, and the translucent blue and yellow flame sputtered upward. He held it out.

Danny had seen it done so many times that the movement didn't feel strange. *Cigarette between lips, fingers angling the shaft down into the flame, breathe in, watch the flame lick the end of the cigarette like a smoldering kiss, inhale, exhale, breathe life into a coffin nail.* He expected the bite of bitterness, but after the first puff, all he could taste was success.

Danny leaned back and savored the rush. His eyes narrowed as he met their stares. He put the cigarette back in his mouth and let it dangle from the corner of his lips as if glued there, as if he'd done it a thousand times. Then he reached into his pocket and pulled out the watch.

"Catch," he said, tossing it to Chad. Danny smirked when Chad had to scramble to catch it before it fell into the snow. Chad pocketed the watch without looking at it.

"Congratulations. You're in." Chad cracked his knuckles and pushed himself away from the railing. "Party Saturday night at Todd's. BYOB." He turned his back and strolled away.

"Second house down from the gas station," Todd said. The boys turned to follow Chad, but not before Danny noticed some admiring glances shot his way.

He was alone. He puffed on his cigarette, breathing deeply, the smoke burning in his lungs, the nicotine coursing through his veins like defiance, straight to his heart.

"Hey boy," Danny said. Buddy approached warily, muzzle to the ground, and backed up before Danny could touch him. The dog's nose twitched as he smelled the cigarette smoke that clung to Danny. "What's up, Bud?" he said, reaching to ruffle the dog's fur. Buddy thrust his muzzle repeatedly into the palm of Danny's hand – the one that had held the cigarette. Danny realized he had a problem. No, two problems. He'd been away too long. He saw a puddle on the kitchen floor. And if Buddy could smell the smoke, so could his mom.

Being late was the easier problem. He'd tell his mom he had to stay to finish a science lab. She'd be happy he was doing his work and wouldn't complain about the mess. But he needed some way to cover up the smoking. Who did he know who smoked?

Papa Joe! He remembered the ash tray on the kitchen table, the lingering scent in the apartment. And he still had Papa Joe's tools. "Let's go visit Papa Joe," he said to Buddy. The dog's tail started beating back and forth.

Papa Joe raised his brows and smiled when they appeared.

"Well, come in," he said, holding the door wide. The smoky air greeted Danny like a gift. He stomped the snow off his boots as Buddy brushed past him into the condo.

He returned the tools and Papa Joe poured orange juice into small knobby glasses. "So," said Papa Joe as they both settled down at the table, Buddy curled at their feet, "your momma decided 'bout me walkin' Buddy?"

"She said she thought it was a great idea," he lied.

"Well, that's wonderful," Papa Joe said. "That's real nice of her."

"She was glad you asked," Danny said. "She was worried about Buddy being home alone all day."

"She's a sweet woman, your momma."

Danny checked his watch and smiled to himself. The school bus should be here by now. Maybe she'd already found the puddle on the floor. Then, if Mom saw him and Papa Joe walking Buddy, how could she say no?

"Wanna go for a walk right now?" Danny asked.

Papa Joe smiled and nodded. "That'd be real nice, David."

Sure enough, he could see Mom through the living room window. Danny gave her a full-faced smile and an effortless wave.

The next day, his mom agreed and said Papa Joe could start walking the dog every noon hour.

# Chapter 19

Saturday morning. Danny lay in bed with his hands sandwiched between his head and the pillow, gazing at the blank ceiling. He was thinking about the party at Todd's. BYOB. Bring Your Own Beer. This was a problem. He didn't know where to get it, his four-dollar weekly allowance didn't go very far, and his mom had completely stopped drinking, so there was nothing to steal in the house. He needed cash.

At lunch, he steered the conversation toward money, and asked his mother what he could do to earn some. His mom smiled and suggested a newspaper route or maybe babysitting. He might be able to make some money shoveling snow.

Danny clammed up. There was no way he was going to do any babysitting. Newspapers or snow shoveling? Fat chance.

"David," she said, not noticing his reaction, "can you come to the store and help carry groceries?"

*Score.*

"Sure," he said agreeably. "Why don't you just give me the list and some money? You don't have to come. I can do it myself."

She smiled at her son. "That'd be great," she said, handing over the list and forty dollars.

He wore his anorak. He scanned the list and planned out the best things to steal – small enough to hide, but worth the most. Maybe the cheese and the canned tuna?

The coat's lining gradually filled. The bottle of vanilla. Paprika. A wedge of cheddar cheese. Sliced ham for his sister's lunch. And a package of gum for himself.

"Well, hello again," said the cashier. "Doing the shopping all on your own now?"

"Yeah."

The cashier rang up the bill. Twenty-nine sixty. Danny nodded to himself. Perfect.

He slipped around the corner of the mall and emptied his coat into the bags. He crumpled the receipt, threw it into the air, and batted it into a trash can. He strode home through the snow, the bag feeling lighter than usual, his mind on the party.

He helped his mom unpack the groceries.

"How much were they?" she asked.

"Thirty-eight sixty," he lied.

"Why don't you just keep the change," she said.

"Sure." He tried not to sound smug.

Mom seemed pleased when Danny told her he was going out with some friends again that night.

"Same as the Hallowe'en party?" she asked.

"Yeah, pretty much."

"At Frank's again?"

"Yeah."

"Okay. Have fun," she said, handing him his allowance.

He tucked the money into his jeans. *One more detail to take care of before I leave,* he thought, *and it'll go smooth and easy.* Danny waited until his mother left the kitchen, then slipped a green garbage bag from the cupboard. He walked to the front door and quickly stuffed in his anorak. He pulled on a short jacket and hurried out the door, shoving the garbage bag under the steps.

The wind shot icicles through him as he turned the corner to Todd's. The house was easy to spot. A couple of cars were parked with one tire on the sidewalk, and footprints crisscrossed the walkway. Lights behind the drapes cast a twilight glow onto the snow. The deep thrum of bass speakers seeped through the walls.

He hesitated at the curb. His hand groped in his jacket pocket and he toyed with the fourteen dollars. He squared his shoulders, lifted his chin, and made fresh tracks to the door.

No one heard the doorbell. He wavered, then grabbed the knob, and pushed. Abandoned boots blocked the entrance and soaked the carpet. Coats sagged on bent wire hangers poking from the closet. Sandalwood incense was burning somewhere, but it was no match for the smell of cigarettes and greasy fast-food containers left too long in the trash. Loud voices competed with thumping rap music.

He plowed through the boots. A gangly youth clutching a beer confronted him. He looked Danny up and down and, satisfied Danny was not an intruder, turned and slunk away.

Danny pulled the money from his jacket and transferred it

to his jeans. Half a dozen kids were sprawled around the living room. He recognized Todd hunched on the floor in front of a blonde girl, his back pressed against the chair. His feet were set shoulder-width apart with his knees pulled toward his chest. The girl's hand dallied on his head. Her fingers combed through his hair, a lit cigarette pinched between her first and second fingers. Two opened cans of beer sat at his feet. He'd balanced a cigarette on an ashtray full of stubbed butts.

"Davey-boy!" Todd called over the music. "Where's your beer?"

Trying to look cool, Danny reached into his pocket and produced his cash. He held it up and stared back. Todd jerked his head to the side. "Back door. Next delivery in 'bout an hour." He closed his eyes and leaned into the girl's caresses.

Danny turned toward what he figured must be the kitchen. He could hear voices. One of them was Chad's.

There he was, leaning against the counter. His feet were spread apart, and between them, with her back to Danny, stood a girl. She was bending forward, as if about to kiss him. Looking over her shoulder, Chad spotted Danny and grinned.

"Davey," he said, as he raised his arm in the air. "Right on time."

Danny made a show of lifting his left arm and pulling back the sleeve, revealing the identical watch. "Right on time," he agreed.

Chad put his hands on the girl's shoulders and roughly pushed her aside. "Got yer brewski?" Chad asked.

"Next delivery," he replied, as if this were all as familiar as old news.

Chad gave him a greasy smile. "Let me front you one," he said, turning to the fridge. Cheap brands packed the shelves. Chad tugged a can free from its plastic ring. He kneed shut the door, snapped the tab, and handed it over.

"Helena," Chad said to the glassy-eyed girl, "meet Davey-boy."

Helena giggled and raised her hand to play with her long black hair. The whites around her green eyes were bloodshot and she blinked slowly. She started shaking beer cans and draining the dregs.

Danny lifted his chin and took a long drink. The beer bubbled bitterly on his tongue, reminding him of molasses. He'd tasted beer before, of course, but it had been crisp-tasting, more like ginger ale. He swallowed quickly, not letting it linger in his mouth. He lowered the can and wiped the back of his hand across his lips, as if he drank beer every day.

They stood staring at one another. Danny wondered what to do next. Sit down? Leave the room? Talk to Chad? Do nothing? He noticed the cigarette pack tucked up under Chad's T-shirt sleeve.

"Gimme a fag," he said, in a voice he hoped sounded commanding.

Chad's eyes swept deliberately from Danny's head to his feet, sizing him up. He flipped the pack from under his sleeve and tossed it to Danny. Danny downed half his beer and opened the pack. He plucked out a cigarette and the lighter and casually lit up. Leaving the cigarette dangling from his lip, he reinserted the lighter, closed the pack, and chucked it back to Chad.

Chad caught it and twisted it into his sleeve. He leaned forward and sucker-punched Danny on the shoulder. A beer in one hand and a cigarette in the other, Danny felt like he'd arrived at his future.

At some point the supplier arrived, slipping in and turning off the back light. Danny traded his fourteen dollars for three cans of beer, four cigarettes, and a lighter. He moved through the night on an alcohol and nicotine slick. Someone hooked his arm around Danny's neck and pulled him into the kitchen, and he didn't notice when the beer can disappeared from his side. By the time Danny had finished the last cigarette, the booze had dulled his brain and his mouth tasted like tar and ashes.

His muddled mind wondered where Todd's parents were, how he managed to have the house to himself.

*Parents. My mom. She's expecting me at ten thirty.* Danny blinked at his watch. It was already eleven fifteen. *Damn.*

He rose woozily. He wove his way past sprawled bodies, and pawed through the closet until he found his jacket. By the time he dug out his boots, his socks were soaked. No one noticed him leave.

Hard pellets of snow fell like hail from low clouds. The temperature had plunged, but at first Danny felt warm, as if he'd swallowed an antidote to ice. He pushed on through the snow-hushed streets until he saw New Haven. He stopped, scooped up a handful of snow, and crammed it into his mouth. He spat it out, grabbed another handful, and did it again. One more time, and then his lips were blue and his teeth hammered together. His tongue felt thick and seemed to fill up the whole of his mouth. He raked wet fingers through his hair, trying to force out the smoke that clung to it.

He reached the steps and hauled out the bag. His anorak fell into the snow. His fingers felt like sticks as he clawed off his jacket and pulled on the stiff anorak, the nylon sliding like cold steel against his skin. He was shivering now, his wet socks draining the last warmth from his body. He kicked his jacket under the steps. His fingers were paralyzed and he couldn't unwrap the gum he'd stashed in his pocket.

The curtain was closed but the light was on. His mother was waiting up for him.

He tried to be silent when he opened the door, but Buddy was right there waiting for him. Buddy's tail swept back and forth, but his nose twitched, taking in the smells Danny couldn't get rid of, on his pants, his shirt, his boots, his breath – smells clinging to him like a shadow.

He didn't hear anything from the living room. With exaggerated neatness, he draped his anorak over a hook and set his boots on the rubber tray. He peered around the corner and saw his mother asleep on the couch, wrapped in the thin gray blanket from Value Mart. The book she'd borrowed from the school library lay beside her.

He crept up the stairs, slipped like a spider into his room, and closed and locked the door.

His mom opened her eyes, took a deep breath, and turned out the light.

His head was still pounding when his bladder forced him out of bed the next morning. He felt like someone had shoved a rasp down his throat, and his mouth was as dry as sawdust. His arms and legs felt too heavy to move. He returned to his room, locked the door, and fell back to bed.

The vacuum cleaner woke him the second time. His sinuses stung like he had an infection. He waited until his mother had finished in the hallway, before stumbling into the bathroom. He swallowed three aspirins, hurried through a shower, and put on clean clothes. He slipped back into his room to wait for the pills to work.

His mom knocked. "I'm collecting laundry," she said to the closed door. He massaged his temples. He had to open the door.

She stepped in and eyed the jumble of clothes piled against the dresser. He couldn't smell anything, but she could. He could only hope she wouldn't catch on about the beer. She stood quietly, then said, "David, please don't make bad choices."

He looked away.

"We've come so far...all of us," she said. "We've all made sacrifices greater than any we thought we'd ever be called on to make. Our old lives were worth nothing. It's in this new life that we can thrive and shine. Come with us, David. Change with us."

He gritted his teeth. *It's a change, all right,* he thought. *Like a butterfly into a caterpillar.*

# Chapter 20

His report card came in the mail – with a letter.

November 2002

Dear Ms. Mayer,
I have enclosed a copy of your son's report card.
It is school policy when students receive failing
grades that we send it directly to the parent or
guardian.

David's record shows a large number of excused
absences. Please review the dates and times to
ensure our records are correct.

I invite you to make an appointment for a parent-
teacher conference. I also ask that you encourage
David to resume his appointments with Mr. Ishii.

Finally, I have also enclosed a letter from Social Services Income Support which is self-explanatory.

I look forward to hearing from you.

Sincerely,

Conrad Kindermann
Principal

Mom flipped to the Social Services letter.

Dear Ms. Mayer
Your son David has missed the hot lunch program more than 7 times. It is our policy that more than five unexcused absences disqualify your son from continuing in the program.

If your son was required to attend appointments during the lunch hour, please provide copies of documents showing the time, the date, and the name of the person with whom your child had the appointment. Acceptable appointments include doctor or hospital visits, counseling sessions, special educational requirements, and legal counsel.

Unless we receive copies of these documents by November 29, your son's eligibility for the hot lunch program will end on November 30.

Yours truly,

T. Timm
Income Support Worker
Social Services Income Support

Susan opened the report card:

| | |
|---|---|
| Mathematics | D |
| Social Studies | D- |
| Science | D+ |
| English | F |
| Health/Phys Ed | C- |
| Computers | D+ |
| Art | C |
| | |
| Absences | 36 |

The teachers' comments were variations on the same theme:

"David is an intelligent young man and just gets by on his in-class work. If he applied himself, he could be an honors student."

"David does not do his homework."

"David does not participate in class."

"David has the potential to be a strong athlete but he does not try. Make an effort, David!"

She shook her head, then straightened her back, and got on with her work.

While Danny gulped down his stew, his mother's eyes alternated between her son and the envelope on the counter. She waited until Julia was settled at the table with her homework and Danny was in front of the TV. She went downstairs, turned on the standing lamp, and turned off the TV.

He straightened up. "Hey! I was watching that!"

"You watch too much TV," she replied sharply. He scowled and slumped back. He'd seen the envelope in her hand.

She sat and turned her body so she could look him in the eye. "I got your report card today." She paused and bit her lip. "What's going on?"

"Nuthin'."

"Nothing. You call this nothing?" she bristled. She dumped the envelope onto the couch. She grabbed the report card and read out the marks.

He shrugged and looked at the blank TV.

She read out the absences.

He ignored her.

She took a breath and toned down her voice. "Look, Da –" She stopped saying his name. "I know you're not happy. And I know it's going to take some time to…to find your feet again, to find your way. But this –" she gestured at the papers, "you've taken a wrong turn. Education is important. You need to look ahead to your future. You're going to need a good job to support yourself, and to get that job you need an education. These marks, skipping school – you're throwing away your future."

He slowly turned to face his mother. His eyes were hard, his voice sharp. "How can I throw away what I don't have?"

"Danny! Don't you ever say that!"

"Why not?! It's true!"

"It is *not* true! Because we're here and *have* a life, because you're David Mayer and not Danny McMillan, *that's* why you have a future!"

"That's crap! Then why did you just call me *Danny*?" He leapt up. "You got us into this mess! You let this happen!" His finger stabbed out each word. "This-is-all-your-fault!"

His mom froze. Her wide eyes focused on Danny's finger and she went pale. She lifted her eyes to Danny's, and he saw naked fear.

He wanted to run away, but there was nowhere to go. He watched her pupils gradually contract to normal size, and some color return to her face. Then she flushed with anger.

"You will not abuse me like your father did! I will not take this from you! Don't you *ever* treat me like this again!"

Danny's teachers were sympathetic when Susan explained that the move to Winnipeg had been difficult and unexpected. She asked for patience, understanding, and that they focus on her son's strengths.

"He's always loved science," she said. "He collected butterflies, rocks, and books about dinosaurs. And sports – team sports especially – and fishing and camping. If we can just reach him on that level, doing the things he used to like, then I'm sure he'll go back to being the real David."

The teachers nodded and took notes. The art teacher, Mr. Thompson, said, "I'm concerned about his skipping and what he does when he's not at school. David seems to like art. Maybe I can get him to express some of his feelings in a creative way instead of by withdrawing."

The meeting ended with firm handshakes and a plan.

It was the coldest day yet — well below zero. His science teacher asked him to stay in at lunch to set up the afternoon's experiment. The class was studying mineral identification — using tracings and specific gravity to classify rocks. Because he couldn't think of an excuse, Danny agreed.

The forty-five minutes passed surprisingly quickly. Because of the things he had learned from his grandpa, he could already identify about half the samples. He was looking forward to running the tests on the others.

When he handed in his report, Ms. Tollman smiled. "Very good," she said, scanning his conclusions. She wrote across the top: *100% A+*.

There was little flicker of warmth in his heart.

Then he missed his grandpa.

"We're looking for someone to play on the basketball team," Madame Beauregard said later that week. "I think you have talent. Why don't you come to a practice? There are only a couple before Christmas. Mr. Miller starts coaching in January."

Danny looked at his feet. He'd outgrown all his shoes. He'd gotten by in gym class with some second-hand sneakers, but he remembered the expensive high-tops his dad had bought for him in Grade 7. How could he play basketball in worn-out shoes?

When he looked up, Madame Beauregard held his gaze. "The school has a budget for athletic equipment. Why don't you buy yourself some new basketball shoes? Just bring in the bill and we'll give you back the money."

He was too embarrassed to say thank you.

"The school's Christmas concert is next week," Mr. Thompson announced. "We display artwork. It can be anything you've done so far this year, or you can do something new – it's up to you." He circulated, talking to each student about the work he or she would put up. When he got to Danny, he looked through every piece in his portfolio.

"You know, I don't think any of this is your best work. Why don't you try a new piece? Maybe something to reflect the season – a rebirth, the end of the darkest days of the old year, greeting the sun and the lengthening days of the new year – even though in Winnipeg there's still going to be plenty of days cold enough to give us all freezer burn."

He moved on to Nixxie. "It's going to be hard to pick just one of yours," he said.

She smiled. Danny hadn't seen much of her over the last couple of weeks. He was hanging around with Chad and his buddies, and she didn't like Chad, so she kept to herself and her old circle of friends. A couple of times she'd worn the earrings he'd given her, then he hadn't seen them again.

But today he decided to speak to her. He felt more confident since he'd been admitted to Chad's group. Some of the other students even sought him out, wanting to spend time with him. But not Nixxie.

"I think you should choose that one," Danny said, pointing randomly at one of her pieces.

She turned to face him. "Why?"

Not a question he'd anticipated.

"I…I like the colors," he said lamely.

"It's mostly black and white."

"Yeah...well..." he fumbled. *When you don't know what to say, change the subject.*

"So what do you think my new piece should be?"

She shrugged. "How should I know?"

He looked at her, again not sure how to answer.

"What do you like?" she asked.

He barely hesitated.

"You." He smiled.

And it felt good not to lie.

# Chapter 21

As soon as he got home from the store, Danny laced up the black-and-white sneakers and sprinted up and down the stairs. Buddy raced around behind him, barking and leaping from step to step. Danny dribbled an invisible ball and scored in an invisible basket. Buddy's barking rose to a frenzy and finally Danny collapsed on the floor. The border collie was all over him. Happy, happy, happy.

After his first practice, Danny hurt in all the places he used to be strong. His shoulders ached and his leg muscles twitched as if they were going to cramp. The gym, which had seemed so small, turned out to be plenty big enough for a challenging game.

His new runners were perfect. He'd forgotten how good it felt to be part of a team. Although the others were at first wary of him, his obvious talents soon overcame their suspicions. Andy, Rico, and Tom started passing him the ball. No one from Chad's group played on the team.

He told his mom about the practice and she listened eagerly, as if each word was salve on a wound.

⚒

Nixxie finally settled on a painting of the night sky – stars stitched into the Milky Way, shining through a glowing green pinwheel of northern lights. A few stars outshone the others.

"Ah, the Aurora Borealis," Mr. Thompson said. "A wonderful choice. Remember to sign it before you frame it." Danny cocked his head and watched her write *P.S.* in the bottom right corner.

Danny had wanted to make something new like the teacher suggested, but any idea he had fell flat even before it hit the paper. He ended up selecting a fish he'd drawn from a picture in a magazine. It was caught on a line, the hook still in its mouth. He took his pencil and darkened a few spots, then leaned over Nixxie's desk.

"So," he said, pointing at hers, "is one of those the star of Bethlehem?"

"No."

"No? I thought, since it was Christmas…"

"It's not the Star of Bethlehem."

"Oh."

She looked at him. "It's my name."

"Your name," he repeated.

"Yes. My name." Then she turned her back and busied herself for the rest of the period.

⚒

On the last day of school, Danny avoided everyone. Suddenly the students' giddiness and the teachers' best wishes were unbearable. He hated Christmas. As much as he disliked school, at least there were people there. He dreaded the thought of being shut up in his house even more. It was almost enough to make him feel sick.

Almost. But he had a bone-deep, sick-making thought.

Christmas was the time he'd planned on calling his dad. The call that would kick-start his real life. They'd move home. Everything would be okay again. It'd be better than okay. It'd be the way life was supposed to be.

He ignored everything on the way home – his unbuttoned coat, the freezing air leaching the warmth from his bones. He ignored Julia's handmade Christmas decorations taped to the front window: Frosty the Snowman with cotton balls stuck to his body, Santa waving from a rooftop, snowflakes cut from white paper. He chucked his coat and boots at the front entry, trudged up the stairs, and locked his bedroom door.

He buried his head in his pillow and even ignored Buddy scratching at the door. The door stayed locked while Julia and his mom went for a Christmas tree.

They'd always had a perfect tree – a long-needled Scotch pine that barely fit through the front door. Dad would saw the bottom flat and release the fragrance of the forest. Then he'd secure it in the stand and put up his feet while the rest of the family decorated it. Every year, Danny and Jennifer fought over the tinsel. Jen loved it, but he hated it because Buddy would track it all around the house. The first year they had him, he ate it and got sick on the carpet. Dad had banished the puppy to the basement for the next two days, and Danny squirmed as he listened to him whine. Dad said it was the only way he'd learn. And Dad was always right.

Mom found a compromise. They'd have tinsel every second year.

Danny heard the front door open and shut. "Davey!" Mom called up the stairs. "Come down for lunch, and we'll put up the tree."

He waited half an hour before he went down.

It was an artificial tree.

Wordlessly, he snatched his coat and Buddy's leash, and they bolted out the door. They stayed out until Buddy started taking mincing steps, trying to shorten the time his feet touched the frigid concrete. Reluctantly, Danny turned back to the condo and stomped through the door. He could see the Christmas hamper from the food bank on the kitchen floor. Mom had borrowed some Christmas CDs from the library, and Frank Sinatra crooned "White Christmas" as Mom and Julia draped the final decorations on the tree. It hadn't taken long – the tree was already strung with mini-lights when they brought it home. It was obviously a display model. The ornaments were mainly red, green, and gold baubles, made in China out of paper-thin glass. Some of them were still in the box, already broken.

A bargain-basement Christmas.

The jolly Santa didn't look old enough to shave, let alone grow a beard, when he arrived with the Santa's Anonymous delivery on Sunday. They used to donate to the Santa's collection box. Now this pathetic looking Santa left four wrapped packages for Julia and him and one for Mom. Julia shook each one before placing it under the tree. She'd always done that, he remembered, but it had angered Dad, so she'd do it when he wasn't around.

And they'd never had only nine presents under the tree.

He'd never felt this lousy. It was as if the holiday spirit had dried to dust in his heart.

Danny trudged over to the mall. He usually spent his measly allowance as soon as he got it on comic books, gum, pop, and chocolate bars. He hadn't saved up any money to buy his mother and sister a present, and this week's four dollars wasn't going to go very far. He drifted past window displays packed with things he couldn't afford, and the impossibility of having them made Danny want them even more. And there were those TV ads – happy families leading perfect lives chock-full of good times, laughter, comfort, and love. Everyone had what they wanted, and no one ever cried. Danny wanted the TV ad life, but what he lived was the six o'clock news.

Christmas Eve. Walking Buddy, the snow scoured his skin like sandpaper, and when it wasn't snowing the wind hit him dead center. Mom had lit candy cane scented candles around the house and more gifts had appeared under the tree. Danny retreated to the cold basement, cocooned in the old gray car blanket. Inactivity had paralyzed him and guilt had petrified him.

He hadn't bought any presents.

And now it was too late.

Danny stayed under the covers until almost eleven o'clock on Christmas morning. He spent another hour shunning the Christmas music drifting up the stairs. He tried to block the smell of roasting turkey by shoving his blanket against the crack under the door. In the end it was Julia's pounding on his door that got him moving.

"Get up! I've waited all morning for you and I'm not gonna wait any more! I don't care if you stay in there all day!" The words came hard and fast from the nine-year-old.

When he was nine, he'd still believed in Santa Claus. Julia had waited until noon to open her few gifts. He clutched his stomach, went into the bathroom, leaned over the toilet, and retched.

Julia greeted him with her hands on her hips. "It's about time." She'd divided the gifts into three piles. Danny had seven gifts, Julia had eight, and Mom had two.

"Can we start?" Julia asked.

Mom looked at Danny. "Do you..." her voice faltered.

He looked away.

"Sure, Jewel, go ahead," Mom said.

Julia picked up the first box and shook it. It was large, rectangular, and flat, and made a faint rattling sound.

"It's a board game," she announced, as she ripped off the *To Julia from Santa Claus HO-HO-HO* tag and paper. It was a board game – Sorry. She bit her lip and began to sniffle. She already had the game, but she'd left it in Edmonton.

"Jewel," Mom said softly. "It was fun to play before, and it'll still be fun to play now. Okay?"

"Yeah, Mom," Julia replied, quickly swallowing and setting it aside.

Next was a book – *Walt Disney's Children's Cookbook*, brightly illustrated with Snow White, Sleeping Beauty, and Beauty and the Beast. Julia flipped through and asked Mom when she could start cooking.

"Any time, Jewel," she replied.

"Look!" she said when the third box contained a string of mini lights covered in a rainbow of miniature, Japanese-style paper lanterns.

"Will you help me put these up in my room?" Julia asked, stretching them along the floor.

"Maybe David would help you," Mom suggested.

Danny looked away.

A long narrow box tagged, *To Jewel with love from Mom* held soccer shin pads. She immediately tugged them on. "I can hardly wait for soccer season," she said, prancing around the living room.

*Soccer?* Danny thought. *When had his sister started liking soccer?* He looked over at her, and for the first time in a long time, she was not invisible. It was almost as if someone else's sister – a stranger – had appeared in the house, challenging the memories he had of his real sister.

"Here's some eggnog, Davey-boy," Mom said gently. He reached for the glass and their eyes met. "How about opening some gifts?" When he didn't move, she nudged one over.

He stared at the tag. *To David, Merry Christmas from Santa Claus HO-HO-HO.* A Santa's Anonymous gift for an anonymous boy. He opened it. It was a Teenager's Excuse Ball. Have a problem? Roll the ball for your excuse. Fifteen Options: 24-Hour Flu, Abducted by Aliens, Amnesia, Bicycle Problems, Full

Moon, Huh?, I was Mugged, It's in the Mail, It's not My Job, I've got a Headache, Kryptonite, My Dog Ate It, My Fish Died, The Voices Told Me To, What Homework?

It was Mom's turn to bite her lip.

The next couple of gifts were hits. For Julia, a hot water bottle with a fuzzy cover shaped like a lamb. Danny unwrapped an illuminated Frisbee, deep yellow, and shot through with brilliant white lights. *Fire Frisbee* the label said. He twirled it on his fingertip and Buddy was all over him.

"No, Bud, this one's not for you," he said. *No, this one I'll keep to play with my...friends.*

A box with four movie passes. A red-and-white Canada flag hacky-sack ball.

Mom opened her first gift. *To Mom from Santa Claus HO-HO-HO.* A handmade tea cozy shaped like a poodle held assorted tea bags. She flipped through the exotic names – Formosa Oolong, Jasmine, Lapsang Souchong. Danny knew she was a coffee drinker. "I can serve them when company comes over," she announced. The second Santa's gift was a box of scented bath salts. Danny knew she generally showered. "They'll smell lovely," she said.

Danny and Julia had identical large boxes. He knew what to expect. *To my Son, All my Love Always, Mom.* Socks, underwear, jeans, a T-shirt, and a sweater. All of them new and expensive looking. His hands fumbled with the clothes as he tried to put them back, but the box seemed to have gotten too small. Mom watched silently.

Julia glowed as she reached into a bag she'd hidden under a couch cushion. She handed Danny a surprisingly heavy plastic margarine tub topped with a green and red foil bow. "Don't shake it," she warned. "They might chip."

He hefted the tub up and down, each movement piling lead weights on his heart.

He knew what it was.

He loosened the tape.

She'd nestled at least a dozen painted stones – smooth round ones shaped like flattened eggs – in a tissue-paper nest. She'd painted each one a solid color and then decorated it with a symbol. One had a sun, unmistakable from a million children's drawings, another had a quarter moon. There was an Egyptian eye, a star, a red circle with a green stem coming out of what he guessed was an apple. One of the larger stones was painted light blue, with a black-and-white patchwork. He held it in his hand.

"It's supposed to be Buddy," Julia said, "but it didn't come out so good."

He swallowed. *Stones can help you be strong.* He hadn't seen Grandpa's stone in months. He looked down, squeezed his eyes and his heart shut.

"And what have we here," Mom said loudly, drawing Julia's attention away from her brother. She made a show of shaking a box by her ear. "Hmmm, what can it be?" she mused, reading the tag aloud. *To Mom from Jewel.*

"Open it, Mom," Julia said impatiently.

"Okay, okay, let me enjoy it," she laughed. Inside were two stud earrings with glittering artificial garnets and a bottle of matching nail polish labeled, *Red Dawn.*

"I bought the earrings for you," Julia said, scooting over to sit beside her mother, "and then I thought I could paint the nail polish on you and you could paint it on me."

Mom looked at her hands. Her nails still didn't show much visible white. She looked up and smiled at Julia.

"Maybe I could help you grow your nails again, Mom."

"That'd be great, Sweetie. I'm going to make it my New Year's resolution." She hugged her daughter with a tenderness that made Danny ache.

Julia still had her large box. "Clothes," she announced, ripping off the gold bow. Fruit-of-the-Loom socks, days-of-the-week panties, jeans, a T-shirt, a hoodie. Without pausing, she scooped up the clothes and dashed upstairs.

That left Danny and his mom alone. Mom put on a new CD. He started to tug at his box of clothes. Then he blurted, "I didn't get anything."

She nodded. "I understand. But I'm not sure Jewel will." She paused. "I have to go baste the turkey," she said, leaving him alone to face his sister.

Julia bounced down and trotted into the kitchen. He imagined her pirouetting before their mother, showing her the new clothes. He heard both of them laugh, and he pictured Mom pulling his sister into another tight hug, the love between them bringing out the best in each other.

Julia returned to the living room, where Danny had not moved. She confronted him, hands on hips.

"You didn't get us anything, did you?"

He stared back at her.

"At least you could have made an effort."

"What'd ya want me to do? Go steal something?"

She curled her hands into fists. "You treat me like I'm invisible. You're no different than dad."

With calm deliberation she said, "You are an asshole."

# Chapter 22

Danny heard the doorbell from his bedroom. After a few moments, his mother called.

"David, we have company! Come on down."

He opened the door and looked down the stairs. It was Scott. Danny's stomach lurched.

"Hi, David," Scott called, his voice cautious.

"David, Scott has something for us."

*Surely, on Christmas Day, it couldn't be.* His mind raced. He took each stair gingerly, as if it might suddenly slope and pitch him to the bottom.

"Come in and sit down," Mom said, motioning toward the living room.

"Oh, no thanks." He shifted his weight from foot to foot. "I have to get back to my family."

Danny swallowed and stayed at the base of the stairs.

Scott unzipped his parka and pulled three envelopes from the inside pocket.

"We took up a collection at the office. These are for you." He thrust them awkwardly at Susan.

She looked at the names written on each one. "There's one for each of us," she announced. Julia came up to take hers, but didn't open it right away. Mom held out Danny's envelope. He shuffled forward and took it.

Julia opened hers first. Inside was a stiff piece of cardboard with red and green holly printed around the border. "It's a gift certificate," she said.

> Lloyd's Cycle
> Gift Certificate for Julia Mayer
> Two Hundred and Fifty Dollars
> $250.00
> Merry Christmas!

She looked at the certificate, then over at Scott.

"It's…it's for a bicycle," he offered, stubbing his boot into the carpet. "I know how hard it is for kids to get around when the family doesn't have a car and you want to visit friends and stuff."

Danny pushed his thumb under the flap and slowly tore his open.

> Lloyd's Cycle
> Gift Certificate for David Mayer
> Two Hundred and Fifty Dollars
> $250.00
> Merry Christmas!

Scott smiled. "It won't buy a fancy bike, but you'll be able to get around."

"Wow," said Julia. "Thank you."

"Yeah, thanks," Danny mumbled.

Susan fumbled with hers. It unfolded into a full-sized sheet. Santa Claus flew his reindeer over a glittering Christmas tree.

Susan Mayer.
Five Hundred Dollar ($500.00) Gift Certificate
Murray's Department Store.

She was speechless. "1 – I don't know how to thank you."

Scott rubbed his hand along his cheek and turned to go. "We think of you often and hope this helps. Merry Christmas," he said, and hastened out.

No one moved. Susan looked at Julia, then at Danny. She sat on the couch, holding the certificate in front of her as she read and reread it.

"Oh, my God," she said, "There aren't many people in those offices. They must have contributed...a hundred...or a hundred and fifty dollars each."

She didn't try to hide her tears.

Danny heard the sharp rap at the back door. It was Papa Joe. Buddy's body gyrated against the old man, his tail threatening to beat Papa Joe's legs out from under him.

"Buddy-boy! Hey, take it easy." Papa Joe smiled at Danny. "Look here! Brought a little somethin' for the pooch," he said, offering a small, loosely wrapped package. "T'ain't much, but I sure 'ppreciate havin' your dog with me on my walks."

Danny unwrapped a cherry-red cotton headscarf with a black border.

"Used to get them for my Ranger," Papa Joe said. "Seemed to make him feel special, all dressed up." He folded the scarf in a triangle and tied it loosely under the dog's chin. His arthritic fingers struggled with the knot. The tip of the scarf lay jauntily across Buddy's shoulder. The dog dashed back and forth between Danny and Papa Joe, his tail beating like a round of applause.

For as long as Danny could remember, they'd hung their stockings from hooks permanently screwed under the fireplace mantel. This year, Mom had improvised and had propped them up against the wall behind the tree.

Traditionally, they'd opened the stocking gifts first. Everything was small enough to fit inside, but some of the contents were expensive: a compass, a fossilized shark's tooth, or a Swiss Army knife with a dozen attachments. And always, a Christmas orange in the toe.

This year they opened the stockings after lunch. Everything was from the dollar store, even the stockings. Small pads of pink post-it notes shaped like hearts for Julia and yellow rectangles for Danny. Miniature chocolate bars left over from Hallowe'en. Julia got some costume jewelry, lavender-scented bath oil beads, and a deck of Winnipeg souvenir playing cards. He opened a pair of socks, another hacky-sack, and a mechanical pencil.

"Thanks, Mom," Julia said after she'd unloaded her stocking. Danny mumbled something that could have been a thank you as he stuffed the items back into the stocking.

"Wait, there's one more," Mom said. "I didn't want to put it out because I thought it might cause problems." She went to the kitchen.

Buddy's nose began to twitch. The dog's stocking was larger than theirs and was crammed full. Dog biscuits, dog bones, squeaky toys, and a new brush. A length of rope for tug-of-war dangled over its top. The biscuits were unwrapped and irregular in shape. It was clear Mom had baked them herself.

"Here you go, Bud," she said, tossing him a biscuit. He caught it in mid-air and settled down beside the couch to crunch his treat.

"No stocking for you, Mom?" Julia asked.

"Next year," she replied.

Danny decided to walk Buddy. He found himself passing Nixxie's house. Although the walk was cleared of snow, it seemed no one was at home. Only a few cars drove the streets. The snow crunched like icing sugar under his feet. Each footfall was like the ticking of a clock.

His mother had made an effort. Right now, she was cooking Christmas dinner, just as she had all his life.

Julia had made an effort. She'd crafted decorations and presents. She'd been patient when he deliberately overslept. She'd taken the time – a lot of time – to find and paint the rocks. She'd saved her allowance and bought Mom a gift to help her heal. Except when she'd told him off, she'd been polite and cheerful. She never let up on the spirit of Christmas.

And she was only nine.

And they'd never before received the kindness of strangers – the people at NIVA who gave them so much when they didn't have to give a dime. Volunteers who delivered donated gifts and food. The good wishes and gestures of neighbors and friends who made his family feel special. He now saw that their last Christmas with Dad had been solitary and isolated. The piles of gifts had masked the lack of friends and relatives. They were good Christmases, even great ones, but maybe not the kind you'd want every year for a lifetime. Before today, he'd never considered there might be more to Christmas than gifts.

Mom had planned every detail for Christmas dinner. She'd picked up an old pewter candelabra at a garage sale and placed three elegant, slender red candles on the snowflake-patterned table cloth. Julia had cut the white paper napkins into matching snowflakes. Christmas crackers waited on each plate. Sparkling apple cider the color of champagne filled three borrowed wine goblets.

Julia's eyes sparkled as she tucked into the food. "Can my bike be red, Mom?" she asked.

"I don't see why not," she replied. She reached out to cover her daughter's hand with her own, but her eyes were fastened on Danny.

"Can I bake something from my cookbook after supper?" Julia asked.

"Well, Jewel, I was hoping you'd both help me do dishes. Maybe it'd be better for tomorrow. And," Mom continued, "this week we'll all get new skates, because – I got the job!"

"Yes!" Julia yelled, pumping her fist. "Does that mean I can go to soccer camp in the summer?"

"Sounds good, Jewel." She turned to Danny. "What would you like to do?"

"I dunno," he mumbled. "Haven't thought about it."

"Well, you can start thinking about it now, Davey-boy. Let's plan ahead. It's going to be a great year."

# Chapter 23

Laughter woke Danny on Boxing Day. Julia made a cookbook-recipe breakfast – Goofy's scrambled eggs with diced red and green peppers. Mom and Julia painted their nails and baked gingerbread men. Julia spent time with Emma or played fox and geese in the snow with the other kids.

Danny wasted most of the week in his room. Other than placing the tub of rocks on the dresser – and installing the lock – he'd done nothing to fix it up. Scuff marks and plaster holes still marked the walls. The black bodies of dead flies lay inside the 60-watt ceiling fixture. The curtains hung crookedly from a sagging curtain rod. He lay on the bed and daydreamed about the past.

As New Year's approached, Julia alternated between wanting to go back to school to see her friends and not wanting the holiday to end. "I'm going to make a New Year's resolution this year," she announced at supper. "I'm going to make a new friend every month, and I'm going to score the most points on the soccer team."

Susan ruffled her daughter's hair. "That sounds wonderful, Jewel."

"What're you gonna do, Mom?"

"Other than grow my nails? I'm not sure yet. I've always wanted to take a sewing course so I can make more than just Hallowe'en costumes. Maybe I can get a used sewing machine and start learning."

"Will you make me a dress?"

"I could try," she replied.

Both sets of eyes turned to Danny. He scowled. "I've never made a New Year's resolution and I don't see why I should start now," he said, as he scuffed the chair back from the table.

New Year's Eve dawned clear and cold. Danny stayed in bed even later than the lazy winter sun. He made it down just in time for lunch.

"We're all invited to the condo complex's New Year's Eve party," Mom said. "There's a candle parade around the common area at midnight. What do you think?"

"Sounds like fun!" Julia said.

"David?" Mom asked. "Be a good chance for you to meet some more of the neighbors."

"Aren't we going to move out of this dump now that you've got a job? So what's the point in meeting the neighbors?"

"I hope we *do* move sometime in the new year. But in the meantime, we can't put off living now because we think it'll be better or different later. We need to enjoy ourselves — have fun — *now*."

He stared at his mother. *Now there's a good New Year's resolution,* he thought. *I'm going to have fun.*

⚖

He wasn't invited, but Danny knew there'd be a party at Todd's. He dropped his new basketball shoes into a plastic grocery bag and snuck out at nine thirty. Sure enough, the lights blazed and the music roared from the untidy bungalow crouched in the snow.

He sold the basketball shoes for twenty dollars. Then he got blind drunk.

Danny had no memory of how he got home. He did remember his mother holding his clammy forehead as he retched into the toilet. He did remember the glass of water she forced him to drink before he passed out on the bed.

In the morning, Danny had never felt sicker. His clothes clung to him like dead skin. His nose was so congested he had to breathe through his dry mouth. Every heartbeat throbbed in his head until his skull was ready to explode.

And he couldn't even remember if he'd had fun.

⚖

Four days until school started. Julia avoided Danny, and Danny avoided his mom. Tension hung over the house like a chronic illness, like there wasn't enough oxygen for all of them. Danny took Buddy for long walks until the dog shivered with cold. He threw away the rest of his time at the mall.

Chad expected him after school on Monday, but half way to the mall Danny paused and then veered home. He heard Buddy scratching, even before he got the screen door open. He cast off his backpack and snapped on the dog's leash. They walked away from the mall.

He needed time to think. The best thing about school was art class, mainly because of Nixxie. The next best thing was Chad. There was no third best thing.

But Nixxie didn't like Chad, and Chad couldn't care less about Nixxie. And Danny wanted them both.

"Davey-boy! Missed you yesterday." Chad's voice had an edge to it. "Busy with your girlfriend?"

"Don't have a girlfriend," Danny mumbled.

Chad chucked him under the chin. "Glad to hear it," he said.

Well before basketball practices resumed, Danny started feeling sick. He skipped the first one with a stomachache, the second with a headache. By the time he'd missed three practices, his mom said, "Maybe we should take you to the doctor."

But Danny already knew what was wrong, and his mother put it together the next day. "I tried to find the receipt for your basketball shoes," she said. "I couldn't find it, and I couldn't find the shoes."

"They're in my gym locker."

"Your Phys Ed teacher said they're not."

"He *called* you?"

"He phoned to remind us the school would pay when we bought the shoes. I told him you already had them."

"So. I lost them."

"You lost them," she repeated flatly.

"Yeah, like *you've* never lost anything." He saw her face fall. He looked away and his neck began to flush.

"Oh, Danny," she whispered.

That evening, while Danny was out with Buddy, Mom searched his dresser. She took the gift certificate and hid it in her room.

---

The new kid in class had shiny pumpkin-colored hair. Even though he cut it short, Everett couldn't get it short enough to avoid Chad's spiteful eye. He might as well have had a target on his forehead.

"Hey, pumpkin head! Anybody ever carve you up at Hallowe'en?"

"Hey, pumpkin head! I bet we could cook you into a great pie."

"Todd! Ever feel like smashing a pumpkin on the street and watching a car drive over it?"

Everett ducked every time Chad came near, but when he walked past the mall one day, he didn't spot Chad soon enough. Chad leaned carelessly against the rail at his usual place. The smoke from his cigarette mixed with the vapor of his breath on the frigid late-January day. Todd and Danny loitered to his right. Some of the gang shared a couple of smokes, the top of their jean jackets unbuttoned to expose thin T-shirts.

"Hey, pumpkin head!" Chad called.

Everett dropped his eyes and picked up his pace.

"Pumpkin head! Pay attention! I'm talkin' to you!"

It was Todd who tackled Everett from behind. Danny rose on the balls of his feet and followed. Todd rammed Everett's face down and ground his knees into the boy's ribs to keep him down. Everett worked his arms loose and his fingernails clawed at Todd's hands, but Todd grasped Everett's hair and yanked it back until the boy started to choke. Danny slammed his knee onto Everett's raised elbow, pinning it to the ground. Todd forced the side of the boy's face deeper into the packed snow until his teeth bit open the insides of his cheek.

Danny watched Chad advance until he planted his feet close to Everett's face. He spat in the snow by the terrified boy. Danny couldn't take his eyes off Chad. He'd seen that look before – on his dad on the last day of the trial.

A creeping numbness started from the soles of Danny's feet and wormed its way up through his body until he couldn't tell the difference between his knee and Everett's elbow, between his body and the snow. He froze in place, stopped blinking, stopped breathing. He couldn't move his arms or legs anymore. He felt like he was floating up, looking down from above. He saw his body kneeling on Everett. He saw the other boys begin to draw their circle tighter around Everett, like mourners around a coffin. Everett had stopped squirming. He breathed through his mouth like a fish gulping in the air that could only kill it, his eye circling wildly in its socket, searching desperately for help. Danny's vision began to narrow, until all he could see was Chad slowly pulling a lighter out of his pocket. His eyes zeroed in on the lighter while Chad placed his thumb on the igniter and rolled down the small wheel. Danny could hear it grind against the flint, *phut, phut, phut,* like a series of barks. Chad struck it again and Danny could smell the sharp flash of flint. On the third try, the flame flickered blue and yellow in the cold air. Chad adjusted the flame to its highest setting. He crouched like a spider and moved it toward Everett's hair.

Everett's howl released pain stored like a memory in Danny's bones. He felt himself snap back into his body like a taut elastic suddenly cut. He lifted his knee off Everett's elbow and lurched to his feet, knocking the lighter out of Chad's hand. Danny took one, two, three steps back, turned, and bolted away, his feet pounding through the snow like pistons. He ran until he thought his heart would burst.

The police were already at Danny's house by the time he got home.

# Chapter 24

"Order in Court! All rise!" called the clerk. About two dozen people rose from low-backed swivel chairs strung in uneven rows across the back half of a small courtroom. Danny sat at the end of the third row with his shoulder pressed against the wall. His mother sat beside him. Her thumb rubbed back and forth across her scar.

A slight woman in a beige suit took her seat behind the bench. Her Honor Judge Nelson wore round black-framed glasses that made her look owlish and magnified the crow's feet around her eyes. Danny couldn't tell her age, but she was certainly older than Grandma.

"Court is now in session. You may be seated." Chairs squeaked as people settled.

"How many on today's docket, Madam Clerk?" asked the judge.

"Seventeen, Your Honor."

"Any adjournments?"

Several lawyers in suits stood up. One by one they addressed the judge and stated their reasons for requesting adjournments. Most were granted and several trial dates were set. Teenagers shuffled out with their lawyers as Danny watched nervously, trying to pick up pointers on how to act when his turn came. This time he wasn't a spectator – he was a player.

When his name was called, he couldn't move and he couldn't breathe. His mother put her hand over his and squeezed it quickly, and gently pulled him up with her. She led the way to the front and stood beside her son.

"Are you David Perry Mayer?" the clerk asked.

Danny swallowed and nodded.

"David Perry Mayer, you stand charged that you did unlawfully assault Everett Sanderman and thereby cause him bodily harm. How do you plead?"

"Just a moment, Madam Clerk," the judge said. She peered at Susan. "Are you his mother?"

"Yes."

"Where's his father? Is he here?"

Susan cleared her throat. "Dead."

The judge looked at the prosecutor, Ms. Samos. "How old is this young man?"

"He's –" Ms. Samos flipped through the file. "He's thirteen."

Mr. Berg, the duty lawyer, intervened. "Ma'am, given the boy's young age, even with this serious charge, the case should be dealt with outside of court."

The judge looked at Ms. Samos. "Why haven't the police recommended extra-judicial measures?"

She scanned the forms. "The crime was one of deliberate violence. A boy was held down and his hair set on fire. Mr. Mayer was

one of the gang that attacked the boy. Given the victim's burns
and the element of gang violence, the police are reluctant to take
the case out of the court process."

"Mr. Berg, what do you say about this?"

"Just a moment, Ma'am." The duty lawyer turned to Danny,
and, lowering his voice, asked, "What did you do?"

"I didn't do it," he whispered. "I left before they burned him."

Mr. Berg straightened. "He says he wasn't involved in the
burning. He left before it happened."

The prosecutor held up the notes. "The police say there are
witnesses who saw him participating in the assault."

The judge pursed her lips. "This is a very serious matter. But
given this youth's age, I don't think it would be in his or society's
best interest to force it through the court process just now. Mr.
Berg, Ms. Samos, what are our options?"

Susan stepped forward. "Your Honor, may I speak? David has
been seeing his school counselor for some…adjustment problems
our family's had since we moved here. Perhaps if he committed to
see the counselor on a regular basis…?"

"Your thoughts, Ms. Samos?" the judge asked.

"He lives with his mother. As long as he stays there, observes
a curfew, and doesn't contact the victim or associate with the other
gang members, I won't object."

"Very good. Mr. Mayer, I'm going to reserve your plea and
adjourn the case for six months. During that time you are to see
your school psychologist – what's his name?"

"Mr. Ishii," Danny mumbled.

"Mr. Ishii. As many times as he feels necessary. He'll prepare a court report with recommendations for your case. Do you
understand?"

"Yes," he said, eyes on his feet.

"Curfew for one month from 6:00 p.m. to 6:00 a.m.?" asked the prosecutor.

"So ordered," replied the judge.

"You're lucky," his mom said when they returned home. "It could have gone much worse. And it can get much worse, if you let it."

Danny rubbed his fingertips across his lips.

She waited another moment, then reached into her pocket. "I found this in the laundry room. It had slipped behind the washer."

It was the worry stone.

"What would Grandpa say if he knew you're on your dad's path – only you've started much younger?"

The psychiatrist's words from his father's trial brought him up short. *He's a bully. He's a dangerous man.*

"Where will you go from here?"

*Once a bully, always a bully. The bully always falls back into the same pattern. The best predictor of future behavior is past behavior. If he's done it before, he'll do it again.*

"Jail time?" his mom continued.

*Make no mistake. If you come before this Court again, convicted of a similar offence, you may well spend the rest of your life behind bars.*

"I heard your boy's in a bit 'a trouble," Papa Joe said, reaching down to snap on Buddy's leash. "Anything I can help with?"

"I don't know," Susan replied, wiping the back of her hand

across her forehead. "I'm worried. He's so distant. He wastes his time in front of the TV, or locked in his room, or even worse – at the mall."

Papa Joe ruffled Buddy's ears as he nodded.

"We don't have any relatives, and he hasn't made any friends – not good ones, anyway. He's been smoking and drinking."

He nodded again.

"He doesn't want to be part of our family," she said, wringing her hands. "It's like he lives by himself. If he had a place to go, I think he'd run away. Or worse."

"Well now," Papa Joe replied. "Let's just see if we can give him a different place to spend some time."

She turned and called, "David, there's someone here to see you."

Danny reluctantly unlocked his door and stood at the top of the stairs.

"Papa Joe would like to speak with you."

"About what?"

"Come down and ask him yourself."

"I came to invite you and Buddy over tonight. Hockey Night in Canada. Thought maybe ya'd like to keep an old man company."

Danny looked at his mom. He would be out past curfew.

"It's fine with me, if you want to go," she said.

Her answer surprised him. *Of all the people to break the rules,* he thought, *his mother was the least likely.*

At school, red and pink tissue paper hearts alternated with cupid cutouts up and down the hallways. The student council sold

Valentine's candies and flowers. Danny seized the opportunity to get Nixxie's attention. Since his arrest and Chad's transfer out of the school, Nixxie had shunned Danny. She avoided eye contact and crossed the hall when she saw him coming.

First thing Friday morning, he bought a bag of cinnamon hearts and a pink rose. He slipped the rose stem through her combination lock and hung the candy bag from the locker handle. Then he fidgeted until art class.

She ignored him.

"I'm afraid your participation in these counseling sessions is no longer voluntary," Mr. Ishii said. "Now I have a job to do. At the end of these sessions, I must write a confidential report so the judge can decide how best to deal with you."

Danny angled sideways on the chair and stuck out his elbow.

"Would you like to tell me what happened?"

"What for? You've already got the police report."

"Yes, I do. But I'd rather hear it from you."

"Read it yourself."

"Very well." He sat back and read the two-page typewritten report. He took his time, leaving Danny to stare awkwardly around the room. Finally, the counselor looked up. "You may go."

The second Saturday night at Papa Joe's was much like the one before. They discussed the players and their records. Papa Joe knew more than Danny did. The potato chips were his favorite kind, and

Buddy wolfed down crunchy doggy treats. Danny was surprised how soon it was time to go.

"The police say you reacted very negatively when they arrested you. They describe you as an 'angry young man more interested in being belligerent than in taking any responsibility for his crime.' Do you agree with that?"

Danny glared at the counselor. "They were jerks," he said.

"So…they failed to treat you with courtesy and respect?"

He tossed his head. "*Yeah.*"

"Is it possible they were just doing their job?"

"I thought their job was to *help* people."

"Even people who commit crimes?"

Danny said nothing.

"Is it possible they *were* helping you?"

"What is this, like, a cross-examination? Am I on trial?"

"Should you be?"

"Yeah, right. Why me?" He lifted up his palms. "Why me and not all the other criminals out there?"

"Do you mean you shouldn't be accountable for your actions?"

Danny licked his lips.

Mr. Ishii tilted his head. "It sounds like you've had some negative dealings with the police."

"They've never done a thing for me."

"I see. So, at some time in your past, the police failed you. Is that what you're saying?"

"They destroyed my life."

"Ah, yes. And you're still angry about that?"

Danny bristled. "You would be, too."

Mr. Ishii pursed his lips. He rose slowly. "Well, David," he said mildly, "our jails are full of angry young men." He paused. "You may go now."

⚖

On Sunday night Danny talked himself into asking Nixxie out. On Monday morning his voice caught in his throat and his courage deserted him. On Tuesday, Danny missed art class for his counseling session.

Mr. Ishii wrote the date on his notes. April 1. Session 3. "Do you shoplift a lot, David?" he asked.

Danny's eyes widened, and then narrowed. "What makes you think I shoplift at all?"

"Your mother told me."

"My *mother* told you?"

"Yes."

Danny twirled his baseball cap around and around.

"Do you know why you do it?"

He thought back to the watch and to the easy money for cigarettes and beer and forgetting and belonging…

He snorted. "No money."

Mr. Ishii nodded and put down his pen. "So you steal because you're poor?"

"Well I wouldn't *have* to steal if I had money, would I?"

"Ah, yes. Well, there are a lot of poor people who don't steal.…"

The counselor's words felt like weights.

"Do you think it's a way to get ahead?"

Danny spun his cap on his index finger. Parties and feeling

good. Shortcuts to relaxation. "Sure, why not?" he replied.

"I understand your mother's working now."

"She told you that, too?"

"Yes." He paused. "She's very anxious to help you. She knows things haven't gone very well, and it's been hard on you."

"At least she's got *that* right."

Mr. Ishii pressed his fingertips together. "You're angry with your mother, too, aren't you?"

"*She* got me into this mess."

"And how did she do that?"

"By making poor choices."

"Just like you?"

Danny's face hardened. "She shouldn't have let it happen."

"Well, whatever '*it*' was, it sounds like she's trying to fix it." He picked up his notes. "Before Christmas you were on social assistance, and now she has a good job."

Danny didn't say anything.

"And your sister has taken the Red Cross babysitting course."

"Nobody told *me*."

The counselor paused. "Yes. Well. It sounds like your sister's making an effort, too." He put down the papers and looked squarely at Danny. "So, David," he finally said. "And what are *you* doing?"

# Chapter 25

The thermometer plunged. It was bitterly cold with a relentless wind. Danny appeared at Nixxie's locker at lunch time, leaned his back against the wall, and slid to the floor. "Hey," he said.

"Hey," she replied. She popped the lock into its slot and sat beside him. Shy silence separated them until she said, "It's sure cold out."

"Uh, yeah," he replied. He busied himself with his lunch bag. "Want an apple?" he asked, holding one out.

"No thanks." She opened her bag. "Want an orange?" she offered.

They both laughed, and it was as if the months between them had melted away.

"Are there more reasons you've been stealing other than being poor?" Mr. Ishi asked.

Danny cracked his knuckles.

"What kind of activities do you have outside of school?"

Danny thought about the basketball team he'd quit after Christmas. He remembered the coach's invitation to try out for the volleyball team. He remembered the library card his mom had propped up against his clock radio and that he'd abandoned under a pile of unwashed clothes. He couldn't remember the number of hours he'd spent in front of the TV.

"Everything's boring," he replied. "My life's boring."

"Do you mean there are obstacles to getting out and doing new things?"

"I can't even buy any stuff."

Mr. Ishii paused. "Have you considered volunteer work, to help people less fortunate than you?"

Danny started spinning his cap.

"You can work toward your future without first solving every obstacle in your path."

Silence.

"There is a minimum amount of time you are required to spend in our counseling sessions. However, there is no maximum. You have a lot of work to do."

⚖

Danny and Nixxie agreed to a matinee that weekend. He let her pick the movie. He asked his mom for an extra two dollars for bus fare.

She handed him a five. "What're you going to see?"

"It's a western. Nixxie likes westerns."

Her eyebrows raised. "Nixxie?"

"A girl from school," he replied, as if it were the most ordinary thing in the world.

⚖

The movie wasn't going to win any awards but as far as Danny was concerned it could have been a blank screen. The important thing was to be with Nixxie. After the movie they wandered into McDonald's for some fries.

"What're you doing for Easter?" Nixxie asked.

"Just hanging around." He shook the ice in his cup. "What about you?"

"Going out to the lake. We have a cabin on Lake Winnipeg."

"Go there often?"

"Most holidays."

"Is that where you were last Christmas?"

"Part of it."

"Where else did you go?"

"Same as always. Mom and Dad take me to the reservation to see my mom for my birthday. Then we go to the lake for the rest of the holiday. The lake's the good part of the holiday."

"Did you see her?"

She shrugged her shoulders. "Not this year." She held up a french fry and picked off the salt grains.

"When were you adopted?" he asked.

"When I was two." She idly swirled the fry in some ketchup. "Denise raised me for the first year and a half. Then she started dropping me off with my grandparents. At first it was just week-ends, but then it was more and more often. One day she never came back, and my grandparents adopted me too."

"Why did your grandparents adopt your mom?"

She sat very still and her eyes unfocussed. "It's a long story. Ever since Canada became a country, the government thought First Nations people were a 'problem' and needed 'fixing.' So they forced kids from their homes into boarding schools run by churches. The white teachers were supposed to teach them to be ashamed of their culture. The government wanted to 'kill the Indian in the child.' It was child abuse."

Danny felt a noose tighten around his chest.

She picked up a napkin and started twisting it through her fingers. Her hair fell forward along the sides of her face. "They didn't have families to protect them and couldn't protect themselves. For some, it was a death sentence."

He crushed the empty chip box between his fingers.

She started shredding the napkin. "My mom, my mom's mom...for them it was a life sentence – of killing the pain with alcohol and drugs."

He swallowed.

"My grandparents are always trying to help others. They adopted her because she had nowhere else to go. When my mother got pregnant with me at sixteen, they already knew they'd end up raising me, too. But they never complain. They never give up hope Denise will change. So, every year we trek out to the reserve. Every year she disappoints me."

Her words sent his mind racing. He had to change the subject. "You said your painting was your name. And the initials you put on it were *P.S.* I don't get it. What does the *P* stand for?"

"Phoenixx," she replied.

"Phoenix, like the city?"

"No, Phoenixx like the bird, but with an extra *x*."

"Bird?"

"A mythical bird, the only one of its kind. A bird that lives for five hundred years, then burns to death and rises again from its own ashes. A bird so beautiful that astronomers put it in the night sky."

He frowned. He didn't remember a constellation named Phoenix in the stars stuck to his ceiling. "Where is it?" he asked.

"In the southern hemisphere. My mom said a person didn't have to see it to know it was there."

"What's it like, knowing you're adopted?"

"Sometimes I feel sad, like a piece of me is missing – like I've lost something, and I don't know where to find it. Sometimes I feel lucky I have my grandparents and they're always there for me. And sometimes I want to scream and scream, or crawl into myself and never come out. It's all so unfair. I wish I had a normal family like yours."

"Your mother says you spend a lot of time locked in your room," Mr. Ishii said.

"So?"

"Is it true?"

"Maybe."

"And when you lock the door, what are you trying to do?"

"What do you mean?"

"Are you locking yourself in, or locking the world out?"

"I need my privacy."

"Of course. Everyone does. But is privacy the only thing you need?"

Danny's eyes shifted around the room.

"If you're like most teenagers, you want to have friends, you want to have the freedom to make choices, and you want to be loved."

Danny's knee jiggled. He thought about the friends he'd made. He'd gotten along with the boys on the basketball team, for a few days. He'd probably been in Chad's group too long. Papa Joe was a friend, but not the same kind of friend. Even Buddy, who never judged or complained and was always happy to see him, was sometimes more excited to see Papa Joe than him. Except for Nixxie, it had been a year and a half – no, longer – since he'd had a true friend.

"Do you think you can make friends from behind a locked door?"

No answer.

"Perhaps it's time to stop locking and start unlocking. Perhaps it's time to let go."

"Let go of what?"

"I think you already know."

"How well are you and your mother getting on, David?"

Danny shrugged his shoulders.

"Your long silences worry her. She's afraid for you."

"So. And just *what* have you been telling my mother about me?"

"I haven't told her anything. She tells me things and I listen."

Danny crossed his arms.

"The judge and the police will keep the report confidential.

It won't be read in open court, and the court file will be sealed at the end of the case."

"So now I'm supposed to trust the judge and the police?"

"It wasn't the failing of any one judge or any one police officer that resulted in your being here. And it was not just your mother's failing, either."

Danny narrowed his eyes.

"Let's take a hypothetical situation. Let's say there's a small child – three or four years old. And let's say that child found some matches."

Danny stayed silent.

"And let's say that child was striking those matches and watching the little flames – playing with fire. And the child was having a good time."

Danny chewed his lip. He started to see where this was going.

"And then, before he got burned or set the house on fire, his mother came by and pulled the matches from him. Do you think that would be the right thing to do? Even if you cried over the injustice of losing your plaything?"

The question bore into Danny's consciousness like a drill. *Ishii knows. If she can tell, then I can tell*, Danny thought.

His curfew had ended and Danny was free to meet Nixxie for a movie on Friday.

He spent the half-hour bus ride trying to keep his hands steady. He hustled off the bus ahead of Nixxie and looked quickly right and left, then right again.

She cocked her head to one side. "It's this way," she said, pointing.

"No. We need to talk."

"Talk?" She paused. "What about the movie?"

"It can wait," he replied. He remembered a park bench in a coin-sized green space between two office towers. "This way."

The temperature dropped with the sun and the park had emptied. Danny hoped Nixxie would think his hands were trembling with cold.

"What's wrong?" she asked. "Did something happen? Are you all right? Is something wrong with your mom?"

"No, nothing like that." He paused. "Well it kinda is."

"Is she sick? Was she in an accident?"

"No."

The concerned look on Nixxie's face turned to puzzlement.

He interlaced his fingers to stop the shaking. He leaned forward and rested his forearms along his thighs, and started talking. The story spilled from him like blood from a wound, pumped until there was nothing left in the hollow muscle that was his heart.

Danny talked with Nixxie almost every day. He told her what Mr. Ishii had said, trying to focus his thoughts by talking them out.

"My mom – Denise – had a lot of good intentions," she replied, "but she couldn't follow through. She didn't know who to be, so she ended up being nothing."

"Do you hate her?"

"Sometimes, but not as often as I used to. She used to say she'd visit me all the time, we'd go places, and do fun things together. She told me I was lucky because I had *two* mothers. She said she'd teach me how to be Native, but she couldn't because she didn't know how to be one herself. When we went to the reserve, I didn't want to see her. I started resenting her more and more, and my parents stopped taking me see her so often. And now, I don't know if there's a future in being Native."

"But you *are* Native," he replied.

"Sometimes I *wish* I were, but most of the time I don't. I just want to be Nixxie, be my own person, but it's not easy. It's complicated."

"You sound like Mr. Ishii."

Nixxie stared straight at Danny. "That's because he counseled me, too."

"He *did?*"

She nodded.

"Why didn't you tell me?"

"He asked me not to. He said it was better that way." She rubbed her arm. "He was Denise's school counselor. Later, when I needed someone to talk to, Mr. Ishii was there."

His face was rigid when he met the counselor. As soon as he sat in the chair, he confronted Mr. Ishii. "You know, don't you?"

"Yes," Mr. Ishii replied.

"How long?"

"Your mother told me a while ago."

"After she told us — no, *lectured* us — *everybody* lectured us —we could never tell, never breathe a word?!"

"Your mother moved you here to give you a better life, but she's afraid she'll still lose you. She told me because she thought it was the only way to save you. Not from your dad this time, but from yourself." He paused. "Don't you think you can trust your mother, David?"

"My name's not David. And it's *her* fault."

"Are you sure?"

"How could she let it happen?"

Mr. Ishii put down his pen. "Maybe that's not the right question."

"What do you mean?"

"It's easy to blame the victim. I'm sure some people thought Everett – and your mother – 'had it coming.' But isn't the real question, 'Why did the abuser do what he did?'"

"But she *lied* to us."

"Your mother made an error in judgment. Haven't you ever done that?"

"What, like the shoplifting?" Danny challenged.

"And the bullying?" Mr. Ishii countered.

Danny was silent.

"So. Why did *you* do it?"

This time, Danny asked the questions. "How can I be sure my dad really did all those things that Mom said?"

Mr. Ishii tilted his head. "How long had you lived in your Edmonton house?"

"All my life."

"Did you ever worry about it blowing up?"

Danny bit his lip. "No."

"There really isn't any question he did it, is there?"

"I guess not."

"And if he did that, isn't he capable of anything? Including murder?"

*My gut tells me Mr. McMillan is one of the most dangerous men I have ever met.* "I guess." Danny speared his fingers through his hair. "But *why* did he do it?"

"Anger is a choice. Bullying is learned. Your dad believed your mom was worthless, and neither the law – nor society – stepped in to stop him. And he didn't destroy just your mother. He destroyed all of you."

"But I *loved* my father!"

"Every person in a family can have different relationships with the other people in that family. Your dad was kind to you, gave you opportunities to thrive. He supported you – or so it seemed. But in the end, when he couldn't mould you into him, he threw you away."

*Suppose the blow to her head killed her instead of just knocking her unconscious. You would be here today being sentenced for murder, and you would be in jail for many, many years. Had that happened, Mr. McMillan, your children would be no better than orphans.*

Danny sat thinking, then got up and quietly left the room.

Mr. Ishii reached into a drawer and pulled out a form: *In the Provincial Court of Manitoba, Judicial District of Winnipeg. Report of Psychologist.* He flipped to the last page, where a dozen blank lines followed *Conclusions and Recommendations.* He wrote, "David is a bright young man at a difficult point in his life. Like many other teenagers, he is a work in progress. I believe he will go on to live well. He has attended every counseling session. I recommend the Court consider it 'time served' and the charge be withdrawn."

# Chapter 26

"You told him!"

"Yes," his mother answered. She stopped wiping the table. "Do you understand why?"

He paused. "Maybe."

She pulled her chair beside him and reached for his hands. "When the police showed up at the door, I knew I was on the brink of losing you forever. Things were spiraling out of control – again. I know how I spent so many years lying to myself about your father that I started to believe the lies myself. And those lies nearly killed me. This time, it was you. You couldn't seem to stop lying to yourself about your dad either. If I hadn't done something, those lies might have killed you too. Telling Mr. Ishii was a gamble. I knew I was risking Jen's life – and mine – but I decided it was worth it. And it was."

He shifted his feet. "Mom...I told someone too."

She stroked his arm. "It's okay. We're going to take one day at a time."

↖

Buddy lay down after his walk, and quiet settled over the condo. Danny's conversation with his mom left him unsettled. He headed for his room, but suddenly angled into hers.

She'd decorated. She'd pinned up their school pictures in their cardboard frames. She'd hung a colorful scarf – a Picasso print he'd given her one year for her birthday – across the plaster holes in one wall. She'd arranged a bouquet of silk orchids on her dresser, and an amateur painting of a rose garden hung above her bed.

He knew where she kept them – on the floor in her closet. He'd seen Mom and Julia pull them out from time to time, but he'd not looked at them since they moved. He opened the closet door, and there they were – the photo albums.

Mom kept them in order, each spine numbered. He lifted the first book and flipped through it.

There he was. A chubby blue-eyed baby in a blue carriage. Standing in his crib in his duckling-yellow sleepers, both hands firmly grasping the bars. Sitting cross-legged in his first bed – a mattress on the floor – the navy blue striped duvet snuggled up under his nose. The bathtub shot, a white bubble beard hanging from his chin. He pulled out the second album. Now Julia appeared, red-faced in a rocking horse print blanket. Julia taking her first shaky steps around the coffee table. Her pink heart-shaped birthday cake with one burning candle. Danny and Julia in bathing suits in the sandbox, throwing sand with a green pail and matching shovel. The Hallowe'en when he was four and his mom had sewed the purple and green brontosaurus costume. Now he started having his own memories – Mom holding the camera and telling them to say *pleeeease* instead of *cheese*. Mom snapping

pictures as they tore through gifts on Christmas morning. Mom
showing off her Mother's Day tea towels, Julia on one knee and
Danny on the other. Mom demonstrating proper Hula-hoop
technique in the back yard. Mom leaning over to write his name
in the sand on the beach. He remembered her holding his hand.

He started the third album and leafed through the pages.
Mickey Mouse towering over Julia in Disneyland. Julia skipping
rope on the front lawn. Julia sticking a stone smile on a snowman.
Julia with her friends, playing the game of all-hold-hands. Julia
holding up a painting of a beaver she'd done at school. Danny
thought about the container of rocks on his dresser, and decided
he'd carry the Buddy stone in his pocket.

He didn't need to look at the rest of the albums. He knew
what they held – the history of a three-person family.

⚖

Nixxie had invited him to the lake for Canada Day. Their log
cabin nestled in a snug semi-circle of evergreens and smelled of
the forest. The kitchen windows faced the gray lake.

"Have a seat anywhere, David," Mrs. Solem offered. "Don't
worry about your shoes."

He looked about, uncertain. His hand automatically went into
his pocket and he rubbed the two stones.

Nixxie rescued him. "Come n' see my room."

The air smelled faintly of old leather. Sunlight touched all corners of the room. She'd placed a flat-lidded red cedar chest under
one window. A bentwood rocking chair with a pair of beaded
moccasins on the seat waited in the corner.

Nixxie ducked her head and sat on the patchwork quilt

covering the bunk bed's bottom mattress. A jumbled zoo of stuffed animals nested on the top bunk. "Like it? My home away from home."

Danny nodded.

"My favorite thing is the cedar chest," she said, pointing. "We brought it back from Vancouver. It was made by a First Nations artist. It wouldn't fit in the trunk, so I had to squeeze in beside it in the back seat for the whole drive home. Our car smelled like a hamster cage for weeks."

The chest's elaborate black metal hinges matched the front latch. When she went to open it, her body casually brushed up against his.

Layers of folded clothes lay inside. "I keep my favorites in here," she said. "The cedar keeps the insects out." She pulled out a striped sweater and pressed it against her face. Her eyes closed as she inhaled the spiced-earth smell.

Danny explored the room. She'd thumb tacked posters on the walls – *54 Ways to Lighten Up* by NACM, the Native Alcohol Counselors of Manitoba, and a *Don't Worry, Be Happy* photo of three tabby kittens curled into a ball. Another one of those willow hoops with the web-like sinew hung in the window. Its downy white feathers were like the ones he and Grandma had collected underneath the owl's nest.

He was distracted by sounds from the kitchen – the murmur of voices, the slow scrape of cupboards and drawers being opened and shut, the crumpling of bags, and the monotone hum of the refrigerator now brought to life.

"Come and have a snack," Mrs. Solem called.

Nixxie grinned. "Every time we get here, it's the first food we have. It's Mom's little ritual."

Mrs. Solem had laid two place settings – a full glass of milk beside a plate with a slice of bread, thickly buttered and spread with amber honey.

"My mom calls this the Land of Milk and Honey," Nixxie said, pointing to the lake. Mrs. Solem laughed as she wiped her hands on her apron.

The milk was ice cold, just as he liked it. The bread was soft and white and his teeth left indentations in the butter. Honey dripped onto his fingers as he rushed to finish it without losing a drop. They were done in minutes. Mrs. Solem cleared the table and said, "Nixxie, why don't you show David around outside? We'll have our Canada Day dinner later, around seven."

"Sure, Mom."

"Take your jackets. It gets chilly when the wind blows off the water."

Evergreens and saskatoon bushes twice Nixxie's height screened the Solems' cabin from its neighbors. The branches hung low with clusters of ripe purplish-blue berries. A flagstone path led to the lake. Metamorphic rock. The name popped into his head. This was his first trip out of the city since...

He pushed the thought aside.

The beach faced south, and wave-tumbled stones caught the sun's heat. A weathered cedar plank led to a boat ramp extending into the water.

Nixxie hadn't said much. They strolled along the water's edge, heads down, nudging the stones with their toes. Nixxie spoke first. "Sometimes my mom – Denise, I mean – used to come here to be with me. She always told me how we'd do the same things she did when she was growing up – learning to swim, canoeing, ice fishing. About fifty times she told the story how one winter they caught so many perch it seemed like they were jumping out of the hole."

She stopped, bent, and chose an oval stone. She used a slow, underhanded toss and watched it plop softly through the water's surface. "But she never did."

"And this is still your home-away-from-home?" he asked.

"If I store the sad memories here at the lake forever, I'll *never* have a home-away-from-home. That's why Mom put a dream catcher in my window."

"Dream catcher?"

"Yeah. The circular web that hangs there. Natives have a legend that a little boy once threatened to kill a spider while she was making her web. An old woman saved the spider, and the spider thanked her by giving her a gift. The spider wove a web where moonlight would glisten on the magical silvery threads. The web snared bad dreams. Only good dreams could pass through the small middle hole. Mom says it will help me remember only the good things about Denise and leave the bad ones caught in the web."

He reached into his pocket for the two stones. As he touched the white one, he remembered Grandma's words: *Live the best life you can live, Danny-boy.*

"Do you mean in your culture the spider can give you good dreams?"

"Of course. Everything can have a good and a bad side."

He clutched the worry stone. "I used to do a lot with my grandma and grandpa. They were always taking me outside and it seemed like Grandma never stopped talking. When she showed me things – the edible parts of a thistle, the way fish breathe in water, and why sunflowers turn their heads to the sun – I thought

I was going to be a biologist just like her."

"Do you think about your grandparents very much?"

"I – I try not to. I miss them."

He kicked at a piece of driftwood while she threw another stone. "Whenever I was with Grandpa, he'd look at every rock as if it held a secret and he wanted to pry it loose and share it with me. He always looked at the whole world and how it worked. For him, petrified wood was more interesting than a live tree because it had been there longer and had more stories to tell. He taught me what the moon was made of, and the planets, and we'd look at the stars...." He paused a while, then sat on the beach. "So I wanted to be just like him.

"And then we stopped seeing my grandparents so much, and I spent more and more time with Dad. He taught me soccer and hockey and how to shoot a gun." He grabbed a handful of rocks and tossed them into the water. "And then I wanted to be just like my dad."

Nixxie tilted her chin to her chest. "I don't know if I ever really wanted to be like Denise," she said, raking her fingers through the pebbles at her side. "I guess what I wanted was for her to be more like Mom – my grandma – and take care of me, and love me, and be with me." She turned to Danny. "Do you think your father loved you?"

He thought a while. "I guess so. At first," he finally answered.

"I was never sure about Denise," she replied. "I think she *wanted* to love me, but she didn't know how, and so all sorts of other things got in the way."

Danny considered this. "I guess it's kinda the same for my dad. What he did to my mom got in the way – and in the end he couldn't love me anymore."

They sat in silence, watching the seagulls wheel lazily through the sky.

Nixxie spoke. "You'll need a dream catcher," she said. "You can keep the good memories and leave the other ones in the web." She smiled. "I brought one for you."

"You did?"

"It was Mr. Ishii's idea." She jumped up. "Let's go see the town."

The 'town' was a small grocery store, a gas station, and a cube van selling hot dogs and ice cream from a roll-up side. As they walked along the dusty road, Danny shifted a couple of steps toward Nixxie and intertwined his fingers with hers.

The roasted turkey smelled and tasted wonderful, and by the end of the meal Danny felt himself relax.

"Margaret?" said Mr. Solem. "That was delicious. Thank you."

"Thank you, Mrs. Solem," Danny said. "It was the best meal I've had…in a long time."

"Glad you enjoyed it. When we're here at the lake, we focus on the simple moments. Later, they're the memories that keep you strong through the bad times. They're the stories you'll tell your family and friends. They'll stay with you for life." She lifted a bag from the counter. She reached in and pulled out the dream catcher. "This is for you. We hope your time here is the start of many happy memories."

He accepted the gift with a smile. "Thank you."

They were quiet for a moment, then Mrs. Solem said, "I think Dad and I can handle the clean up."

Mr. Solem started piling dishes and rose. "I've stacked wood and kindling outside by the fire pit, Nixxie. You and David start up a bonfire, and as soon as you have good roasting coals, we'll bring the hot chocolate and marshmallows."

Nixxie crumpled a yellowed newspaper. She pushed a few sheets of curled birch bark over the newspaper and then methodically arranged a loose layer of twigs across the top. Danny sat on an upturned log with rings worn smooth by time. He clasped his hands. Unconsciously, he rubbed one palm across the top of his other hand and moved it in a circle, as if washing under an invisible stream of water. Nixxie tended the fire until the small, tipi-like structure started to burn from within. The birch bark sparked with a violence that seemed out of place amongst the languid flames pulsing out slowly from the fire's heart. In time, the larger branches fed the flames, and then the entire fire settled down on itself.

Nixxie sat on a log to Danny's left. They both stared at the fire, the sparks dancing up and disappearing, some of them seeming to go high enough to join the stars. He looked out to the dark water. Beneath the sound of the fire's erratic crackle he could hear the waves stroking the shore, as regular as a clock counting out eternity. The fire was remarkably smokeless, burning clean and hot. The heat shimmer made the stars dance. The Milky Way showed itself, dressing the black velvet sky with a soft, white scarf stitched of stars, its pattern unchanged in a billion years. His grandfather's words echoed soft and clear: *It's time, Danny. It's time to go.*

He rose, stepped around the fire, and began moving toward the lake. He reached the boat ramp, and jumped on the cedar planks.

Now the stars shone more brightly than ever. He moved to the end of the dock, and his feet were sure on the weathered grain of the old wood. He felt lighter now, like the times he woke up in the morning and the answer to a problem had come to him overnight.

He reached into his pocket and pulled out the two stones. He looked at them both and then slipped the Buddy stone back into his pocket.

He swept his thumb back and forth across the worry stone. *Take this with you, Danny-boy. Keep it with you, and hold it when you need help. Stones are strong, and they can help you be strong too. Use it when you need to, and when you're ready, you can let it go.*

Danny straightened and squared his shoulders. He threw back his right arm and flung the worry stone far into the lake where it dropped from the darkness of the sky into the darkness of the water.

*Grandpa would approve.*

# Chapter 27

Two months before, Mom had planted bare-looking sticks at both ends of the tiny flower bed under their front window. "Do you expect those pathetic things to grow?" Danny had asked at the time.

"Just watch them, Davey-boy," she'd replied. "By summer, they'll be the most beautiful flowers in the world."

And they were. Danny bent to smell the roses, and a ladybug flew onto his hand. It tickled up his arm and flew away. Grandma had told him an old French saying – if a ladybug lands on you while you're sick, when it flies away it will take the sickness with it. He tugged out tendrils of chickweed that had started creeping around the corners of the bed, and smoothed the soil with his hand.

They'd just finished a long session with the Frisbee, and Buddy lay panting on the grass. "Let's get you some water, Bud," Danny said.

His mom had already set the table for their holiday dinner – early, just like Grandma used to. He went to his room and the dream catcher caught his eye. When he'd explained it to his mom, she'd listened eagerly and insisted on hanging it right away. They put it in the window, where the beads would catch the moonlight.

He looked through the window onto the common area. Mom was sunning herself in a lawn chair out back. Buddy had dropped into the chair's shadow. Julia was kicking around a soccer ball. The outdoor season started in two days.

Danny retrieved a second lawn chair from the basement. He unfolded it beside his mother's. They watched Jewel dribble the ball around the common area. "She's pretty good," he said.

His mom looked at him and nodded. "She's come a long way," she replied. "So have you."

He observed his sister's footwork. "Maybe I could teach her a few moves." He swallowed. "Do you think she'd let me?" His knee jiggled up and down.

"I know there's a lot you could teach her," his mom replied. "She just might need a little time...to trust you to follow through." She reached out and put her hand over his knee. "You'll need some cleats."

He willed his leg to stay still. "Do you think I can still get a paper route? It'd get me back into shape, and taking Buddy would make it fun." The dog's tail thumped. "I could make a little extra money."

His mom smiled. "We could phone tomorrow and see."

He nodded.

They watched Julia kick the ball towards them, and Danny didn't try to move his mom's hand from his knee. Julia was sweaty when she stopped in front of them.

"When's dinner?" she asked as she tossed her head and pushed her bangs away from her forehead. "I need to jump in the shower first."

"You have at least an hour," Mom replied. "Your brother has offered to help you practice some moves."

Julia narrowed her eyes. "You?" she asked.

His Adam's apple moved up and down. "Sometimes your stance could be better," he said. "You can react faster if you keep your weight on the balls of your feet."

She pursed her lips and then relaxed her shoulders. "Show me," she said.

He stood and planted his feet shoulder width apart and parallel. He bent his knees and drew his shoulders over his knees. He kept his head up, and his mind automatically shifted to the next move. "You have to 'think yourself tall.' When your mind is ready, your body will be too." He smiled. "It just takes practice."

He turned to his mom. "We'll need about half an hour, 'kay?" he asked.

She smiled with her mouth and her eyes. "No problem. Take your time."

"Grab that ball," he said to his sister. "And by the way, you can call me David."

It takes only one abuser to endanger a whole family. In some cases, conventional laws (restraining orders, criminal proceedings) cannot keep victims safe. In 1997, the Alberta Government began a program of last resort. It was called NIVA – New Identities for Victims of Abuse. The program operated for ten years, assisting about five hundred people, some of whom received complete identity changes. Canada's federal government then took over the program, which is now called the Confidential Service for Victims of Abuse (CSVA). Other countries have similar programs for victims and their families.

## ABOUT THE AUTHOR

Rosemarie Boll has been practicing family law for more than twenty years. She has written extensively on how the legal system affects families. She is committed to educating the public about the complex network of laws that govern our everyday lives, and explaining what the justice system can and cannot do. Rosemarie lives in Edmonton, Alberta and currently practices with the Family Law Office of Legal Aid Alberta. This is her first book.

## ACKNOWLEDGMENTS

I'm grateful to Marsha Mildon, who urged me to write this book all those years ago and helped me with an early draft. I'm indebted to editor Carolyn Jackson and Doris Rawson for gently nudging my manuscript into a novel. Thank you to publisher Margie Wolfe and the Second Story Press staff for the opportunity to tell this story in the hope that society progresses past the need for a program like NIVA.